Matt couldn't believe what he'd heard.

"What are you saying?" he asked.

"Joe wasn't Shawn's father," Tessa said quietly.

The silence stretched out to painful tightness, turning him inside out.

"I am," Matt said. He didn't know where the knowledge had come from, but there it was. The certainty of it stunned him, taking his breath away.

"You never told me," he said. "Why not?"

"You didn't want to stay here. All you ever talked about was leaving," she said. "How you were going to blow this old burg and see the world."

"What the hell did you expect me to say? That this would be home forever? I never belonged to anybody. I didn't know I had anything to stay *for*."

Dear Reader,

Welcome to the Silhouette **Special Edition** experience! With your search for consistently satisfying reading in mind, every month the authors and editors of Silhouette **Special Edition** aim to offer you a stimulating blend of deep emotions and high romance.

The name Silhouette **Special Edition** and the distinctive arch on the cover represent a commitment—a commitment to bring you six sensitive, substantial novels each month. In the pages of a Silhouette **Special Edition**, compelling true-to-life characters face riveting emotional issues—and come out winners. All the authors in the series strive for depth, vividness and warmth in writing about living and loving in today's world.

The result, we hope, is romance you can believe in. Deeply emotional, richly romantic, infinitely rewarding—that's the Silhouette **Special Edition** experience. Come share it with us—six times a month!

From all the authors and editors of Silhouette **Special Edition**,

Best wishes,

Leslie Kazanjian, Senior Editor

P.S. As promised in January, this month brings you Curtiss Ann Matlock's long-awaited first *contemporary* Cordell male, in *Intimate Circle* (#589). And come June, watch what happens to Dallas Cordell's macho brother as . . . *Love Finds Yancey Cordell* (#601).

ANDREA EDWARDS
Places in the Heart

Silhouette Special Edition

Published by Silhouette Books New York

America's Publisher of Contemporary Romance

To Megan,
for her meals and her attempts at silence
so we could finish the book
when school was no longer in session.

SILHOUETTE BOOKS
300 East 42nd St., New York, N.Y. 10017

ISBN: 0-373-09591-0

First Silhouette Books printing April 1990

Printed in the U.S.A.

ANDREA EDWARDS

is the pen name of Anne and Ed Kolaczyk, a husband-and-wife team who concentrate on women's fiction. "Andrea" is a former elementary schoolteacher, while "Edwards" is a refugee from corporate America, having spent almost twenty-five years selling computers before becoming a full-time writer in 1982. They have four children, two dogs, four cats and live in South Bend, Indiana, in an old home on the edge of the University of Notre Dame's campus.

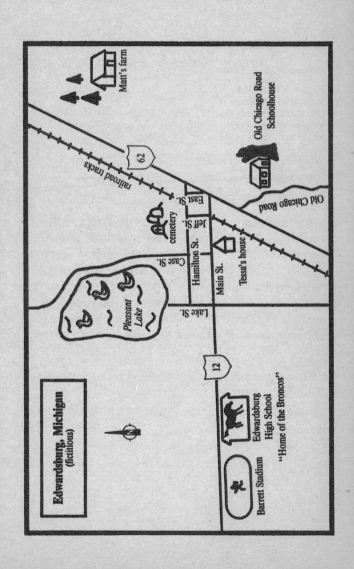

Chapter One

"Shawn," Tessa Barrett called sharply. "Come here, please."

She waited a moment as her thirteen-year-old son rounded the corner of the two-story building that was their home and her place of business. She actually wanted both of her boys, but knew if she called Shawn, eleven-year-old Jason would follow.

Shawn was tossing his ever-present football up in the air, wearing what had lately become an ever-present scowl. Tessa set her own jaw firmly. She'd raised two brothers and three sisters after her mother's death, and had learned that you never backed down from a kid.

"I thought I'd told you boys to put that brush over near the edge of the property," she said, pointing at a pile of newly cut branches.

Jason looked blandly at the pile while his brother shrugged and said, "We're going to burn that stuff anyway."

"It's too green to burn well," she said. "In the meantime, rabbits are going to nest in that pile and it's too close to my garden. So move it out to where I told you in the first place."

"An extra fifty feet aren't gonna strain a rabbit," Shawn said. "They're still going to steal from your garden."

The logic of her son's words didn't soothe Tessa's irritation any. Nowadays Shawn appeared to take great joy in poking holes in any idea she advanced.

"It doesn't look neat there," she snapped.

A smirk appeared on her elder son's face. "Lennie Barnes has had a car in his yard for over a year. And the Widow Crenshaw has that big garden with pinwheels, a scarecrow and bells hanging all over everything to keep the crows and rabbits away."

Tessa clenched her teeth hard. Edwardsburg was a little country town, and people left their large rambling lots in every stage of informality there was. Like all country folks, people here easily tolerated different styles of landscaping, but recently her older boy had been losing a lot of the tolerance that should have been part of his heritage.

Although maybe he was staying true to his heritage, she thought, watching Shawn with a new uneasiness. Maybe his restlessness wasn't due solely to his age, but was in his blood. Even as she had the thought, Tessa clamped a lid on it. Matt Anderson might have fathered Shawn, but the boy was her son, not his. Matt had been long gone from this town and her life by the time Shawn was born.

"I want that pile moved over to the edge," Tessa said, keeping her voice low and calm. "And I want it moved right now."

Shawn's mouth opened, ready to spill out more words of argument.

"I'll make you a deal." Tessa smiled grimly. "You move that pile like I told you, and I won't ruin the rest of your afternoon by making you stay in your room."

Storm clouds gathered in Shawn's eyes, dark like the clouds that were now threatening far to the west of them, but Tessa stood and matched his stare, waiting to see which path he would choose: further rebellion or compliance.

"It's not that big a pile," Jason said. "Let's get it moved quick or we won't get any playing in before the storm hits."

Shawn paused only a moment—long enough to shoot Tessa a quick glare—then he moved quickly to help his brother, who'd already started on the branches and brush. Tessa watched them for a few minutes, not really to supervise, but to show Shawn that she was not running away.

Tessa sighed. Two sons, so different from each other. Shawn was big and husky for his age, while Jason was of average height, but thinner than most. Where Shawn was strong and powerful, her younger son was quick and wiry. Jason was easygoing and conciliatory. Shawn had always been quiet and inclined to moodiness, though that was now rapidly growing into surliness.

She turned to go into the house, walking slowly so the grass could caress her bare feet. Jason was nearly a carbon copy of his father, while Shawn seemed to have inherited all of her knot-headedness. She wished Joe was still around to help her with the boys.

"We're gonna play over back of the ad building after we're done. Okay, Mom?" Jason asked.

"Sure. Just let me know when you're going."

She shook her head and smiled as she climbed the stairs to their apartment. How many hours had she, Joe and Matt spent at the field in back of the old administration building when they were growing up? Playing touch football, base-ball and just weaving dreams for the future. She was going to be a C.P.A. and work in Chicago or New York, Joe was going to be a starting halfback for the Chicago Bears, and Matt was going to see the world. Had he been the only one with luck enough to buck the odds?

It had been such a shock when Joe had a heart attack a year and a half ago. Things were starting to fall back into place now, but Tessa would always miss him. For herself, but especially for the boys.

Boys or girls, kids were pretty much alike until the teens, then the hormones kicked in and the differences widened. She sighed. Boys going into their teens could really use a man in the house. Or maybe it was the mother of boys going into their teens that could really use a man in the house.

But Joe had laid a solid foundation in the time the Lord had given him, and she was just going to have to finish the job. She'd done it with her brothers and sisters, and she would just have to do it again.

The rental car sputtered and gagged, its steady rhythm lagging as the car slowed slightly. The cornfields no longer whizzed by at the same speed.

"Don't you dare die," Matt Anderson muttered under his breath, pumping the gas pedal over and over again. "Not unless you want to be left out here to rust."

The auto quit its sputtering, thanks to either the threat or the gas, and the cornfields once again became a blur. Waves of heat shimmered before Matt on the highway and he re-laxed, letting the warm summer air steal away some of his irritation.

Once the irritation was down to a manageable level, Matt let his eyes wander about. Gently rolling green fields inter-spersed with clumps of woods filled the frames made by the front and side windows of the car. After his two-year stint in the deserts of Egypt, the green scenery was a little disconcerting, but habits built up in one's youth never totally disappeared. It wasn't long before he was wrapped in a feeling of cool comfort.

Maybe he was just a Midwest country boy at heart. Matt swatted that thought aside like a pesky bug. He had enough things to deal with at the moment and forced his attention back to the godforsaken landscape.

Though obviously this country wasn't really forsaken. Not that he could speak for God's interest in it, but people seemed to like this little piece of southwestern Michigan. The area around Edwardsburg had grown. A number of new brick ranch-style bungalows filled in the open spaces that had lined Route 12 when he was a boy, especially in the wooded areas. A house on a wooded lot must still be part of the American dream, he thought, though he wondered how much happiness prevailed during the leaf-raking time of the fall.

Although most houses were more than a stone's throw from their neighbors, almost everyone who lived here could at least see the place next door. That was more than could be said for the farm he'd grown up on. Now that *was* forsaken country, both by God and man.

The car missed a couple of cylinders and shivered. "Don't even think of it," Matt warned. "I'm not in the mood." He glared at the hood until the rhythm sounded smooth again.

Shaking his head, Matt sighed and let his eyes wander back to the road. Damn new cars with all their gidgets and gadgets. The shiny piece of junk should have at least had the decency to start acting up while he was near the South Bend Municipal Airport. Then he could just have traded it in for another. No, the damn thing had to wait until it was out here in the wilds of Cass County. Machines were getting so complicated they were becoming as contrary and ornery as people. If he had had time he would have found himself a beat-up old Jeep.

Matt sighed again. There wasn't one single reason for him to be in such a bad mood. He was just coming back to get rid of his aunt and uncle's Christmas tree farm, cutting his last ties to this old burg. Aunt Hilda and Uncle George were dead now. And once he'd sold those three hundred acres of sand, there would be no more ties between himself and Edwardsburg. No reason at all to feel guilty about not visiting.

That was stupid, he thought, letting his eyes wander over the rolling Michigan countryside. He didn't feel guilty. Hell, he'd never been part of the town anyway, not in any way whatsoever.

Matt grimaced slightly in the rearview mirror. That wasn't entirely true, there had been some that accepted him. Okay, one person in particular who had shared his dreams. But that had been only for a short time. A very short time. And then once he was out of sight, he was out of mind.

Squeezing the steering wheel hard brought his mind back to the matters at hand. Sell the farm. That was all he'd come into town for. Clean the place up, find a real estate agent and sell the farm.

He forced a smile to his face. Actually, he didn't even have to stick around for the sale. All he had to do was find a good agent, give some lawyer power of attorney, and everything would be taken care of, whether he was there or not. And it wasn't as if he needed the money, so the damn place could sit on the market as long as it had to.

Fir Road approached and sped past; he was only a few miles outside Edwardsburg now. The storm clouds from the west that had been following him all along sent a few scouts ahead to nip at his heels. A spattering of drops fell on the back window, then stopped.

Matt sighed for the umpteenth time since he'd slipped into this shiny heap back at the airport. Damn, damn. There was no reason for him to feel gloomy. His aunt and uncle hadn't been bad to him. He and they just hadn't gotten along. People whom circumstances had thrown together for a short time, like passengers scrambling for lifeboats off the *Titanic*. They should just have stayed at arms' length, tolerated one another and then gone their separate ways when fate rescued them. But none of them had been made that way.

Matt suppressed the urge to sigh. After all, they were family, sharing the same dominant stubborn genes. He shook his head, as though to clear it of the images of the past.

His Uncle George had been short and solid, like an oak stump. His aunt had been Matt's mother's sister, twelve years older. Nature, in its infinite wisdom, had chosen not to distribute some of the other genes equally. His mother had been given brightness and laughter, rose-colored vision to give color to the darkest storm clouds. His Aunt Hilda had gotten height and broad shoulders, the better to carry the many burdens that life sent her way.

Hilda and George had been his closest living relatives, so when his parents died in an accident in the Rocky Mountains, the court in Denver had decided that he should go to live with them on their farm in Michigan.

Matt scowled. They just never seemed able to get close to one another. He'd been twelve when he arrived, and they'd been childless for the twenty-five years they'd already been married. Oh, he'd been fed, clothed and sheltered, and his aunt and uncle had gone to all his school functions and sports. The form had been there, but somehow the spirit hadn't made it.

Back in those days, he'd blamed everything on his aunt and uncle. Now that a few gray hairs had found their way to his head, though, he knew better. In his memory's eye, he could see the three of them dancing. When they had reached out, he had pulled back. When he had reached out, one or both of them had pulled back. It must have been hard for them to take in a child who was almost a teenager. They'd missed out on all the early years when both parties had a chance to get used to each other.

"Oh, damn." The car was gagging and sputtering again. He'd been willing the thing along the road, and once his attention drifted, it had decided to quit.

"Not now," he warned. "You've only got a few more miles to go."

He was on the western edge of town, near the Old Chicago Road School, which had been the only school in the district back when his mother had gone there, but was now an administration building, replaced as a center of learning by three modern complexes stretched out in a long row down Section Street: an elementary school, a junior high and a high school.

The car sputtered again. "Come on," he said through clenched teeth, trying to will life into a motor ready to lie down and die. But it was no use. The sputtering and shaking increased. Matt quickly threw the gears into neutral and turned the wheel to let the car coast over to the side of the road. Damn.

He got out and locked the car doors, then wondered if people here still left their doors unlocked the way they used to. Somehow he doubted it. Distrust thy neighbor was the philosophy of choice these days. Edwardsburg wasn't that isolated. He glanced back at the storm clouds bearing down on him. If he walked fast, he might make it downtown before the storm hit.

"Hey, mister."

The kid's voice caught him unawares and he looked around. Two boys, about ten and twelve years old, were coming across the field behind the old school.

"Could you throw us the ball?"

Matt looked down and saw a football lying at the side of the road. A smile twisted one side of his mouth. Some things never changed. Running to catch a pass was fun. Shagging a ball lying on the ground was work. He picked up the ball and gave them a perfect spiral. The smaller boy caught it expertly, and they moved away from the road. Matt paused to watch them.

How many boys had run across those fields? The old school had to be at least forty or fifty years old. He and his best friend, Joe, had been in that long line. Football, baseball, kite flying, they'd done it all on this field.

Memories brought a smile to his lips. Of course, boys weren't the only ones to use this field. Girls had been in the minority, but there had always been a group of them who would push their way in.

Tessa Wolarski had been one of those pushers. She'd been a couple of years younger than he and Joe, but neither that nor her sex had stopped her. They'd laughed at her, but she'd never quit or gone away. A pug nose and a determined scowl had topped a sturdy frame, and eventually they'd let her into their friendship. She'd even played toss up and tackle with them.

As the years passed, the sturdy frame got wrapped with womanly curves. She'd still come out to play catch with them, but toss up and tackle had gone by the wayside. The games of catch also had gotten less and less attention as the threesome became a pair. Joe took his athletic talent to camps and extra practices after school. Matt and Tessa took to lying on the little knob of a hill over on the far side of the park on warm, muggy days like today. They'd lie on their backs and look west down Route 12.

He turned and stared down the way he had come. Folks had said back then that all a person had to do was follow Route 12 and they'd wind up in Chicago. Chicago. With its bright lights and people, fine restaurants and theaters. With its glamour and excitement.

It was everything Edwardsburg wasn't, and Tessa and Matt were going to experience it all. They'd get those old diplomas, step off the stage, hike on out to Route 12 and point their thumbs west. It'd be goodbye Edwardsburg and hello Chicago. Goodbye, dull and hello, excitement. Had it worked that way?

"Mom wants us home before it starts storming," the younger boy was saying. Matt turned to watch them again.

The older boy, obviously his brother, though not sharing a strong family resemblance, scowled. "Mom always wants us doing things her way."

"You ought to quit fussing with her," the younger said, zinging a neat spiral to his brother.

"She ought to get off my back," the older snorted as he reached up to catch the ball.

Some things never changed, Matt thought again. A distant rumble of thunder demanded attention, and Matt looked up to see the storm clouds getting closer. He had to agree with their mom; they should get home before the storm hit.

"You boys best be getting on home. It's going to pour," Matt called out, then almost burst out laughing. He'd spent more than a decade traveling the world, yet five minutes here on the edge of Edwardsburg had him talking like a Midwest farmer, accent and all.

The older boy had the ball and interrupted his passing motion to look back. "Skin don't rust," he said and completed his pass.

Matt shook his head, remembering his own smart mouth. Must be something in the cow patties that fertilized the soil here. "Water may not hurt you," he said, "but a bolt of lightning, put in the right place, can sure scorch your butt."

When the younger kid had returned the pass, both paused to look west. Some god or other hurled a bright, jagged bolt toward earth. The noise of thunder followed soon afterward, so they knew the rain was close. The bigger kid tucked the ball under his arm and both walked toward Matt, stopping at the other side of the ditch.

"Something wrong with your car, mister?" the older boy asked.

Matt nodded. "Yeah, it up and died on me."

"You know anything about cars?"

"Not this kind," Matt replied.

The younger one didn't say anything. He was probably at an age when he was more cautious about talking to strangers, Matt thought. "My Uncle Henry can fix anything that eats gas," the older one said. "Come on to our house and you can call him from there."

"Okay," Matt said with a nod.

The boys moved forward, then the older one paused. "We're going to run home, mister. I doubt you'll be able to keep up, so just look for the blue, two-story house with a store in front. We'll be around back."

They took off and Matt glared after them. He wouldn't be able to keep up? That little punk! He had a good mind to run them down.

Matt continued gazing after them. The younger one was a real speed merchant, and even the older one was having trouble keeping up with him. Matt settled into an easy trot and followed along after the boys.

"Tessa Barrett," the woman said, almost in exasperation. "You sure you want to make all those paper roses by yourself?"

"I've got almost two months," Tessa answered. "And they're not that hard to make."

Sandy Michaels, the decorations chairperson for September's high school homecoming dance, shrugged. "I'm not about to argue when it saves me finding more volunteers, but let me know if you change your mind." She walked across the gravel driveway to her compact station wagon and looked up at the sky, turning toward Tessa. "It's going to be a rough one when it hits."

Tessa let her eyes go skyward. Things really were looking dark and ominous. "The boys are playing in back of the Old Chicago Road School," she said. "I hope they're on their way home."

"They probably are." Sandy got into her car. "See you Tuesday," she called out the window.

Tessa waved and hurried through the athletic uniform store she ran out of the first floor of her house. She had clothes drying on the line out back that she had to take down or they'd be soaked. Just as she reached the back door, the phone rang.

"Darn," she muttered, picking up the receiver. It was Bruce Moran, one of her better customers, checking on a shirt order.

Tessa gripped the telephone as she stared out the window. "I'll give you a call tomorrow, Bruce, but I don't see any problem with having all those shirts done by Friday. The only thing that would stop me is if I don't have all the numbers in stock. I'm still restocking after doing the softball uniforms.''

"Let me just check that we covered everything," the man said slowly.

Dancing from one bare foot to the other, Tessa watched as the tree branches were whipped by the wind. The storm was going to be here in a matter of minutes, and her clothes would be soaked. Bruce was great and he gave her a lot of business, but he was as slow as molasses going uphill in January. Right now she knew he was checking all his forms, making sure everything was in order. She knew there was no hurrying the man, but she really didn't want her clothes wet. Then she'd have to throw them in the dryer and they wouldn't smell fresh anymore.

"We got twenty red, twenty green and twenty blue shirts," Bruce said.

"In the usual assortment of sizes from youth large to adult medium," Tessa agreed.

The lightning also worried her, but she was sure that the boys were on their way home. Shawn might get involved in a game, but Jason was a sensible sort. She wished that they'd get here soon, though, so they could help her strip the clothes off the line.

"Three striped goalie shirts," Bruce was going on.

"And three pairs of gloves."

There was a long moment of silence, broken by a faint sound of rustling on the line that was either static or Bruce and his papers.

"Okay, Tess," Bruce said in his slow drawl. "I think that should do it."

"Good, Bruce. Real good."

"So how is everything with you?" he asked.

Drops were hitting the windowpanes. There was no way the boys would make it before the deluge hit. She just had to get off the phone. "I'm fine and I'd like to chat, Bruce, but I have clothes hanging on the line and it looks like it's about to storm."

"Oh, I'm sorry," he exclaimed. "You should just tell me if you have something else to do. It won't bother me none. Our business is pretty much done and—"

"Bruce."

"Oh, yeah," he said with a laugh. "Goodbye."

"Goodbye." She slapped the receiver down and raced outside. The rain had started, but the initial drops were spread wide apart. She started taking down the clothes.

"Mom."

"Get these clothes down," she shouted, snatching garments off the line as she darted a quick glance at Jason. Shawn was coming into the yard behind him. Neither looked as if he'd drowned or been hit by lightning. What a worrier she was turning into, trying to raise the boys by herself!

Jason pulled the clothespins off the towel next to her. "There's a guy following us."

"What?" She paused, clothespins in one hand and a pair of swimming trunks in the other, to stare at Shawn and then Jason.

"His car's broke," Jason said.

"Yeah," Shawn added. "We said he could call Uncle Henry from here."

"Oh." The rain began to come down in earnest, stirring her into action. "Take these in the house," she said, handing Shawn the basket. "Jason, get the other basket from the porch."

A tall, rugged-looking man stepped around the corner of the clapboard building, sliding around the crabapple tree so that its branches, hanging heavy and low from the rain, wouldn't soak him more.

Tessa's heart skipped a half beat, but she forced her attention to the clothes. It was just what Granny always said— young widows tended to get horny on sultry days just before a thunderstorm.

"I'll be right with you," she called over to him. "I need to get these clothes off the line before they get soaked clear through."

"No problem."

His voice teased at memories hidden deep in her heart, bringing back visions of long-gone friends and days of wild dreaming. It wasn't possible. He had left years ago. But her heart didn't seem to be listening. The rain all but forgotten, she turned slowly, clutching a pillowcase in her hands.

The man standing at the corner of the house had flecks of gray in his hair and he looked harder, but she recognized him at once, her eyes as well as her heart. Matt Anderson was home at last! Her gaze ran over the muscles bulging in his arms and trembled slightly at the toughness added to his face. He hadn't carried that at eighteen or even twenty-one, but the brown eyes still flashed in that special way and his lips still carried the little smile that Tessa had so loved. Her astonishment was echoed in his eyes.

"Matt. Oh, Matt, is it really you?" she cried, dropping the pillowcase and clothespins as she ran into his arms.

"Tessa? I don't believe it!"

His arms reached out to catch her, swinging her high in the air as their laughter danced around them. The years melted away and it was just the two of them again, clinging together and standing firm for their dreams.

Her feet came back to the ground, but her heart didn't. Just gazing into his eyes sent it soaring. Tessa threw her arms around his neck and he pulled her close. For a long moment, they read each other's eyes, then his lips drowned out all thoughts and questions, even as the rain poured down in earnest. It was a gully washer, filling every crevice. It molded their bodies into one, while thunder and lightning crackled around them and the wind flapped the clothes still hanging on the clotheslines.

Nature itself seemed insignificant compared to the emotions raging in Tessa's heart. She and Matt separated slightly, and they gasped hungrily for air.

"Looks like you guys sort of know each other," Shawn said.

Chapter Two

Tessa started and turned to see two solemn faces staring at them. She sprang out of Matt's arms with a laugh, but the sound came out nervous and a tad screechy. She cleared her throat and tried again. No better.

"Yes, we do know each other," she said, managing to keep her voice low and brisk. "This is Matt Anderson. He and I went to high school together."

The boys nodded and continued staring. Water puddled at her feet and Tessa was wondering what to say next, when a humongous bolt of lightning shook the earth around them.

"Get in the house, guys," Matt commanded. He grabbed the remaining basket and shouted at Tessa over the storm, "Let's go."

The lightning and his voice shook the bonds of wonder from her limbs and he moved to take the rest of the clothes off the line.

"Leave them," he shouted over the wind and rain. "They're already soaked."

"It's only a few," she shouted back. "And I can put them in the dryer."

"Damn," he muttered, as he slammed the basket down and moved to help her. "You're as stubborn as three mules. Haven't changed a bit."

"I don't remember you as any shrinking violet," she snapped back.

He sent a glare her way, but concentrated on dumping waterlogged items into the basket. Tessa almost laughed out loud. It had been over ten years, and here they'd been doing some passion-pit groping, then finishing up with an argument, just as if they were still meeting behind the school before classes.

The four of them looked like drowned rats when they stepped into the back entryway. Tessa felt suddenly confined in the small space. The baskets of wet clothes, the boys' bicycles and Matt's broad shoulders made the area feel smaller than it ever had. Her breath was coming rather short, and it was either start blathering like an idiot or retreat into her mother role.

"Shawn, Jason," she said briskly, and pointed at the baskets of dripping clothes. "Take these things downstairs and throw them into the sink. I'll come down and squeeze the water out before putting them in the dryer. Then change into something dry. There are some clean clothes down there that haven't been sorted yet."

"Okay," Shawn replied, as they nodded in unison.

"And bring up one of—" She hesitated and swallowed. "One of Daddy's robes and a pair of his shorts. They're in some boxes behind the water heater."

Her elder son just stared at her, eyes wide.

"Mr. Anderson needs some dry clothes, too," she said. "And Daddy won't be needing them anymore."

The muscles danced in Shawn's forehead, then he nodded grudgingly. "Okay."

The boys disappeared down the stairs, leaving Matt and Tessa to a heavy silence between them. The stairs to the basement loomed next to her, inviting her to escape down into its cool dampness. She should have gone for the clothes for Matt herself, then she wouldn't have been standing here with him, wondering what to say, or noticing how his shirt had molded itself to his chest.

Tessa glanced around quickly, at the puddle under her feet, at the jackets hanging all askew from the hooks next to the door, at Matt watching her.

"Good thing I don't have air-conditioning," Tessa said quickly with a short laugh. "We'd be chilled to the bone waiting for those guys to get back."

"Weather report on the radio said a cool front is following the storm."

Tessa brushed some drops from her curls. "That's good. It's been on the hot side this past week."

He turned to stare out the door at the rain washing over the backyard, the vegetable garden and the big cherry tree in the back. "Looks like you could use the rain."

"It's been dry," Tessa said, nodding in agreement.

Having exhausted their store of conversation, both stared out at the yard. Tessa's gaze went past the cherry tree to the tall hedge lining the back of her property. The downpour had slowed to a steady soaking rain. The tomato plants in her garden seemed to be reaching up into the moisture, shivering under its caress and begging for its life-giving kiss. Tessa shook herself and moved over to straighten the jackets. She toyed with the idea of throwing Shawn's jacket over her shoulders.

"You cold?" Matt asked.

She started, then realized she'd been holding on to the jacket. "Uh, no." She put it back on the hook.

No, far from it. Based on her own body heat and what she felt coming from Matt, Tessa was surprised there wasn't steam rising from them. Right now she'd rather throw off her clothes, rip his off and wrap herself around those hard muscles. Granny sure had been right. Nothing like a good summer thunderstorm to make a young widow horny. Damn, where were those kids?

"I don't think they could have gotten lost." Tessa knew her laugh sounded nervous, but there wasn't anything she could do about it. "The basement isn't that big."

"They'll be up when they're ready," Matt replied.

"Why don't we go on up to the kitchen?" she suggested and led the way up the stairs to their apartment above the store. The kitchen was at the top of the stairs, a big room that didn't seem all that much larger than the entryway all of a sudden, not with his eyes following her everywhere she went. She stopped at a cabinet by the sink and reached for the coffeepot. "I could make us some coffee."

"None for me, thanks," he said, standing awkwardly in the middle of the floor as if he was trying not to drip too much. "It was so hot, the rain felt good."

"Some lemonade then, or iced tea?" she offered.

"I think I'd rather get rid of the wet outside me before I put any more wet inside me," he said with a laugh.

"Yeah. True." She listened for the sound of steps on the stairs, but heard none. "Maybe you should go ahead and get out of those things."

The smile that came was broad and vintage Matt. "Sure."

Tessa paused to take a firm grip on herself. "I mean before you get chilled."

"My thoughts exactly."

They exchanged smiles. The look in his eyes awoke more than just memories. It awoke the longings to be held, to have someone to confide in and share dreams with, and the need to belong to someone. Longings that had caused her trouble in the past and that she should know better than to think about now.

"Go down the hall to the bathroom." She pushed at his shoulder, but quickly removed her hand. The muscles beneath her fingers felt so good and familiar. She settled for a wave at the hallway leading off from the kitchen door. "And take your clothes off."

His smile reminded her of those of her sons when they were told they'd be alone for a while and in charge of the freshly baked cherry pie.

"I'll find the boys," she said, "and see why it's taking them so long to bring you something dry."

"Maybe you'd better come with me." Matt paused. "Just to show me where the bathroom is."

Being alone with him up here was the last thing she needed. "There aren't that many rooms," she replied. "Just look around. It's the room with the tub and shower."

"You're very trusting. Letting me wander around your house, unescorted."

It was herself she didn't trust. He made her feel young again, young and so very much alive. "I don't trust anybody." She moved toward the stairs. "I'll find something nice and dry."

"I'll be waiting," he replied. The smile on his face glowed with a soft warmth.

Tessa padded quickly down the wooden steps. Matt Anderson. She had just been getting her life settled and smooth. And now Matt Anderson was in town. She tried to frown, but her face never made it.

*   *   *

Matt wrung out his shirt over the bathtub, then laid it on the pile with his other clothes. With its molded tub and shower the bathroom looked very modern for what was obviously an old building. His engineer's eye saw that someone had done a good remodeling job recently. Probably Tessa's husband.

He brushed off the feeling of annoyance at the thought. Those two boys didn't exactly drop out of the sky, and what the hell did he expect a pretty young woman to do? It suddenly struck him that there was no masculine presence in the bathroom. There were the boys' toothbrushes, but no shaving paraphernalia, no large bathrobe. He frowned. Tessa had sent the boys downstairs for one of their father's bathrobes, not one of their father's old bathrobes. Maybe she was divorced?

Matt shook his head sharply. What difference did it make? he tried to ask himself.

He looked in the mirror and felt the earth pause. Fourteen years ago, the only person he could really talk to in this burg had been Tessa. She'd understood him better than anyone, even Joe. Now he came back, and she was the first person he ran into.

He closed his eyes, hearing the rain beating against the side of the house but seeing, in his mind's eye, Tessa as he'd seen her by the clothesline, with her jeans rolled up to her knees and wearing an Edwardsburg Junior High School T-shirt. The pouring rain had worked its magic like a sculptor, showing that the years had improved her womanly curves, softening but at the same time accentuating.

A lump blocked his throat. They'd had such dreams, but they'd both been determined to leave the little town way behind them. He'd traveled the world, but it looked as if she hadn't made it past Three Oaks. Which of the fates had played this cruel joke on little Tessa Wolarski?

But then, she wasn't Tessa Wolarski anymore, was she? Of course not—she was the mother of two young boys. Suddenly he frowned. He didn't remember seeing any gold wedding band. He'd better get his clothes dried, call Uncle Henry and get out of there before he forgot just how much things could change in fourteen years.

Where the hell was that robe and stuff?

As if in answer to his question, there was a sharp rap on the door. Then it was opened slightly and a boy's arm dumped shorts and a robe on the floor, quickly closing the door again.

"Thank you very much," Matt muttered to the door before bending to pick up the dry clothes.

He put the shorts on and pulled the robe over his shoulders, trying not to notice that his shoulders were a bit wider than Tessa's husband's, then went down the hall to the kitchen. The boys were there, but Tessa wasn't.

"Where's your mother?" he asked.

"Downstairs," replied the older and sour-looking one Matt thought was Shawn. "She's getting into some dry clothes."

Matt sat down carefully, keeping his shoulders still so as not to strain the bathrobe cloth. The bigger boy was staring at him. Matt figured the kid was about twelve, but he had a glare on him that would have done a KGB interrogator proud.

"You're bigger than Dad was," Shawn said.

Was? Matt felt like asking the kid if his father had shrunk, but Shawn didn't look like the joking type, so Matt just answered, "Yeah. I was a lineman. Not too fast but big enough to push people around."

"Our father was a halfback," the younger one, Jason the friendly, said quietly.

Matt stared at him for a moment. The sharp features beneath the light brown hair stirred something in Matt's memory, but nothing came forth. He pushed the feeling back and looked around at the large country kitchen. An old gas stove, wooden cabinets, a butcher block in the center and a round table by the wall. Worn, in a comfortable sort of way.

"You know my mother real well?" Shawn's penetrating brown eyes stared at him. The kid would also do well at poker. Never cracked a smile.

"We knew each other from school." Matt nodded. "She was a couple of grades behind me."

Both of them stared at him and Matt turned away. Actually he and Tessa had been more than just classmates, but that wasn't something he wanted to get into with the young lads.

His eyes took another pass around the kitchen. Clean wallpaper. Pots and stuff hanging from the walls. A real pleasant place to spend a stormy evening, either in January or July.

He and Tessa had been more than classmates, a lot more. But they'd also been best friends. There hadn't been anyone else he could talk to about blowing this crummy little town, especially once the college scouts were swarming over Joe. No, he and Tessa had shared the same dream, out there on the little hill back of the old school. A dream of traveling to far places, seeing the world.

He glanced at Shawn, who was still checking him out. "What grade are you in?" Matt asked.

"I'm going into seventh grade," Shawn replied.

"I'm gonna be a sixth grader," Jason added.

The older kid was about twelve or thirteen. It didn't look as though Tessa had gotten far out of Edwardsburg at all. Shawn had to have been born a year or so after she graduated from high school.

Matt wondered if she'd ever been outside of Michigan. Well, she had to have been, living this close to the Indiana-Michigan state line. The better question was had she ever been outside Michiana, as the area was known.

He matched eyeballs with the two lads. Healthy-looking kids. But was that enough? Enough for a lifetime of Friday night fish fries at Calico Jack's and Saturday afternoons at the University Park Mall in South Bend? What had Tessa done with her dreams? Had she stored them someplace, only to bring them out on a long boring day, like in the middle of February when the rain mixed with snow for days on end? Or had she killed them and buried them deep within her soul?

"Think she got lost?" Matt asked, looking toward the door at the head of the stairs.

"Nah." Both boys shook their heads, but it was the older who spoke. "Women just take their time dressing." Jason nodded his solemn agreement.

A smile flickered on Matt's lips, but he controlled it. When did one lose that wisdom about the opposite sex? Probably around junior high, when the hormones started agitating more. It was totally lost when the girl you loved ignored your very existence.

Of course, that kind of pain always hurt something special, no matter how old or experienced you thought you were. He'd tried keeping in touch with Tessa, but it just hadn't worked out. His letters had been long and rambling as he searched, mostly for himself. Hers had been short and curt. Telling him to set simple, straightforward goals and go

for them. Her advice had been good and he'd been success-
ful. He sighed inwardly. What had he given Tessa?

"Hi, guys."

Tessa appeared in the doorway. She was wearing a long-
sleeved, long-bodied shirt over some shorts.

"You combed your hair," Shawn said.

Matt thought the kid's tone sounded accusing, but Tessa
just laughed. "It was wet and yucky. And, thank you, I
think it looks nice, too."

Nice? Nice didn't begin to do her justice. The firm,
tanned skin, the bright smile, the sparkling eyes—she looked
even more beautiful than he had remembered.

"We're not going to eat for a couple of hours, guys," she
said to the boys. "Why don't you go and watch TV?"

They quickly exited, taking some cookies to sustain them
on the journey. Matt and Tessa were left alone. Alone, except for the awkward silence hanging heavily between them.
Matt stayed seated at the table and Tessa remained standing in the doorway while the hands of the clock crept forward, minute by agonizing minute.

"I'm still the same old country girl," she said, laughing
and wiggling her bare toes. "I almost never wear shoes in
the summer."

Matt looked at her brown feet, unmarred by any shoe or
sandal lines, and nodded. A voice inside him teased, asking
whether Tessa was brown all over, totally free of any stripes
of winter-pale flesh? He slammed the door on that question.

"Want some lemonade?" Tessa asked.

"Yeah. That would taste good."

Matt watched as she glided across the tile floor, strong yet
graceful as he imagined Artemis, goddess of the hunt, would
be. Her smile was cool, but friendly. The lemonade was

sweet, but tart. Two of the few things where nature could combine opposites in such beautiful harmony.

Tessa sat down at the table across from him. "What have you been doing with yourself?" she asked, sipping at her glass of lemonade. "I remember the last time you came through after you got out of the Army. You were packing it up for college."

"Oh, I studied civil engineering. Always liked building things." He drank some more of his lemonade. "Then after graduation I caught on with Bechtel, an international construction outfit based in San Francisco."

She nodded, but Matt wasn't sure if she really had heard of Bechtel. It was a large company, but few outside the industry knew about it. It didn't really matter.

"My first assignment was in Saudi Arabia, working on a hospital complex. Then there was a bridge in Denmark, a dam in the Sudan, some roads in the Amazon." He shook his head. "There were so many projects that they sort of blend together. The last one was a dam in Egypt, and I'm going on to a bridge in Australia." He paused a moment. "Or maybe it was a bridge in Egypt and a damn in Australia." He grinned to show he was teasing.

"Any family?"

Tessa's voice was soft, but her eyes were penetrating, he noticed. She appeared to be a bundle of compatible opposites. He checked his glass. It was empty except for the ice cubes. "A rolling stone gathers no moss."

Nodding in apparent understanding, Tessa emptied her glass, then she, too, examined her ice cubes.

The wind had died down to a shy breeze, but it was still raining, a gentle tapping on the windows—the kind of rain his mother used to say was carried down by angels and laid gently on the ground, so that nothing on earth was bruised.

"I came back to sell the farm," he said.

Tessa nodded. "That's what I thought. It's terrible about your aunt and uncle." She shook her head. "Killed together in an accident, just like your first parents."

His only parents, Matt wanted to reply, but he just nodded. It would sound childish, as if he were still fighting them after they had died. So she wouldn't think him callous, he explained, "I was way out in the boonies. It was a couple of days before they found me, and would have been two weeks after their death before I could have made it back here." He shrugged. "I would have missed the funeral anyway."

"Everyone understood," she assured.

Matt's jaw clenched momentarily. What did he care what anyone in town understood? Everybody and his brother damn well knew that he and the old folks hadn't got along. There weren't any secrets in a place like Edwardsburg. But Tessa's eyes lay gently on him and he forced himself to relax.

"What happened to the gang?" he asked. "They scattered all over?"

"Some," Tessa replied. "Mike and Ryan moved to Chicago and Linda's in Detroit. I think Jerry and Vi are out west. But most are around. If not in town, then in South Bend or Niles. Pretty close."

Matt nodded. It was said that apples fell close to the tree. "Whatever happened to Joe?" he asked. "Did he make it to the pros like he always said?" He drained some ice water from his glass. "I lost track of him."

"No, he didn't play in the pros."

"Too bad," Matt said softly. Was he the only one who had reached for his dreams? "He wanted that pretty bad."

"I guess," Tessa replied. She moved her glass in slow circles on the tabletop.

"I guess not everyone's dreams come true."

"Or they change."

The sounds of the television floated into the room. "So what did he do? Did he graduate?"

"Not from Michigan State." She got to her feet and wandered over to the refrigerator to pour herself another glass of lemonade. Then without asking, she poured more for him. "He hurt his knee."

"Bad enough to end his playing?" He paused long enough for her to nod. "That must have destroyed him."

She just shrugged. "I don't know. He came back home and commuted to Indiana University at South Bend."

Poor Joe. Since junior high on, he'd talked of nothing but the pros.

"He got a degree in physical education, then he taught health and driver's ed at the high school. And he coached football and baseball."

"Hope he likes it," Matt said. But what a letdown that must have been! "So, is he still around here? I'll have to look him up."

Tessa rattled the ice cubes in her glass, looking as if she hadn't heard him, as if she were off in some distant world that he couldn't inhabit. "We were married as soon as he came home from Michigan State," she said.

Joe and Tessa were married? Matt stared at her, the raindrops echoing in his ears. But all he was conscious of was an awful pain, the sense that while he'd been out chasing dreams, life had been passing him by.

"So your last name's Barrett now." A really clever thing to say. He swallowed hard and tried again. "You have nice-looking kids."

Tessa had taken the lemonade back to the refrigerator and was now staring out at the rain. "Joe had a heart attack early last year." Her voice was quiet, walking the tightrope between pain and control. "A few days after New Year's, in fact. He was dead before he got to the hospital."

Matt felt as though he'd been hit from behind and plunged into a deep, dark abyss. "I'm sorry," he blurted out before he was completely gone.

"He was always in such great shape." She shrugged, but the gesture tore at him for all the pain she was trying to bury. "The doctors said that things like that happen. There's no way to predict it."

The room seemed stuffy. Matt found it hard to breathe but he was climbing back up into the real world. Joe Barrett, the lean, mean running machine, dead from a heart attack, leaving a wife and two kids. God, he couldn't believe it. It had to be a dream. Some kind of a nightmare.

"I was going to grill a steak and bake some potatoes for dinner."

Matt shifted his gaze to stare at Tessa, forcing his eyes to focus. Her eyes seemed a tad damp, but the smile was beautiful. Where did she get such strength?

"I made a lot of salad," she said. "Want to stay for dinner?"

He nodded.

"Your clothes should be dry by now. I'll get them," she said. "You'll be more comfortable that way. Joe wasn't as deep in the shoulders and chest as you are."

The soft pitter-patter of her bare feet disappeared and Matt sat there, staring out the window. The rain seemed to be picking up again. It didn't sound like it, but the window had gotten more blurred. A lump bounced in his throat. Joe Barrett, gone. He'd seen young men die on some construction projects, but Joe had been in Edwardsburg, a quiet little place, teaching school and taking his sons fishing on Pleasant Lake. Young men didn't die in a place like this. It wasn't right.

Chapter Three

Did you play varsity all the time you were in high school?'' Jason asked.

Tessa leaned back in her chair as Matt smiled. He was spinning yarns about his and Joe's high school days, and the boys, rapt, were staring at him. Well, Jason was rapt. Shawn had his usual scowl in place.

She checked her older son's features closely to see if it was his normal scowl or a special one for Matt, but she quickly gave up on that. It was hard to tell with the kid. Teenage boys were a special breed, and it hadn't made it any easier for Shawn to have lost Joe like that.

This was really a treat for the boys. Tessa swallowed the little tickle in her throat. She had brothers and cousins all around the area who gladly spent time with the boys, but somehow Matt's attention seemed special. Maybe it was because he and Joe had been close and he could tell the boys personal things. Then, too, it could be the way Matt told the stories, as if nobody had listened to him with such intensity before. Had that exciting life he'd left Edwardsburg to find given him everything he needed?

"Your dad and I were both on the varsity team," Matt replied. "But we didn't start doing much until our junior year."

"Weren't you guys good enough?" Shawn asked.

"Shawn," Tessa scolded.

"That's all right." Matt turned back to the boys. "No, we weren't good enough. Most boys go through a growing spurt about that time. You usually grow tall first. Then your muscles play catch-up. Most freshmen don't do well against juniors and seniors."

Shawn turned toward Tessa. "I thought you said Dad played right away."

"He played some in his freshman year," Matt explained. "A little more in his sophomore year, and then first string in his junior and senior years."

"How come?" Shawn asked. "Was Dad better than you?"

Tessa nudged her son with her foot. "Tact isn't one of Shawn's heaviest attributes, and lately he's been even less so."

Matt laughed. "I can relate to that." He took a swallow of his iced tea. "I was a lineman and I needed to bulk up before I could do any good, and that didn't happen until my junior year." He leaned forward and looked directly into Shawn's unblinking brown eyes. "But, in answer to your question, no, I wasn't as good a player as your father. He was much better. That's why he got an athletic scholarship to college and I didn't."

"You don't have to answer all his questions," Tessa said softly. She enjoyed having him here, too. It didn't matter if he talked about Joe, his projects around the world or the price of corn on the open market. It was just so nice to have a man at the table. No, it was just so nice to have this man at her table, as if she were offering him a moment of rest between the races he chose to run.

Matt gave Shawn a conspiratorial wink. "I don't mind your questions." He smiled at Tessa. "I like his no-nonsense approach. It's a lot like you."

"Thanks," Tessa replied, while keeping Shawn under a stern gaze.

"Don't mention it," Matt said with a snicker.

"Jason's a lot quieter," she said.

"Like Joe." Matt's voice was soft, and they exchanged silent glances.

Poor Matt. Tessa knew that he'd have to go through a grieving process for Joe, just as she and the boys had.

"Your father was something else," Matt said, continuing with his stories. "The other guys on the team used to call him 'the Ghost.'" He shook his head. "Didn't seem to need more than a few inches of space and he'd slip through. Then once he was past the linebackers, he'd turn on the afterburners. Darn few people could catch him."

"Jason's fast like Dad was," Shawn said. "I'm slow like Mom."

Matt was laughing again. "She's not slow in everything."

Tessa gave him a fierce glare, but it did nothing to dampen his smile. Or to dampen the glow in her heart. It wasn't as if she'd lived her life under storm clouds, but suddenly sunshine seemed to fill every corner of her being.

"Mom's slow in running," Shawn pointed out. "But I got her muscles."

"Don't knock that," Matt said. "She used them to keep everyone in line back in high school."

"She still does," Shawn grumbled.

Tessa gave each of her cherubs a tight smile. "Thanks a lot, guys. Now, if you're through picking on me, why don't you clear the table?"

They grimaced ever so slightly but got to their feet and went about their tasks. Tessa led Matt into the living room, feeling suddenly tongue-tied and awkward. Time seemed to melt away between them and she was that young high school girl again, treating the angry football player with half adoration, half easy familiarity. She had loved him so much back then, and from that love had risen a fierce sense of protectiveness. He had been desperate to escape Edwardsburg, and she hadn't been going to let anything stand in his way. Shawn's voice came floating in from the kitchen and her heart trembled. Not anything.

"You've got nice kids," Matt said, moving to an overstuffed chair in the corner.

She dashed over and grabbed a sneaker from the seat. "Could be a little neater," she replied, waving the errant shoe and looking around for its mate.

"They've got good hearts. What else is important?"

"Yeah." The other shoe was nowhere to be found. Hopefully, it was someplace in the house or yard. Tessa dropped the one on the floor and pushed it under the lowboy. "I think it's Jason's. He's probably outgrown it anyway."

"Won't need new ones until September," Matt said.

Tessa searched his face briefly. Was he making fun of her country ways? Well, she didn't care if he was, but she slipped her bare feet under her as she sat down on the sofa.

The boys had left the television on, and a surfing competition was on the sports channel. Tessa and Matt stared at it for a while as the murmur of voices and the clatter of dishes drifted out to them. She began to relax. The past was the past.

Suddenly Matt yawned. "Excuse me," he said.

"Tired?"

He blinked a long moment. "I guess." He shook his head. "I'm not sure what time zone my body thinks it's in right now."

"Poor baby."

"You always were generous with sympathy."

She stuck her tongue out at him, and he returned a smile of what appeared to be contentment. Probably the steak and wine. Men were like wolves and lions. Give them a full stomach and they were ready for a nap.

Tessa watched his eyes flutter to half-mast. It was like the old days. With each other, they could be themselves—angry, frightened, tired. Hungry for love.

"So how long do you plan on staying this time through?" Tessa asked.

Matt opened his eyes. "Long enough to get the farm on the market."

"And then?"

"On to that dam in Australia."

Not exactly an unexpected answer, but fair warning to her heart. Listen up, you silly old thing and stop fluttering every time he comes near! This time's no different than any other time Matt Anderson's been in town. He's counting the days until he's gone from a place that only means unhappiness to him.

"Speaking of the farm, could I persuade you to give me a ride out there?"

His head was still lying back on the chair but his eyes were wide open. Hard brown eyes like some kind of guard dog. He wasn't as easy to read as he had been back in high school. Now those eyes told her nothing that he didn't want her to know.

"You could," she said.

"Thanks." He turned his half attention back to the television. "Any time you want is fine."

How about midnight, after the boys have been asleep for a few hours? Tessa put a frown on her face and forced the thoughts out of her head. *Get real, kid.*

"The electricity's been turned off there," she said.

He shrugged. "I have a flashlight."

"It's a farm," she reminded him. "Without electricity the pump won't work. And if the pump doesn't work, you have no water."

"Oh, yeah."

"Nothing to shave with and nothing to drink."

"Hmm."

"No refrigerator for food."

"Doesn't sound good," he muttered.

"The place hasn't been cleaned in a month."

"Oh, yucky."

"Field mice and bats have probably taken over."

"Ooo, that's scary."

"Fine, smart aleck. Sleep out there if you want. I don't care."

She paused, then added, "I'm sorry."

He had his little-boy smile on. "No, you're not," he said. "I remember you as being more accepting."

"I remember me as more naive."

On the TV screen, hunks in wet suits were hopping about and waving their fingers. Someone must have won something.

"Then can you give me a ride to a motel?"

"You can sleep here if you like." Now why in the world had she said that? It was obvious that this Matt Anderson could more than afford a few nights in a motel room, and she probably needed some distance between them until she regained her equilibrium. She put some snap in her voice. "You can sleep on the sofa."

"No way I could turn down an invitation like that."

Fortunately, the boys strolled in before things got out of hand. That had been the story of Matt and Tessa. They could converse pleasantly enough about running away from Edwardsburg, but anything else was an argument—full of fire and passion. And if they weren't arguing—

She stood up. "Let's go with Mr. Anderson to get his suitcase, boys." Apparently they still had the fire and passion.

The bugs were screeching their nightly symphony, and once in a while a car would come roaring down Route 12, its headlights sweeping across the ceiling of Tessa's bedroom like a lure trying to pull her from her complacent life. She turned over in bed and stared at her clock. The numbers changed with diabolical slowness.

Her eyes wandered around the room. It was the smallest of the bedrooms, but she and Joe had taken it because it was at the front of the building. They gave the boys the bedrooms in back, away from the noise and headlights of Route 12 at night.

The bedroom's small size meant they didn't need much furniture, which they hadn't been able to afford anyway. Joe's parents had given them the bed and bureau. She'd bought the ladder-back, woven bottom chair at a garage sale in Sturgis. And the Christmas before Joe died they'd given each other a new spring and mattress set from Sears.

Sighing, Tessa rolled over onto her back. All their furniture was on the worn side, but she regarded it more as comfortable than as shabby. She and Joe hadn't had an abundance of money, what with his being a teacher, but they'd always had enough. That was the way things had always been for her anyway. There had been just enough to go around, but she remembered her childhood as happy. She was sure it was the same for her boys.

From a financial point of view her life wasn't any harder without Joe than with Joe. Just as before, she had just enough to make ends meet. And, as before, her days were filled with work, family and her boys. But the nights were another story. Then in the quiet all the goblins came out of the closets deep in her psyche. Loneliness and need were the worst. On a lazy summer night like this, with a cool breeze pushing past the curtains, Tessa would have given almost anything for a loving man at her side. And tonight it certainly didn't help to know there was one in the next room.

It wasn't just the snuggling that she missed. In fact, she missed even more the lazy words wrapped in sleep. The short simple sentences dissecting the day, looking at the tiny islands of happiness that luck let drift into their life. That was what everyone needed to give their life purpose. Or was it? Matt seemed to be doing very well without someone to share those little pieces of life with.

Damn. Tessa rolled over, threw off her blanket and punched her pillow. She was getting along just fine. What did Matt Anderson have to come back to town for anyway?

The answer was obvious. George and Hilda were gone, so he'd come to sell the old family farm and then run off to some far corner of the earth. The least he could have done was to wait until she was gone on vacation. Of course, since a vacation for her usually turned out to be a three-day trip to the Cedar Point Amusement Park in Sandusky, Ohio, it would have been a little tricky for Matt to schedule his own trip within that kind of a time span. But why not? He'd always been a smart one in school.

They'd been friends for many years, but since she was a couple of years younger it hadn't been until Joe and Matt were seniors that they'd really become close. Matt had been the driven one. Good student, ambitious, going to make it big outside of Edwardsburg. Joe had been the quiet one. A great athlete, but he didn't seem to have any ambitions; he'd been content to drift with the flow. Everyone talked of his dream to play in the pros, but sometimes Tessa wondered whether he'd really had that dream.

Sometimes it had been hard to know what he really wanted. His father had put him on the football and basketball teams. His coaches had put him in track to stay in shape. His teachers had carried him through classes, not really greasing his way through school, but taking care of him more than they had the average student.

Fate had always seemed to carry Joe. His knee injury had put an end to his collegiate football career and killed his chance for the pros, but he had liked athletics and kids so he'd drifted into teaching. The store had been her idea to supplement his teacher's salary. As it turned out, it was a good thing that she'd pushed for it, or now she would have had nothing but a small social security pension.

And who was she? Tessa remembered herself as the one who was always running things. The student council, the Christmas turkey drives for her church, her own brothers and sisters after Mom died and finally Joe. She'd shared Matt's dreams of running away. She was going to study accounting and law. After graduation she was going to run a big company, but—

She sat up straight in bed. If she wasn't going to sleep, she might as well make use of all this free time. She slipped out of her room and down the hall. Pausing in the living room doorway, she listened to Matt's breathing and watched him sleeping in the moonlight shining through the front window. She smiled when she saw he was wearing swimming trunks. Apparently Mr. Hunk didn't sleep in pajamas. Her cheeks warmed and she hurried downstairs to the store. Bright fluorescent lights and the cool tiled floor beneath her feet put things back into perspective.

She'd get those soccer shirts done and maybe even start taking inventory of the numerals and letters she had in stock. Tessa was pulling a stack of shirts off the shelf when the back stairs cried out in protest. She turned to see Matt coming slowly down into the store.

"Hi," she said.

He blinked, waiting for his eyes to adjust to the light. "You working the night shift?"

"I have some orders to catch up on." She carried the shirts over to the appliqué iron and the waiting pile of numbers.

"Nice outfit," Matt said, his eyes losing their sleepy look as they slid over her shortie nightgown. "You always dress like that for work?"

Tessa could feel her face grow hot, but she concentrated on smoothing the top shirt on the pile and refused to look down at the cotton nightshirt. "I wasn't expecting company."

"It's still nice."

"The boys gave it to me for my birthday." Her voice was brusque. It wasn't any of his business anyway. "This is a fairly quiet operation, so I think you should be able to finish your sleep undisturbed."

Matt didn't reply, but moved over to get a stool, leaning on the bingo table that served as a counter as he sat down. "Place has atmosphere," he said, looking around at the bare blue steel shelves and banks of fluorescent lights.

"I don't do any retail," Tessa said. "It's all telephone orders from teams and leagues in the area."

"Didn't know Joe had an interest in the business side of sports."

"He didn't," Tessa said with a laugh. "This was my idea."

"I should have known."

Tessa didn't know whether his words were of approval or disapproval, but then she decided that she really didn't care. She tested the iron with a moistened finger and was disappointed to find it still not hot enough.

"I take it you never got to be a C.P.A."

She paused a moment. Did she really want to get into one of these what-have-you-been-doing-with-your-life chats? But then, what difference did it make? And anything was preferable to having him just sit there staring at her.

"Nope," she replied.

"Too bad," Matt murmured. "With the way American industry is going they sure could have used you."

"My family came first."

He stared at her uncomprehendingly.

"Remember that summer you were here last? You'd just gotten out of the Army." His face remained bland as he nodded. "Mother got real sick soon after that."

He shook his head. "I'm sorry. She'd been sick for so long, I guess I didn't think it was anything different."

Tessa shrugged. "She died late that summer."

He didn't say anything, but his eyes were full of sympathy.

"It hit Dad hard." She swallowed at the memories and looked back into the past. "He was working overtime at Indiana and Michigan Electric, and there were five more kids behind me. I just sort of took everything over. Even when he was home, he couldn't seem to make any decisions."

Matt nodded his encouragement for her to continue.

"Dad had enough to do with supporting us. The raising and caring was asking for more than he had available."

Matt remained silent.

"Things worked out fine. Jenny, she's the youngest, finished high school last year. She's working at a YMCA camp this summer and then is going to Western Michigan in the fall. Paul will finish veterinary school next year. Martha's a teacher in Mishawaka, but still lives in Edwardsburg. Dan's at Michigan State on a baseball scholarship, and Louise is waiting for her first baby."

Matt's face seemed to darken with an inner storm.

"Things worked out well for everybody," she repeated firmly.

"You never told me any of this."

Tessa checked the iron again. Another few minutes.

"I did write," he said.

"I know." She forced a smile to her face. "But you had your own thing. I mean, you'd just started college. It didn't seem fitting to bother you about things you couldn't change." Besides, she wouldn't be the one to drag him back, to imprison him in a place he hated.

Matt looked away and little tremors of unease shook her foundations. "You wanted to see the world," she reminded him. "I mean, that's all you ever talked about. Right?"

He nodded, looking around at the shelves.

"So things worked out the way they were meant to be," she said, hoping her voice was brisk enough to close the subject.

The iron was hot at last, and Tessa turned her attention to the shirts and numbers that had to be put on. She checked her list, put a twelve on a shirt and brought the iron cover down.

"How is your father?"

Tessa watched the timer and when it buzzed she removed the shirt. "He died about three years ago." She put the next shirt on the iron, then carefully laid out the number fourteen on it. "Just three months before he was supposed to retire."

"Too bad."

Shrugging, she pulled the cover down. "I don't know. He was never the same after Mom died. He was always one to laugh and joke around, but after she was gone he hardly smiled. I sometimes think he waited around long enough to make sure we'd all be okay, then he just let go."

She took the shirt out and put another in its place, number fifteen.

"Can I help?" Matt asked.

Tessa shook her head. "I've been in business more than six years now. I've got this down to a real science." As one shirt was bonding, she found the next numerals she'd need. The buzzer would sound, she'd lift up the cover, pull one shirt out and put another in, then close the cover and set up the next. She could do this in her sleep.

Actually, if Matt wanted to know the truth, he was more of a hindrance than a help. She felt naked in her nightie, but she wasn't about to go upstairs and change, thereby letting him know that he still had an effect on her. She'd just grit her teeth and ignore him, just as her mother had told her. Mom had said that all little boys, no matter what their age, had a short attention span. Ignore them and they'd soon go away. Tessa didn't have to look up to see that Matt was still there. She could feel him.

"Got any more to do?" Matt asked as she put the last shirt on the finished pile.

"Nope." She turned the iron off.

"Guess you'll have to go to sleep then."

"In a while." Tessa rolled the pile of shirts and stuffed them into a large clear plastic bag. "I like to wait for the iron to cool."

He nodded. "Good idea."

"You can go to bed though. I'll just read for a while."

Matt shrugged. "I'm not really sleepy. It's probably eleven o'clock in the morning in Egypt right now."

"I see." Tessa pulled over a stool and sat down, struggling in the silence as she watched one wall while Matt watched the opposite. As long as they were trading memories, was this a good time to tell him? Would there ever be a good time?

"It's really too bad about Joe," Matt said. "He was so talented. You name a sport and he could do it."

Tessa nodded slightly in agreement.

"Wasn't he in some kind of tournament when I was home from the service? I don't remember seeing him much."

"It was a Memorial Day baseball tournament," Tessa replied. "In Kalamazoo."

"Yeah, right." He nodded. "I guess if I had waited, we could have gotten together. As I remember, I didn't stay around too long."

Long enough, Tessa thought. *Long enough.*

Matt was shaking his head. "Hurting his knee like that must have really ripped Joe up."

Tessa shrugged. She didn't remember Joe talking about it much. He'd left in August for preseason practice and had come back for the Labor Day weekend wearing an elastic bandage around his knee. He'd come home for good a few weeks later.

"It didn't seem to bother him," Tessa replied. "I mean, not even physically. He played softball, basketball with the guys. He jogged regularly." Tessa stared down at her toes. "He just didn't play football."

She hadn't started to show yet when Joe had come back that weekend, but she'd had no doubt that she was pregnant. She hadn't told her father; he just hadn't seemed able to handle surprises well since Mom had died. Her sisters were too young, and she wasn't sure what her aunt would say.

Since she and Joe used to hang around together, and most of their friends were away at school, they'd spent that weekend together. Then Sunday night, coming back from a movie in South Bend, they'd stopped at the Dairy Queen on Route 31. The tears had started suddenly, and she had blurted it all out.

"Maybe it was one of the ligaments," Matt said. "Could have affected his cutting."

"Yeah, could be," she murmured.

That night was the only time she'd ever seen Joe take charge. He had said they were getting married, and by the beginning of October they had been. Later, everybody had known she was pregnant at the time of the wedding, but it hadn't mattered—just a few winks at Joe and some sly jokes about rushing the starter's pistol. People had laughed, in a friendly kind of way, telling them that the first baby always came quickly; all the others took nine months. The country folks around there were very accepting toward the passions of youth.

"And Joe wasn't the least bit bitter?"

Tessa shook her head.

"Yeah, I can believe that." Smiling Matt slowly shook his head. "Joe seemed to be able to float through life without getting a single bruise. Just like when he carried the ball on the field." He looked up at the far wall. "Sometimes I wished I could do that."

Once they were married, Joe had never taken charge again. Not that he had been a bad man, or lazy. He'd just been Joe.

"I've probably always been a little too intense about life," Matt said.

Her brothers and sisters had loved Joe. He'd always been there for them to talk to, to play a little catch with or to sit around with and watch the traffic zoom by on Route 12. She couldn't have handled them all on her own. And then when Shawn came, Joe had loved him as his own. When Jason, his own son was born, he loved them both equally, playing for hours with them, teaching them how to swim, taking them fishing and playing catch.

"But we are what we are," Matt said. "I guess the secret is accepting that."

She'd accepted Joe wholeheartedly. He hadn't been exciting, but he sure had been good to her. And if he hadn't worried, well, she'd always worried more than average, so things evened out. He'd brought his paycheck straight to her, and she'd managed their books. When she saw things getting too tight, she'd started the sports store. He'd gone along with it. He'd gone along with anything she wanted. All she had to do was tell him what to do.

Matt was looking around the store, the shelves filled with shirts, hats and socks, finished orders sitting on the floor in clear plastic bags. "Hard to picture Joe in business," Matt said. "I don't remember him being much into arithmetic and stuff like that."

Tessa laughed. "That never changed."

He looked at her, his eyes filled with unspoken thoughts, but she wasn't in the mood to decipher anything and turned away. "He was good at meeting people. You'd be surprised how many people remembered him and would drive over just to talk with him." She wet her lips a bit. "It brought business."

"You're quite a lady," he said quietly.

"Joe was quite a man," Tessa said. "He was there when I needed him."

Matt's eyes gentled as he stared at her, seeming to reach out and wrap her in a soft embrace. *Joe was there when I needed him and when your son needed him.* Tessa didn't know what would have become of Shawn if it hadn't been for Joe. Joe had given them a name, and he had given Shawn a father's love.

Matt's big brown eyes, which were usually so tough, softly lingered, and Tessa wondered, just for the moment, whether she should tell Matt about his son. But as she looked, the eyes seemed to grow harder again. He'd had a dream to travel the world and he hadn't satisfied that yet. Besides, Shawn adored Joe. How could she take away her son's idol for a father he might never see again?

She stood up. "I'm going to bed. We'll take care of your car in the morning."

Chapter Four

Good morning," Matt said as he came into the kitchen.

Tessa looked as bright and cheerful as a little bird that had slept all night. She was wearing cutoff jeans and a plain green T-shirt. The boys were in swim trunks and T-shirts. Life hadn't changed much since he was a boy, Matt thought; they'd all worn swim trunks in the summer then. With so many lakes close by, a kid could take a dip whenever he felt like it.

"Want some waffles?" Tessa asked.

"That's okay," he replied. "I don't go in for heavy breakfasts."

Shawn glared at his mother. "You said to make extra," he said.

"Shawn." Tessa's returning glance wasn't any too friendly, either.

"Well, we certainly can't let the batter go to waste," Matt said. Waffles weren't of any consequence compared to the undercurrents he was feeling.

A smile returned to Tessa's face, but her eyes for Shawn were still sharp. "Would you like to make Mr. Anderson some waffles, Shawn?"

Her son matched her innocent smile. "Sure. Glad to."

The kid would be a handful in a year or two, but Tessa seemed up to the challenge. Raising her brothers and sisters had probably toughened her. Still, doing it without a husband wasn't going to be a picnic, Matt thought. Parenting was meant to be a two-person job. He wished there was something he could do to help.

"Jason and I are going downstairs," she said. "We need to unpack some stuff and put it away."

"Okay," Matt said, as he sat down.

"Want me to get someone to take care of your car?" she asked.

"It's a rental," he replied. He didn't want to put more burdens on her. "I'll just call the company."

"I don't think they'll do much about it right away," Tessa said. "Henry might be able to get it going for you."

"Is that the Henry who can fix anything that eats gas?"

Tessa looked at him sharply. "He's a good mechanic. He's Martha's husband."

"Yeah, give him a call."

She dialed without looking up the number and had a murmured conversation with somebody before hanging up. "He wants to get someone started on a brake job," Tessa said. "He'll be by in an hour or so."

"Thanks," Matt said with a nod.

"You can put your dishes in the sink when you're finished." Then Tessa turned toward Shawn. "Come down and help when you're finished here, please."

"Okay," the boy murmured as he kept an eye on the heat indicator on the waffle iron.

The soft slap of bare feet disappeared down the back stairs with Tessa and Jason. Matt and Shawn leaned back in their silence. Satisfied the waffle was done, Shawn opened the iron and placed the toasted batter onto a plate. Matt noticed that the boy moved with the efficiency of those who knew they were capable.

"Syrup's on the table and orange juice is in the refrigerator," Shawn said as he put the plate in front of Matt. "If you want coffee, the cups are there and the instant coffee and the sugar are in the pantry. Use the microwave to heat the water."

"Orange juice is fine," Matt said, reaching for the bottle of syrup.

Shawn nodded and then eyeballed the little batter still left in the cup. "Gonna want more?"

Matt shook his head. "This'll do me."

Nodding, Shawn pulled the plug on the iron, spilled the batter down the disposal and then washed the mixing bowl. He put some spoons and such into the dishwasher, closed the door and fixed Matt with a hard stare. "I'm going down to help Mom now. You don't have to leave your dishes in the sink, even though she said to."

"Righto, Governor," Matt said with a quick salute.

A smile flickered on the boy's lips, but he didn't say anything, going downstairs instead. Matt shook his head as he slowly chewed a mouthful of syrup-soaked waffle. The kid certainly knew how to take charge. Older-child syndrome probably. No doubt he could be a pain without half trying.

After finishing breakfast Matt rinsed his dishes and put them in the dishwasher, then cleaned up the table and the counters. Shawn was probably going to run a white-glove inspection when he came up, and Matt certainly wanted to pass. He might get thrown out on Route 12 if he didn't.

The creaking stairs announced Matt's descent to the store, and Tessa had a smile for him when he entered the store-room.

"Need any help?" he asked.

She shook her head. "No, we've got everything under control. Why don't you wait over by the door? Henry should be by soon."

Matt took a seat on the ledge by the plate-glass window. It was pleasant right now, but he guessed that in another hour or two this southern exposure would be boiling in the July sun.

"Going to be a hot one," Tessa said.

"It'll still be a mild spring day compared to what I left."

"That was Egypt, right?" Shawn asked. He was pulling shirts out of a box and folding them without needing to give the task much of his personal attention.

"Right," Matt replied.

"Probably better than this old town," Shawn said.

Matt stared out at the tree-lined street. Two people were chatting down by the post office, a big brown dog was checking out the area around the porch at the house across the street, looking for a cool spot to spend the day.

"That's hard to say," Matt replied, surprising himself. " 'Better' depends on what you want."

"There's more to see than around here," Shawn said.

The big trees, branches of green dipping over the two-lane road, rolling green lawns, day lilies splashing color around, all blended into a landscape reminiscent of an Impression-ist painting. Not harsh like the desert Matt had left in Egypt.

"Yeah, there's the pyramids, the Sphinx, the Nile River, camels." He nodded. "Lots of new and exciting things for a farm boy from Michigan to see."

There were also the children begging in the streets and families foraging for a living in the garbage dumps on the edge of the cities. He had never gotten used to the extreme poverty that pervaded the Third World countries he'd worked in.

"When I get big, I'm gonna see what's on the other side of the hill." Shawn's determination looked so familiar that it almost hurt. It reminded him of Tessa back in high school. What had happened to her dreams of seeing what was on the other side of the hill?

"That's what your mother used to say when she was a kid," Matt said.

Shawn's quick glance was not quite believing, but Jason just stared at his mother. "Is that true, Mom? Did you really want to leave Edwardsburg?"

Tessa laughed. "Yeah, I guess."

"But why?" Jason asked. "Everybody we know lives here."

She shrugged. "Maybe I just know more people now."

"I like it here."

That was the first time in the several hours that Matt had been there that the younger lad had made a strong statement. It was funny how two kids made out of the same mold could come out so different. Jason was a lot like Joe, while Shawn was like Tessa. Or, at least, like Tessa had been.

What had happened to her? Where was the vibrant, ambitious Tessa he had known in yesteryear?

Although he hated to admit it, there really was no decline in her vibrancy. Her eyes still sparkled. She was still a bit of a smart aleck. And it was obvious she was making a good business of her sports uniform operation.

So what was the difference? Well, for one, she wasn't as dissatisfied as he had remembered her. A sense of irritation pinched at him. Was that the difference between the Tessa of his youth and the Tessa of today? Hell, that just sounded as if today's Tessa had gained some maturity in the past ten years or so. Which was exactly what everyone should do. Especially given the extra responsibilities that come with the years.

His sense of irritation grew with each moment until he could almost feel it overwhelming him. Where did all this leave him? He really had no more responsibilities now than he had then.

Certainly he was managing bigger projects, but that was handling grown men and a few women—people who were taking care of themselves anyway and just needed to be co-ordinated in their work. They weren't really dependent on him. If things didn't work out, they just went on to another job.

A moodiness came to join his irritation. Did that mean he wasn't any more mature now than he had been years ago? Was he still the same headstrong kid of long ago?

He turned to stare at Tessa, who was now counting socks. A mundane task, but she didn't seem dissatisfied. There was a contentment and a sense of control in her eyes. Had she found something that he was still looking for?

Aw, hell. That was a bunch of junk. He was traveling the world and she was stuck in this backwater little burg. She was—

The beep of a horn called for Matt's attention and he eagerly gave it. There was a tow truck outside, with a smiling driver waving out the window. "Looks like Henry," he said. "See you later."

"Hey, Matt," the young mechanic greeted as Matt climbed into the seat of the truck, pushing aside with his foot some tools cluttering the floor. "How you be?"

Matt shook the outstretched hand attached to a bulging-muscled forearm. The driver wore green slacks, a light blue, short-sleeved shirt with Henry embroidered on the left side and a broad smile beneath tousled dark hair.

"Fine," Matt replied.

"You probably don't remember me," the mechanic said. "I was only a freshman when you and Joe graduated. I'm Henry Wade. I married Tessa's sister Martha."

"She teaches in Mishawaka," Matt said, nodding.

Henry nodded as he checked his outside rearview mirror before pulling out onto Route 12. "Yep. And my mom's town treasurer now."

"That's nice." Matt stared straight out the front window, watching the day's early heat waves ripple up off the blacktop before them.

"So what have you been doing with yourself?" Henry asked.

Matt sighed inwardly. How did one condense almost ten years of travel to some of the most exotic places in the world, working on huge building projects, putting up bridges and dams?

"I work for an engineering/construction company out of San Francisco," he said. "They have building projects all over the world."

The rental car came into view and Henry slowed down. "Looks like front-wheel drive," he said.

"Yeah."

Henry made a U-turn, drove past the car and then backed up to it.

"Don't sound like you get much of a chance to stay put."

"Huh?" Matt asked.

"Your job," Henry said. "Sounds like you have to chase halfway around the world and back."

Matt nodded. "That's right, I do."

The mechanic shook his head, then shrugged. "Jobs are hard to come by these days. Man's got to take what he can get."

Warmth flooded Matt's face and he knew it wasn't from the heat of the July sun. He couldn't believe his ears. The guy was making it sound as if Matt had a bad deal. That was crazy! Matt was the envy of lots of people, probably half this old town, if truth were known. He and Tessa couldn't have been the only ones who couldn't wait to get out. Except how many had actually done it?

Henry touched the hood of the car. "Good thing we're getting at it this early," he said. "Another couple of hours in this sun and a body'd be able to fry eggs on the hood."

Matt watched as Henry quickly and efficiently hooked up the disabled vehicle. Once he was back in the cab of the truck, Henry turned on the flickering globe lights on the roof and pulled back onto the road. Traffic was light and they proceeded slowly into town.

"I got me my own garage now." Then Henry laughed shortly. "Well, it's really mine and the bank's. They got the bigger share right now, but I'm my own boss."

"Lot of work running your own business," Matt said.

Henry shook his head. "I work more hours than I thought there was in a day." He laughed again. "But I'm as happy as a hog in slop. Ain't nobody around to boss me."

"Sounds nice," Matt replied.

"That is, nobody except Martha." He turned to wink at Matt. "But she's got a special way of doing it, so it don't bother me hardly at all."

Matt forced a smile to his face.

They went through town and came up to the hill that took them over the railroad tracks. "I got me a good location," Henry said, indicating a service station to the left. "Right on the corner of M-62 and 12. We sell a lot of gasoline in the summer to folks heading for the lakes.''

Matt nodded. Eagle Lake, Diamond Lake. And other lakes, deep and clear. They had just been getting popular when he was growing up in the town. With land being gobbled up the way it was, their popularity couldn't go anywhere but up.

Henry turned into the station. "We'll be another half hour or so on that Escort," he said, pointing to a small red station wagon on the rack. "Once we're done with it, I'll pull yours into the bay and take a look at it. Don't think it should be anything major. Those rental companies keep an eye on their cars.''

Matt nodded.

"If you want to get out to the farm, I'll have Billy drive you. He went for some parts. Should be back any minute now.''

"I don't want to be any trouble—"

"No trouble," Henry assured him. "Then Billy can bring the car out to you. He can haul a cycle behind so you won't even have to bring him back.''

Matt hesitated a moment before accepting. He wasn't doing anything around town, and Tessa sure didn't need his help. Not anymore.

"I doubt there's anything really wrong," Henry said. "Should get it there before noon so you'll be able to go out to lunch.''

"Sounds good," Matt said. "I really appreciate it.''

Henry ignored the praise. "Care for a cold soda?" he asked, as they went inside the station. "Gonna be a hot one.''

Matt was about to say no, when he remembered Tessa's mentioning that the electricity had been turned off at the farm so there was no running water there. And the sweat was already starting to bead on his forehead and around his neck. It would be a good idea to stoke up on liquids. He nodded his head. "Anything but cola would be fine."

After getting two cans from the machine, they went outside and sat on a ledge in the shade, watching the traffic go by on Route 12 and M-62. Someone was mowing a field and a bird in the ditch added his two cents' worth to the song of summer. Getting some work in before the humidity brought on the midday lazies.

"Too bad about Joe," Henry said. "He could have been a great one in the pros."

"Yeah," Matt replied noncommittally.

"You guys keep in touch with each other?"

"Not much." Not at all would have been more correct, but it seemed a shame to say anything negative on such a pleasant summer's day.

Henry took a long drink. "Sure was a surprise when Joe had his heart attack. I mean, he was lean like a racehorse and always running."

"Probably some heart defect," Matt said.

"Yeah."

They watched a semi, pulling a full load of pigs to market, slowly creep over the tracks.

"He was a heck of a nice guy," Henry said.

"Yeah."

"Coached football and baseball. Was made a school counselor the year before he died."

"Oh?"

"Folks sure miss him."

"Yeah, I can see that."

"'Course, Tessa and the boys miss him the most. It's hard to be that young and lose your husband and daddy."

"Yeah."

"Seemed to hit the older boy, Shawn, the most."

"Oh?"

"Yeah, him and Joe did a lot of things together. You know, running and stuff like that."

"I see," Matt said.

"But that's life." Henry stood and brushed off the seat of his pants. "Anyway, he was there when Tessa really needed someone. Lordy, her dad fell apart when her momma died. Wasn't anyone but her to take all those kids in hand. Her and Joe, that is."

Henry walked away toward the repair bays, and Matt leaned back to let clouds of gloom settle over him again. Damn it. He would have been there to help Tessa. All she had had to do was tell him that she was in trouble.

A motorcycle roared by, and he let his eyes follow it until the sound and exhaust fumes disappeared over the far horizon. Her mother's death occurred late that summer. Probably right after he'd started school in Colorado. Would he have come if she'd called for his help? Of course, he told himself angrily.

There was a lull in the traffic, and he listened to some bird in a far field. How could he be so sure? He hadn't left town with the best of feelings. He'd returned after three years in the Army feeling that he was a man. His plans were all made; he'd already been accepted at Colorado.

Uncle George had said he belonged on the farm, that there was no other family and it was his duty to stay on. They'd had a terrible argument. He'd told his uncle that he'd given him and Aunt Hilda his respect for the past nine years and they had no right to hang a millstone like the farm around his neck.

Matt had gone to Tessa that night. Forthright, no-nonsense Tessa. For once she didn't tell him what to do. She just listened. Memories crawled down and shook the dust from themselves. Actually, she'd done more than listen.

She'd . . . she'd taken him in her arms and comforted him, then said he had to follow his heart.

A Jeep pickup truck, with a young towheaded, freckle-faced lad at the wheel, pulled into the service station's drive. That was probably Billy. Matt stood up as Henry walked out.

"We should have your heap out to you before noon," Henry said, leading him out to the truck. "Billy," Henry shouted over the blaring rock music. "Take Matt here out to the Walters' Christmas tree farm."

Billy nodded as Matt climbed in. With screeching tires, they turned onto M-62 and barreled north. The young man appeared more interested in his hard rock music than conversation. Grateful for small favors, Matt leaned back and closed his eyes. He wasn't in the mood for talking.

Yeah, it was a good thing Joe had been around when Tessa needed him. Things had worked out for the best. Still blanketed in gloom, Matt sank farther into his seat.

His mood didn't get any better once they got out to the farm. Weeds filled the yard and the old house looked tired. Billy waited until Matt got out, then was gone in a flash, leaving behind a cloud of dust and strains of rock music hanging in the air.

Matt walked up the steps and pulled out his key ring. The old farmhouse key was still there, like a shadow that had followed him all over the world. He put the key in the lock and opened the door.

The furniture was still there, but covered with dust and cobwebs. Matt shook his head. All a man had to do was turn his back for a moment, and nature was busy reclaiming lost territory. Of course, he hadn't really been a man when he was here before. Just a temporary nuisance. He leaned on the doorway and let silence and depression crowd in on him. Why had he come back? He could have hired people to clean up and sell the place without coming anywhere near it. Nothing had felt right since he'd started back up Route 12 yesterday.

"We all done here, Mom?" Shawn asked.

Tessa blinked and stared at her son.

"I said, are we all done here?"

The question finally penetrated the fog that was her mind. Darn. Since Matt walked into her yard, she'd seemed unable to think clearly. "Yes, Shawn. We are."

"Can me and Jason go swimming?"

The boys were already scrambling upstairs before she had finished nodding. Tessa smiled for a moment and thought of Pleasant Lake, cool water lapping at her feet. Shaking her head, she dropped the smile. The kids were getting to an age when they wanted to do things alone. It wouldn't be long before they were grown and gone. Then she'd be all alone.

Grimacing, she slapped some wrinkles out of a pile of jerseys. Boy, she certainly was a cheerful little camper today.

Dark, brooding eyes floated into her consciousness. She wasn't the only grump on the planet. Matt hadn't been any bundle of joy, either, but then, what did she expect? He was doing something he didn't want to do, in a place where he didn't want to be.

Images of the two of them lying back on that little hill, looking out on Route 12 came to mind. He'd never liked it here, had always wanted to run away. She'd also wanted to travel, but she didn't remember it as running away. More as wanting to see new things. Tessa knew that the sooner Matt finished up his chores in Edwardsburg the happier he'd be. And the more relaxed she'd be.

The phone rang once and Tessa paused, then returned to straightening her merchandise. Either the kids had gotten it on the first ring or no one wanted to talk to them anyway.

"Mom!" Shawn shouted down. "It's Uncle Henry. He wants to talk to you."

Tessa picked up the extension. "Hello, Henry." Tessa forced a strong dose of cheerful into her voice.

"Hi, Tess. Say, ain't no way I can fix Matt's car. The fuel pump is shot. Since it's a rental, I doubt he wants me to go to the trouble of putting in a new one."

"I wouldn't think so," she replied. "Have you talked to him?"

"Can't. He wanted to get out to the farm, so I had Billy drive him out."

"He's out there without transportation?"

"I thought I'd have his car out to him before lunch." Henry paused a moment to answer someone's question. "We're busier than three kittens in a basket of yarn right now. Billy's out putting a new battery in a tractor over at the Fergusons'. I'll send him out for Matt as soon as he gets back."

Poor Matt. He was out on the farm without any food or water. Lack of water would be the worst. There was a stream through the property, but with all the fertilizer and herbicides that drained into it, it wouldn't be a good idea to drink out of it.

"Things are slow around here," Tessa said casually. "I can drive out and get him."

"I imagine he'd appreciate that," Henry replied. "Have him give me a call. I can get the rental company to send another car out or he can use an old truck of mine for free. It's a rusted-out Ford with a stick shift, but it'll get him from here to there and back again."

It wasn't that she really wanted to go out there, but she could hardly let Matt stay stranded. And since it was almost lunchtime, it would only be neighborly to provide him with some sort of lunch. She wasn't jumping at the first chance to see him again, but still, she could feel butterflies of excitement fluttering in her stomach.

"I'll tell him about the car and your truck," Tessa promised, then dropped the phone into the cradle and hurried upstairs. "Boys, we're going out on a picnic."

"Do we have to wear shoes?" Shawn asked.

"Bring some along," Tessa replied. "That's what I'm going to do."

She scurried around packing a picnic hamper. Roast beef sandwiches, potato chips, tomatoes and pickles. Soda for the boys, lemonade for her and Matt and a large container of water for drinking and washing. By the time Tessa was packed and had the car on M-62 headed north, the song in her heart had burst from her lips.

"You sound real happy," Shawn said, suspicion filling each word.

"We haven't been on many picnics this year," Tessa replied.

"Right," Jason agreed.

Shawn kept quiet, but clouds still darkened his brow. Tessa locked her lips and just hummed. She'd always liked picnics, and that was all this was.

The old farm looked deserted as she pulled up. "Matt," Tessa shouted out her window. No answer. She and the boys shouted a couple more times, but there was still no answer. She honked the horn, and he finally appeared from a grove of evergreens behind the old red barn.

"Hey, a rescue team," he said. As he recognized them, a big grin split his face.

"Mom said we had to come," Shawn remarked.

Matt's smile hung on easily and Tessa felt so bubbly that she had no inclination to correct Shawn. She felt like a kid allowed to stay up late to catch fireflies.

"I brought food." Tessa laughed for no reason at all. "We thought we'd have a picnic."

"I'd sure appreciate a drink, ma'am."

Shawn pointed out the large orange container and Matt easily hoisted it above his head and let the water fall into his mouth. The corded muscles in his arms bulged out. Tessa was sure that Matt Anderson could still block for any running back in the country.

"Ah," he said with a sigh as he put the water down. "That tastes so good. I was almost ready to dip my mouth into that old creek in back."

"Hungry?" Tessa asked.

"Sure," he replied. "And I know just the spot. There's a little grove over back of the house. It's got shade from the evergreens and a good breeze. So it'll be cool and hardly any bugs."

"Lead the way," she said.

The grove was only a short distance away and they soon had the picnic lunch spread out. All three of the boys were hungry and silently devoured the food. Once they were down to the ice cream cups Tessa had brought for dessert, Matt leaned back and looked around him.

"The house is run-down," he said, "but the grounds are in good shape."

"The bank hired someone to maintain the trees," she said. "That's money. But no one's put in a crop of seedlings this year. Your uncle started, but no one's followed up."

Matt shrugged and threw his empty cup into the garbage bag Tessa had brought. "I don't think it will affect the sale price any."

He leaned back on one arm and looked down into the little valley below them. Tessa wanted to lie by his side just as she had in the past. Only she wanted to share more than dreams. Once a hunk, always a hunk.

"Want to play some catch?" Jason asked.

"Sure," Matt replied. "I could use a little exercise after that lunch."

Both boys got up and ran toward the car, but slowed down to a stroll before they were halfway back to the house.

Matt chuckled as he watched them. "The old creek's over on that side. I wonder if they'll ever make it back here with the ball."

"Why not?" Tessa was cleaning up the debris from their picnic. "They like sports."

He shrugged as he got up to help her. "Hot day like this, a cool creek is nothing but temptation. It would probably feel good to splash around in it."

Tessa swallowed hard. "I guess."

One hot summer's day so many years back, she and Matt had stumbled across such a stream. They'd splashed each other, drenching themselves to the skin before the laughter had died and they found other uses for their lips. Their passions had run so strong back then; everything had seemed so important, every need so shattering.

"Tess."

She started, looking up to find that Matt was right beside her, that his eyes burned with that same old hunger and that she wanted nothing more than to be held by him.

His arms opened to accept her, to greet her and welcome her back into the mysteries of love. She moved into his embrace, reaching out to hold him closer to her, as they pressed their bodies and their lips together.

The world both stopped and spun ahead. It was better than memories of his touch were, yet tinted with her longings as a woman. Love and needs were more than just kisses and fevered embraces, yet the touch of his lips on hers promised so much more. The insistent blending of spirits said this was more than physical need, more than the raging hormones of youth, but the crying out of one soul mate to another, to the one person in all the world who knew all the secrets in the corners of the heart. Or was it just her own desires, wanting to read so much into a simple kiss?

Chapter Five

A need for air forced Tessa to pull back from Matt's lips, but along with oxygen, she also sucked in a measure of common sense. She and Matt weren't the only two people in the world.

"The boys will be back soon." Her voice came out low and husky as she moved even farther away. The world had seemed so still, so motionless while she was in his arms, but suddenly it came alive again. The birds sang wildly from hidden perches in the trees while the insects hummed harmony. An uneasy shadow fell across her heart, as if the world now knew of her moment's weakness.

Matt reached out his hand to pull her back. "You don't think that cool creek will tempt them?"

"I'm not worried about what might be tempting them." Tessa forced a laugh. "I'm more worried about us." She sat back on her heels, waiting for her heart rate to slow to a mere frantic pace.

Matt let his hand fall to his side, but his eyes still clung to her. Tenderness reigned supreme in his gaze, even as memories of other years and moments in his embrace danced before her eyes.

Tessa cleared her throat and glanced around the clearing. Branches swayed in delicate rhythms, but no breezes seemed to reach her heated cheeks. The air seemed stifling.

"Jason might like to wade in the stream," she said. "But not Shawn. Nothing can distract him from football. He's already decided that he's going to be a great football player. Just like Joe."

A frown creased Matt's forehead momentarily. "He looks a little slow afoot. Jason's the one who moves like Joe. He's got his father's speed and quickness."

Suddenly a pain seized Tessa's throat and she could not reply. Actually, they both had their fathers' build and speed, but that wasn't something she could talk about. She watched a blue jay hop about in the grass under some trees.

Matt got to his feet and stretched. "Shawn's on the big side, though. Probably be able to make it as a lineman."

Just as his father had been. Pain seemed to be everywhere lately, hovering unseen in the air, yet ready to block out the sun at a moment's notice. Tessa turned away quickly and began cleaning up. Crumpled paper napkins, sandwich wrappers and empty pop cans all went into the garbage bag. She set aside the half-empty tin of cookies and the cherries that were left. Oh, God, please don't let Matt come close. Her lips were ready to spill secrets that were never meant to see the light of day, and one more touch from him could wipe out what little resistance she had left.

"Hey, Matt, heads up."

There was a thump of a football hitting Matt's hands, and Tessa breathed a sigh of relief and thanks. The cavalry had arrived.

"Good hands," Shawn said. "For a big guy."

"Shawn." She looked up as she pulled the picnic cooler toward her and fixed her son with a stern glare. "Mr. Anderson is not a playmate of yours and he deserves some respect."

"Sorry."

"Don't worry about it," Matt said. "He's just stating the facts."

Tessa was about to add further words for her son, but Shawn just smiled at her and threw the ball. "Catch, Mom."

It was concentrate on the ball and catch it, or concentrate on Shawn and probably get hit in the face. Tessa chose to catch the ball. From where she was kneeling, she passed it to Matt.

"Nice spiral," he said, his eyes touching her gently.

"I haven't lost a thing," Tessa said.

Matt threw it a little long for Jason, but his speedy legs took him quickly under the ball. Jason threw it to Shawn, who returned it to Matt. By the time Matt lofted a gentle one for Tessa, she had closed up the cooler and taken her place in the square.

Actually, she'd lost a number of things over the years. She threw a high one for Jason while she thought. Her parents. Joe. And Matt. All gone. Sure, Matt was here now, but she knew that was only temporary. All he wanted was to sell the farm, and he probably wouldn't even hang around for that.

"Mom!" Shawn shouted. The ball zipped by her shoulder and she had to run to retrieve it.

"Mom sometimes loses her concentration." Shawn caught a pass from Tessa and threw the ball to Matt. "Dad never did."

That depended on what there was for her to concentrate on, she thought. Football didn't quite make it, not when there was so much else here to distract her. "I'm going to relax for a few minutes," she said and moved out of the game. "Then we're going to have to go."

"See," Shawn said. "No concentration. Dad always said she could have been a great receiver if she practiced."

"I know," Tessa said, laughing. "Just think of all those pro contracts I missed out on."

She sat down in the sun at the far edge of the clearing, where the ground sloped away and acres of Christmas trees were spread out before her. For a few minutes, she watched Matt with the boys as they played their game, increasing the difficulty of the throws so that they had to jump or dive to make a catch. Her boys could play catch for hours and were always trying to press her into service, but it was as Shawn said, she had no concentration. Fifteen or twenty minutes of tossing the ball about and she was ready for some real excitement, like hanging upside down from the cherry tree in the backyard. It was nice to have Matt around. He was a good fill-in.

Turning away to stare out over the trees, Tessa shoved all such thoughts out of her mind. No concentration? She'd show them. She concentrated on the warmth of the sun's rays caressing her face, on the hawk circling high above, watching for the slightest movement under the trees. Every once in a while, she could hear a truck lumbering down the highway, but then it would be gone and peace would return. Just as it would once Matt left again. She stretched out her feet, letting her toes wiggle contentedly in the warm sand like a brood of piglets.

Poor Joe. He'd never understood how her feet had to be free. Every Christmas he'd buy her slippers. She'd wear them for a month or two, then they'd go into the closet with all the others. Tessa decided she'd give them all away to charity. There had to be some women with cold size seven feet who could use them. She forced her attention back to the game of catch.

"I'm going to play halfback in high school," Shawn announced out of the blue. "Just like my father."

Matt paused to give Jason a long, long pass. "Shouldn't concern yourself with what other people have done," Matt said. "I'm sure he'd be proud of you no matter what you did."

That was certainly true. Tessa watched as Jason leaped into the air for the catch, a triumphant glow warming his face as he came down. Joe had loved the boys, both of them equally. He never pushed, yet they seemed to strive and work for his approval, which he was quick to give for even the smallest achievement.

Shawn ran up to receive the pass from Jason. "Yeah, I know," he said, responding to Matt's comment. "But that's the way I feel now."

"It's good to have goals," Matt said. "But don't tie yourself to them with a chain. A man's got to be flexible to make it in this world."

Shawn backed up a few steps and sent the ball soaring into the air for Matt. The boy's look of concentration was mirrored almost exactly on Matt's face. Tessa's heart became a battleground until she closed her eyes to the present, conjuring scenes from the past to look at.

Joe's love for the boys had been returned tenfold, especially from Shawn, since he was the older one. Jason had been more for staying at her side, but Shawn had gone everywhere with Joe—on errands, to football practices and even jogging.

One of the few times Shawn hadn't gone running with Joe had been the day of his heart attack. Shawn had been sick, and both she and Joe had insisted that he stay home. As much as she tried to convince him otherwise, Shawn had blamed himself for his father's death, convinced that if he had been there it would never have happened, or that he would have been able to save Joe. Their minister had tried to help the boy, but at times his guilt would still come rushing back.

Tessa looked at her watch. They really should be going soon. That order of shirts for the Mishawaka soccer all-stars should be coming in right after lunch, and she needed to put names and numbers on them. But the boys had shifted from playing catch to toss-up and tackle, and Matt was the one being tackled, though the boys were having a hard time bringing him down. They were having such fun that she hated to break it up. Little boys needed to roughhouse with a man. *So did big girls,* a little voice told her. Tessa lay back on the grass and squeezed her eyes shut. It seemed almost unfair to Joe's memory for her heart to be so restless.

She owed Joe so much; there was no telling what would have happened to her and Shawn if Joe hadn't come into their lives. Sure, her father would have reconciled himself to her pregnancy, but her family had needed strength back then, something she just didn't have. Jenny, the youngest, had only been five when their mother died and Martha, the second oldest, had been fourteen, with Louise, Dan and Paul in between.

Joe's stepping in had solved everything, had given everyone what they needed, but mostly had saved her from failing her family when they needed her most. The very least she could do was keep Joe's memory alive. True, the project to name that stadium behind the high school for him would help, but she needed to do more. She had to make sure that he lived forever in the memories of his two boys. He had given them so much. And he needed to live in her memory, also. He hadn't exactly shortchanged her.

Tessa stood up. The sooner Matt Anderson cleared up his business and left, the better it would be for everyone. "Boys!" she called. "We have to be going."

There was a flash of disappointment across their faces, even Matt's, it seemed, but they stood up and came to help carry the jugs and portable cooler back to the car.

"I have to put an order together," Tessa explained to Matt, as they trailed along after the boys.

He nodded. "I should get back and do something about getting another car."

"Henry says he has an old pickup he can lend you."

Matt nodded again. "Could you drop me off at the station? I can look into that, then I'll arrange to have the electricity turned on out here. Need that to make the place liveable."

"Sure," Tessa replied.

"And can I mooch off you for another day? I'll be out by tomorrow. Promise."

She hesitated. After all, they were old friends. And what were friends for if not to help each other? But did she really want to spend another night with Matt sleeping in the next room? Wasn't it better to keep her distance from him as much as possible? But though her mind agreed, her mouth forgot how to say the words.

"Sure. No problem," she said. "The sofa's yours as long as you want it."

The boys made race car sounds as Tessa hung a left and pulled into Henry's service station. "You guys can walk any old time you please."

Matt smiled at the growl she'd forced into her voice but had to wipe it off quickly as she turned toward him.

"We're having a plain country dinner," she said. "Chicken fricassee and dumplings, coleslaw and biscuits."

"Can I bring anything?" Matt asked.

"Just yourself," Tessa replied.

"A big package of vanilla ice cream would be nice," Shawn said.

"And a cherry pie," Jason added.

"Boys!" Tessa scolded. "Mr. Anderson is a guest. Besides, we have more than enough of that kind of stuff at home."

"You can never have more than enough dessert, Mom," Shawn replied. "Besides, we don't want him feeling like some old mooch."

"I'm leaving." Matt quickly exited the car, giving them all a wave and smile.

Tessa's face still carried a glare as she pulled out onto M-62. It looked as if Shawn were going to catch a few stern words, but Matt doubted that it would be the first time. And, with the lad approaching his teen years, it certainly wouldn't be the last. He sighed as he walked into the station. Tessa was going to need all her experience from raising her brothers and sisters, and then some.

"Hey," Henry called out as Matt walked in. "Good to see you made it in from the country."

"Yeah, my fairy godmother came out and got me. Fed me lunch, too."

"Sorry about that, sport. I got tied up here."

"No problem. Things worked out fine."

Henry nodded. "Tess tell you that rental needs major surgery?"

"Yeah, new fuel pump."

Henry nodded again. "Seeing as it's a rental, I didn't think you wanted us to do any work on it."

"Nope, they can come out and pick it up. I'll give them a call."

"I got an old pickup you can use," Henry offered. "It ain't a thing of beauty but it'll get you around the block and to church on Sundays."

Matt hesitated. He was sure Henry wouldn't accept money for the use of the pickup, and Matt hated to be, as Shawn put it, an old mooch.

"Old truck ain't doing nothing but sitting in the corner. I'm just keeping it to strip for parts."

"I'm a big boy," Matt said. "I don't need a free ride."

Henry just shrugged. "You see something pretty on one of your travels, why don't you get it for Martha? She likes little things from faraway places."

"It's a deal," Matt replied and they shook hands on it.

"I got to put some new tires on the junker," Henry said with a laugh. "A couple of them are near bald. They pop and flip you in a ditch and you'll be back suing me."

"I'll call the car rental and tell them to get the real junker off your hands."

Henry was gone with a quick wave. It took a few calls for Matt to settle with the rental car company. They said they would send a wrecker out for the disabled car and not charge Matt anything due to the inconvenience. Matt then called the electric company and the telephone company about restoring service at the farm. Because he had no credit rating in the county he would have to come in and leave a deposit for each.

"I need to go to Cassopolis to get electricity and a phone out at the old farm," he told Henry as he came back. "They need a deposit."

"The truck's all ready," Henry said. "The muffler's shot, so it's louder than a Hawaiian sport shirt, but the motor and brakes are good."

The roar of the truck rang in his ears, but it took the hills with no problem and the brakes were indeed good, so Matt felt comfortable with the vehicle. Things had changed in Cassopolis, the county seat, but after he found the offices, his business was quickly taken care of. The electric company would send a man out in the next twenty-four hours, and the telephone would be installed sometime before three tomorrow afternoon.

Everything was settled and it was only four o'clock. Now what should he do? Matt wondered. It certainly was a hot day, but he never had been one to sit in a bar and suck on a cool one. And it wouldn't be right to drop in on Tessa and impose on her for a couple of hours, though that was what he felt like doing most. It was enough that he was mooching dinner and a bed from her.

He leaned against the truck and watched the few people walk slowly along the main street. It was a weekday, but he doubted that the old town was lively even on weekends. Folks wanting to do serious shopping headed for the malls in South Bend or Michigan City. Maybe he should run out to Egypt or India and get that little gift for Martha for the use of Henry's truck.

Suddenly the light bulb went on in his head. Here he was worrying about paying Henry for the use of the truck, when Tessa was giving him a number of meals and a comfortable place to sleep. He didn't have time to rush out to Africa or Asia but he could certainly buy her a gift locally.

But while getting Tessa a gift was the proper thing to do, it was easier said than done. He checked out a dress shop, but realized he didn't know what size she wore or what her tastes were these days. Staring in the windows of some jewelry stores didn't inspire him, either. There was no need to take her any baked goods, because she could make them much better herself and the boys would quickly scarf up something like that by themselves. It was five-thirty by the time he found himself standing in a flower shop, hands in his pockets, glaring all around.

"Can I help you, sir?" a pleasant-faced woman asked him.

"I don't know," he grumbled. "I'm sure she likes plants but she's got flowers all over the yard right now. I mean, the place is filled with day lilies."

"Have you considered cut flowers?"

Matt shook his head. "They'll just die in a few days."

"We have some nice artificial arrangements."

He made a face. Artificial? But Tessa was so...so real. How could he take her an artificial gift? Matt looked at the shelves. A lot of the arrangements were very attractive with silk flowers in handmade baskets.

"How about this cornucopia?" the woman said. "It has such beautiful earth colors."

Matt stared at the orange flowers, mixed in with dry stalks of wheat and brown artificial leaves. It was now five forty-five.

"I'll take it."

The woman wrapped his selection in tissue paper and took his money. "I'm sure she'll love it," she called to Matt as he stepped through the door.

Matt gave her a quick wave. It was pretty, but somehow it wasn't quite right. He put it on the seat of the truck and climbed in. Well, it would do for starters. He'd take some time before he left to find something that really was perfect. Of course, to do that, he'd have to get to know her all over again. It was not an unpleasant prospect.

"You know," Matt said with a sigh. "This is a real kitchen."

Tessa looked up from the pan she was scrubbing to see Matt leaning with his back against the counter, his eyes roaming slowly over the cabinets, the old stove and yellow curtains, faded by a daily dose of sunlight. She wasn't sure what he saw, but she saw the heart of her home, a place where she and the boys gathered with love each day. A place that seemed all too complete now with him here.

"It's a lot prettier now," she said, nodding at the cornucopia basket on top of the refrigerator. "With the present you gave me."

Matt looked up and stared at it. Shawn's words, "what's it good for?" came back to him.

"Don't worry about Shawn," Tessa said, apparently reading his mind. "Boys his age are grumps."

Especially boys who'd lost a father they adored, Matt thought, remembering how he'd felt when his own father died.

"Anyway, the kitchen isn't quite as real as it looks," she said. "I've got to tell you the timer on the stove is broken."

"That's not what I meant." He sounded almost annoyed, and she glanced back over her shoulder at the room, relenting slightly.

"It sure isn't like the kitchens that are written up in the homes sections of the newspapers," she admitted. "You can get faucets now that look like something from outer space, stoves that look like counters and cabinets that have shelves that pull out like drawers."

Matt just shook his head. "Those're all frills. Cosmetics that cover up the fact that most kitchens aren't made for real cooking, like making a Thanksgiving dinner with all the trimmings or canning a bushel of peaches."

"Some people go out for Thanksgiving dinner and buy their peaches already canned," she pointed out.

His eyes came back to hers, alive with some deep, unfathomable fire. "And some people aren't fooled into thinking designer labels are the measure of a person's beauty."

The air in the room seemed to change with the quickness of a summer storm. The comfortable ease of two old friends had been changed into the charged awareness of lovers. The flame in his eyes leaped and flickered.

For a brief moment, her heart cried out with joy at the hunger in his eyes and the tenderness in his smile. She knew, just as she'd always known, what his heart was saying without his mouth having to form the words. Apparently, back here in Edwardsburg, his old fears had returned, his old insecurities and feelings of not belonging. In her arms, peace and security could be found and, for a time, life would seem perfect.

Perfect for her, too, a little voice tried to tell her, but she knew better. She wasn't a young, impressionable girl of eighteen anymore. She turned back to the sink, scrubbing the pot extra hard, as if her feelings and emotions could generate energy. After a moment, she slowed down and sighed inwardly. Her arm was tired, but Matt was still more than just a casual old friend.

"I really appreciate you taking me in like this," Matt said, picking up a serving spoon from the dish drainer to dry.

His fingers brushed her arm in passing, and dreams began to dance and weave in her heart, silly dreams of snowball fights and walks in the spring rains. Year-round dreams that could not include him.

"No problem," she muttered. "And you didn't have to help clean up. The boys could have."

He shrugged and concentrated on drying the spoon. "I don't mind."

"Well, you didn't have to."

The silence got a little heavier. "Did Joe help you with this kind of stuff?"

She didn't answer for a long moment. How far her mind had wandered from Joe, from the determination she'd had just that afternoon to keep his memory alive for the boys.

"I'm sorry," Matt said. "That really isn't any of my business."

Tessa forced a smile to her lips. "Joe would help with anything I asked him to." It wasn't that he hadn't been a helpful person. It was just that he hadn't *seen* things like dirty dishes or dusty shelves.

"Hey, I mean it." Matt took the pot from her hands and let it slide under the soapy dishwater as he turned her to face him. Leaving his hands lightly on her shoulders, he smiled into her eyes. "It isn't any of my business."

"I just didn't want you to think poorly of Joe."

"I know he wasn't perfect," Matt said. "But then none of us are. We've all got good points and some not so good points."

The hands felt so comfortable, and that tempting lure of comfort was more dangerous than the fires of passion. Passion exploded and died down, but comfort, companionship and security, those were needs that lived with her daily, that haunted her nights and brought silent weeping with the early hours of dawn. Tessa wanted nothing more than to lean into the comfort of Matt's arms, his whole body. He bent his head, moved his lips closer to hers. So wonderfully, comfortably closer.

No, a voice screamed inside. She tried pushing herself away, but felt so weak. "Please," she said, barely able to hear herself. "Please."

Much to her relief and disappointment, Matt pulled quickly away. "I'm sorry."

"That's okay," she replied, and turned back to the safety of the sink. She plunged her shaking hands into the water, surprised that it didn't start sizzling. "It takes two to tango."

"I didn't mean to do that."

"I said it was okay." It was easier to talk now that her eyes were on the pot she was cleaning, though her breathing wasn't necessarily any smoother.

"It's just the two of us here," he went on. "My arms were around you." He took a deep breath and exhaled slowly. "For a while I thought it was like the old days, when we could communicate without speaking."

The pot hadn't been so thoroughly cleaned for years, but she put it reluctantly into the drainer. "The old days are long gone," she said softly. "I'm not a single, carefree young kid anymore."

"I'm not sure that anybody is ever really carefree."

Tessa shrugged. "Maybe. But I am a wife and mother—"

He stared at her for the longest moment; she could feel his eyes on her, so sad and sympathetic that she felt like biting her tongue. Joe had been gone almost a year and a half now. So she wasn't a wife and mother anymore. She was just a mother.

"Being a mother hasn't done you any harm," he said. "In fact, I think it's added to your charm, your beauty." He stepped close again as he reached for the pot to dry. "Added to everything that makes you a woman."

Close. He was so close that whiffs of the soap he'd used teased her. It was plain, unscented soap. Nothing special about the smell, just clean. Just Matt. The hair on his arms seemed to tickle her as he reached near her to mop up some water he'd dripped from the pot onto the counter.

All she had to do was lean forward. Lean forward and she would be safe in the fort that was his arms. She'd be warm and safe. There would be no need to shoulder the entire burden of life by herself. She'd have someone to share things with.

Tessa pulled the plug in the sink and moved quickly away. If she stayed that close to him any longer, all the old habits would come back, just as if it was yesterday that she'd lain in his arms and talked about love and dreams. She started washing the counter top almost viciously.

"I was Joe's wife," she said.

"I know. But he's not here anymore," Matt pointed out, his voice so gentle that it hurt. "Through no fault of his or yours, he's not going to be around at all."

A little spot, right near the corner, required her special attention and it got it. She scrubbed and wiped, scrubbed and wiped.

She knew Joe wasn't coming back; that wasn't the reason why she didn't want to get involved with Matt. It was the debt she still owed Joe, but how did she explain that to Matt? Sure, the three of them had grown up together, but Matt had traveled all around the world. He was much more sophisticated now than when he was a part of their simple, straightforward little world. No, he wouldn't understand at all that sometimes a person had to put aside their own needs and wishes for some intangible rightness.

Matt had wanted to leave and he had. Joe had stayed and made Shawn his own son. He had loved and scolded and hugged her brothers and sisters. He had given to their community: counseling kids, coaching teams, getting things started for the new stadium.

No, someone who'd left to chase his own dreams wouldn't understand a man like Joe at all. He wouldn't understand being faithful to memories, the building of traditions. Traditions had been one of the things Matt had hated when he was forced to live here. Falling into Matt's arms wouldn't buy her any more than it had the last time, if she was lucky. This time Joe wouldn't be around to bail her out.

"Joe was younger than most folks when he died," Tessa said. "So it's only right that we keep his memory alive a little longer than normal."

Matt smiled, but Tessa wasn't sure that she liked what she saw in the smile. "Do you think he would have wanted this type of prolonged mourning?"

Matt had stepped back to the other side of the kitchen, and Tessa began to rinse the sink. Same old Matt, smart mouth and all. She squeezed out the dishcloth and hung it over the middle of the double sink.

"If you share our values, you understand," she said. "If you don't, you won't. Joe gave so much to everyone here in town that we have to do something in return."

"Everybody adored the guy when he was alive. Wasn't that enough?"

"We're naming the new high school stadium for him," she said. "He started the project, getting the plans drawn up and the bond issue passed. So after he died, the town decided to name it after him."

"That's great, but what does that have to do with us being friends?" he asked. "If you're still in love with him, I can respect that. But every time I come near you, I feel like you've put up a wall to keep me out. You were the only thing of value in this town for me years ago, yet now you seem to have gone over to the other side."

Some fuse deep inside her seemed to blow, and she spun to face him. "There is no other side, Matt. There never was except in the way you saw things. You left, went looking for your life elsewhere while some of us stayed here. You can't come back now, after all these years, and tell us what we're doing wrong."

"I didn't mean to," he insisted, reaching out for her hand, but she folded her arms over her chest. "I just hate to feel like I'm still on the outside."

"Maybe you are because you choose to be," she said. "For the whole time you lived here and for the past fourteen years, it's been your choice."

She knew that Matt's eyes were locked on her, but she turned slowly and went outside without looking back. It was a nice evening. The kind for taking a little walk over to Pleasant Lake with the boys.

Chapter Six

Damn." Matt glared at the battery-powered razor as it sputtered and gave off sick little groans instead of the powerful hum of a well-charged appliance. Although he hadn't been in the States for a while, he'd known that he needed a sixty-cycle adapter, but he hadn't gotten around to getting one.

He put the electric razor back in its case and dug a disposable razor and shaving cream out of his suitcase. Grimacing at his image in the mirror, he wet his face, then spread on the thick cream. He couldn't remember the last time he'd used a blade on his face. There would be blood flowing in the streets by the time he finished shaving. Not that Tessa would care after the cold treatment he'd gotten yesterday evening.

He'd walked down to the lake with her and the boys, and while the kids were wading in the water, he'd tried to talk to Tessa. He didn't want her to think that he had expected to take up where they left off fourteen years ago, that he had thought the closeness they had before would have lasted through so many years of silence. But then, neither had he expected that their friendship wouldn't have weathered the storm.

He'd felt as if he were talking to a wall. Oh, it wasn't that she'd ignored him. No, she'd been very pleasant and talked about the weather, the prospects for a good corn crop this summer and the repaving project for M-62 that was due to start next month. It was as if he were a stranger.

And maybe that was how she saw him, Matt realized with a sigh. After scraping his face thoroughly, he rinsed off the razor and checked himself out in the mirror. Not too bad, he told himself.

Tessa and the boys were already cleaning up after their breakfast when he walked into the kitchen. Country folks got up with the roosters, even during summer vacation. He smiled to himself. Especially during summer vacation, when there were more interesting things to do besides going to school.

"Good morning, all," he said. "Anybody have anything exciting on the agenda for today?"

"I'm washing clothes later today," Tessa replied. "That's about as exciting as my day gets." That sounded to Matt as if he was still in the doghouse.

"We're going swimming this afternoon," Shawn said as he put his breakfast dishes in the dishwasher. He frowned as he stared at Matt's neck. "You just learning how to shave?"

"No, I'm not just learning how to shave, smarty," Matt said. "I normally use an electric razor, so my skin isn't sensitized to a blade."

The boy continued staring and then turned away with a grunt. "Sure looks a mess," he said as Jason followed him out of the room.

Matt glared at the doorway through which the kids had disappeared. "Methinks the lad has a smart mouth," he muttered.

"He's not the only smart mouth that Edwardsburg's produced," Tessa pointed out as she started taking dishes out of a cabinet.

"Hey, can't blame me for that kid," Matt said. "I didn't have anything to do with him."

Tessa slammed the cabinet shut. Her back was to him, but he could see her shoulders trembling. Damn, everything he said lately was wrong.

"I'm sorry," Matt said. "I don't mean to imply that he's a bad kid. He's just lively, and sometimes us old guys can't cope with too much of that."

Tessa moved over to the stove, her face averted. "We had French toast for breakfast. Would you like some?"

"I can take care of myself," he assured her.

"You're our guest," Tessa said. "And it may be old-fashioned, but us small town folks take care of our guests."

He glared for a moment at her stiff, tense back.

"French toast would be fine," he murmured. "Thank you."

Tessa busied herself with his breakfast without replying. Since her back was still to him, Matt felt free to closely check her out. Obviously the forecast was for a hot day, because she'd pinned her hair up off her neck and had on a pair of light green shorts with a white halter top. The tanned skin, enclosing smooth womanly muscles, contrasted nicely with the light-hued outfit. She was wearing her "country sandals": callused bare feet, the soles darkened from wear.

"Would you like sugar or—"

She turned around to catch him in a full-blown stare. Her face tightened and grew flushed. Matt felt his own cheeks warm with embarrassment.

"I'll just have it plain, thank you."

Staring down at the table, Matt avoided looking at Tessa. Instead, he immediately began attacking the hapless pieces of egg-soaked bread on his plate. Damn. Joe wasn't around anymore, so it certainly wasn't as if they were playing around behind his back. But now she had him feeling guilty.

"Would you like some coffee, milk or orange juice?"

Her voice had softened considerably, but Matt was still carrying his set of grumps. "Anything you have is fine."

"I have all of them. Which do you want?"

"Anything is fine. I don't care."

"Well, since I'm not thirsty I don't care, either."

Matt looked and they exchanged glares for a moment. Then both burst out laughing.

"We still do argue well," she said. "And all these years without any practice."

"When you're good, you're good." This time they exchanged rueful smiles. "A cool glass of orange juice would be a good way to start off the hot day that we're sure to have," Matt said.

Still smiling, but silent, Tessa poured him a large glass of juice, sitting down across from him after she brought it over. The drink's cool tartness was a good contrast to the French toast. They sat in silence as he ate.

"Would you like anything else?" she asked, as he drained his glass.

Matt shook his head and looked out the window at Route 12, his path out of Edwardsburg.

"Did you get very far on that accounting degree?" he asked.

Smiling, she shook her head. "One course cured me."

"I thought you were pretty good with numbers when we were in high school," he said.

Tessa shrugged. "People change. I found that I like living things. Plants are my favorite."

"I guess you should have become a horticulturist then."

"I did," she replied. "I got my degree from Western Michigan. Took me a while, but Joe encouraged me and was always willing to help out."

Just what the area needed, another Saint Joe. As if the area already didn't have a county, a city, hospitals, schools and streets named after the holy carpenter.

"If you spent all that time getting a degree, you should be working in your field."

"I will," she said.

"I imagine you could run a nursery, be a landscape architect."

"I'm sort of working with plants now."

"Sort of?"

She got up quickly and went out of the room, returning with a handful of paper roses. "I'm making these for the homecoming celebration," she said, holding them out to him.

Even his quick glance told him they were well made, things of beauty, but he just grunted. They weren't exactly what he'd had in mind.

"Joe's last game was in the Rose Bowl so we're using the rose theme for the whole homecoming weekend." She paused, then explained, "That's the weekend we're officially naming the new high school stadium after him."

Matt could feel a sourness swirl around in his stomach. "If you sold your business, I bet you'd get enough to buy into a nursery. Or set up a small one of your own."

Her face immediately turned hard. "Boy, you have a one-track mind, don't you?"

"What?" he protested. "I'm just offering some suggestions."

"I've taken care of my life quite well," she snapped. "Without any help from you, I might add."

"What are you so touchy about? You're the one who said you spent so much time getting a degree in horticulture. All I'm saying is you should use it."

"And all I'm saying is mind your own business. I've run the past fourteen years of my life without any help from you and I can take care of the rest of it the same way."

She stomped off back toward her room. Matt stared out the window and fought to control his growing irritation. Tessa had always been hot tempered, but now she was a grump as well. Probably bored to death with this little town. Still, that wasn't any reason to take it out on him.

The phone rang, but it went silent when he glanced at it. Someone else had picked it up, no doubt.

A moment later Tessa was in the doorway. "That was Henry. He's put the new tire on the truck. Said you can come down any time and pick it up."

Although he knew he shouldn't, Matt found himself staring at Tessa, framed like some masterpiece in the doorway. She was so beautiful. She didn't need designer clothes, fancy hairstyles or hours in front of a makeup mirror. There was a beauty that shone through everything she did, a grace and serenity that made him want to hold her and never let her go.

He quickly jumped to his feet, pushing aside such annoying weaknesses. "Thank you. I'll go get the truck now." The words came out curtly, but he had things to do.

"I can give you a ride."

"No, thanks. A walk would do me good."

Stomping down the stairs, he moved quickly out to the road. The sun was already baking the sidewalk, and Tessa's orange juice was beading on his forehead. That woman had better leave the past behind, he fumed, or the world would leave her behind, far behind.

Clenching his teeth, Matt picked up his pace, ignoring the heat. Hell. As she said, it was her life and she could live it any way she wanted. Maybe staying in Edwardsburg was a good idea for her, he thought. The whole damn town was stuck in some sort of time warp.

"How come you're mad at Matt?"

Tessa spun around to look into her boys' wide, staring eyes. They must have come in in time to see Matt stalking out. Or, more likely, they'd been sitting out on the steps all this time and listening.

"I'm not mad at Matt, Jason." She forced a smile to her face.

"Is he mad at you?" Shawn asked.

"No." She didn't bother keeping the smile on. It was too damn much work holding it up, so she began to clear Matt's breakfast dishes away.

"They're mad at each other," said Jason, ever the conciliator.

"Nobody's mad at anybody." The twin stares told her that her voice had come out a tad more than loud. She cleared her throat, put the dishes into the dishwasher and turned to face them with a smile. "Aunt Martha's coming over in a few minutes. I have to go to a meeting at the old school. You boys mind her now."

They stared for a moment. "Can we go to the park?" Shawn asked.

"Ask Aunt Martha when she gets here."

They tried to hide their smiles, but didn't quite succeed. Tessa knew that her sister was easy on the boys, but then, why have a favorite aunt if she didn't spoil you? She was willing to bet dollars to doughnuts that some time that afternoon they'd be over to the ice cream parlor in the minimall across the tracks.

Footsteps came up the stairs. Tessa's heart skipped a beat, though she recognized them as her sister's. It was just as well. She wasn't ready to face Matt again anyway. She wiped off the table as Martha came into the room.

"Hi, guys," the woman said.

"Hi, Aunt Martha," the boys chorused.

"Can we go to the park?" Jason asked.

"Sure," Martha replied. "Soon as I chat with your mom. Wait out in the yard for me." Ever obedient with the park in the near future, the boys raced down the stairs, sounding like a herd of elephants.

"Don't stuff them full of ice cream," Tessa said.

Her sister waved dismissively. "They run calories off quicker than you can blink."

Tessa grimaced.

"Anyway, I don't want to talk about your dirty-faced little kids," Martha said, laughing. "Tell me about him."

"Him? Who are you talking about?"

Martha just hooted as she sank into a kitchen chair, her eyes eager for all the juicy details. "Nice try, Sis. I know he's here. Everyone in town knows that Matt Anderson is back and he's staying with you."

Suddenly Tessa could feel her cheeks blazing with heat. Oh, Lord! What had she done? She had just been trying to be neighborly.

"His car broke down," Tessa said. Rather than face her sister, she checked the houseplants lined up on the kitchen windowsill. She slid a finger under the leaves of each plant, but none of them needed attention. "Over by the old Chicago Road School."

"Uh-huh."

"The boys were playing there." She found a withered leaf and tugged it off. "It started to rain and they brought him home."

"That's nice," Martha said.

"I thought it was the Christian thing to do," Tessa said with a smile.

"The reverend will be pleased with the fine example you're giving the community."

Tessa's smile turned into a glare, but that was only letting her sister get to her. She gave each plant a quarter turn to the right.

"Is he as handsome as he always was?" Martha asked. "I asked Henry, but all he said was Matt hadn't changed much."

"That's right." Tessa wrapped her words in dignity. "He's in his mid-thirties, so one wouldn't expect him to have changed that much yet."

"He's still a hunk, right?"

Her plants taken care off, Tessa washed her hands and dried them before answering. Then she decided that maybe no answer would be most dignified. She gathered up her notes for the meeting from the corner of the counter and slipped them into a file folder. Besides, what could she say? Oh, yes, he's as much of a hunk as ever. Actually, he was more of a hunk now. He'd been good-looking in high school, but a man didn't start to fill out into true hunkiness until his mid-to-late twenties. However, that was probably a comment best left unsaid. Martha had never been a very mature person and she was bound to misinterpret it.

Besides, Matt's real attraction lay not in his appearance but in his understanding—how he knew what was in her heart and her mind, and how he made her feel special. None of which she needed in the least, she assured herself as she slid her feet into sandals and picked up her purse.

"I'll be at the homecoming celebration meeting," Tessa said. "I should be home by lunchtime. If not, I'll call."

"How did you manage to get him to stay two nights in a row?" Martha asked. "Hog-tie him and sit on him?"

Tessa picked up her folder. She'd better leave quickly; Martha's infantile attitude was starting to get to her. "I've been very busy the past few days, what with the homecoming and my regular business and all."

"I'll bet."

Tessa glared. One punch. One punch and her sister would be out like a light, but then Tessa would have to find someone else to stay with the boys. Discretion was the better part of valor.

"The phone number is on the bulletin board, if you need me," she told Martha and hurried down the stairs.

The boys were tossing a football around in the yard and shouted goodbyes to her as she went around front. She paused, trying to decide if she should drive over to the old school, but then shook her head. It was early and she had plenty of time. Besides, she liked warm weather and the walk would do her good.

She walked through the longish grass alongside Route 12, letting the tall blades brush against her legs. It felt good to be soaking up the summer air. There was something so constant about nature. Inside a house you could forget what was important, get blinded by all sorts of new styles, but outside it was just the sun, the wind and the grass.

This was where she belonged; this was who she was. Matt had no right to come back and try to change her. He was like the starlings that flew through town each fall, stopping for a few days to feed and rest before flying on. She was more like the sparrows, here today, tomorrow and always. She could enjoy his company, listen to his stories but remain true to herself.

* * *

"Hi, all," Tessa greeted her friends as she stepped into the cool meeting room. The sun was getting hotter, but the windows were open and an overhead fan was whirring pleasantly in the old classroom.

"Hi, Tessa," they chorused.

"I hope I'm not late," she said as she sat down. "It's such a beautiful day I decided to walk over."

They sat there, still smiling at her. Tessa had to strain a bit to keep her smile on. Friendliness was good, but hadn't they ever heard that too much of a good thing could be bad?

Peggy Smith turned to Claire Daniels and said, "Did you hear the news?"

"What news?" Claire asked, in what Tessa thought was a rather exaggerated show of interest.

"Matt Anderson's in town," Peggy said in a stage whisper.

"No!" the group chorused. Several pairs of smiling eyes turned toward Tessa.

"Did you know that, Tessa?" Peggy asked.

Tessa's cheeks grew warmer as giggles filled the room. She should have driven over, especially on such a hot day. Obviously, she'd gotten overheated from her walk. "Yes." She poured herself a glass of ice water and drank. "He stayed with us." As if they hadn't known.

She refilled the glass and drank more water. "With the boys and me," she added.

The glittering eyes just stared at her. Tessa had never realized before that joy could be such a mean thing.

"He came on Sunday evening," she went on, made uncomfortable by the extended silence.

Several heads nodded.

"You all remember how it stormed. Thunder and lightning."

"Terrible." They shook their heads.

"Well, by the time I got the clothes off the line, they were soaked."

Her companions blinked.

"Matt got all soaked, too."

"Poor fella," someone murmured. Tessa looked suspiciously around the table, but everyone just stared back, eyes full of concern.

"His clothes had to be dried," Tessa said. "And seeing as it was nearly dinnertime, I asked him to stay."

They just stared.

"Seeing as it was Sunday, it was the Christian thing to do," she snapped, sending a glare around the room.

"Absolutely," they agreed.

"He was going to stay at the farm after that, but his rental car couldn't be fixed, and there was no electricity at the farm."

They nodded.

"Henry was going to let him use some old beat-up pickup of his, but he had to put on a new tire."

They shook their heads in commiseration.

"The electricity should be turned on today," Tessa said. "He'll stay out there tonight."

There was no reply. Great, that subject was closed and done with. She pulled out her notes. "Harriet, have you got the wood lined up for the bonfire?"

Harriet stared for a long moment at Tessa, a smile playing on her lips. "Is he still as cute as he was in high school?"

Tessa clenched her jaw. Were they going to have a meeting or were they going to talk about Matt Anderson all morning? Besides, there were more important qualities one looked for in a man than his appearance.

"That man was made to be a stud."

Everyone turned to stare at the woman who'd spoken. It was Mabel Crenshaw, who'd just celebrated her eighty-first birthday last month.

"He just travels all over the world, Mrs. Crenshaw," Tessa said quietly.

"Had me a dog like that once," the woman said. "Traveled all over Cass County."

Tessa smiled. "That's nice."

"Didn't hurt his studding any."

It was really getting quite warm in the room. Tessa looked around at all those disgustingly happy faces and decided she'd better make some things clear right here and now.

"Matt was able to share a lot of stories about Joe with the boys," she informed them all. "I can't tell you how much it meant to them."

"Must have been nice for all of you," Claire said.

"It was," Tessa agreed with a nod, glad that someone finally understood.

"Nice to have someone around with big, strong muscles to open jars," Clair went on to a round of giggling.

"Or somebody tall to reach those dishes in the back of the cabinet."

"Who cares about tall, as long as he's strong enough to catch me when I try to reach them and fall."

Tessa finally let out an impatient sigh. Just because she and Matt had been an item years ago in high school didn't mean they were still one. "We'd better get on with business. I don't know about anyone else, but I have other things that need doing," she said briskly, though it only made the smiles grow broader and her cheeks grow hotter. "Barb, can we have a report from the parade committee, please?"

Barb Zabel started reading her report, and Tessa fought to pay attention. It wasn't a big deal to get the electricity turned on. She was sure Matt would be staying out at the farm from now on, which was well and good. She didn't need the distraction of his constant presence.

Regardless of all the teasing, it wasn't his muscles, his height or his strength that were proving to be the worst distraction. No, it was just his presence. The knowledge that there was someone to talk to, to lean on, to share the days and nights with. That was the hardest thing to fight, and the longer he stayed with her, the worse the temptation to lean on him grew.

Barb stopped talking and put her papers down, so she must have finished. "That's great, Barb," Tessa said. "How about if we go on to the bonfire? Harriet, how's it going?"

Tessa tried concentrating, she really did, but her mind wandered back home. That old sofa was sure going to look lonely tonight, and it wouldn't be the only thing. The boys would miss hearing Matt's stories at dinner, and she'd miss the way his eyes smiled when she came into a room.

Rats. The boys had heard a million stories about Joe already, they didn't need any more. She was getting a little old to care about smiles of appreciation, and as for the sofa, if that looked too lonely, she'd offer it to Harriet for the bonfire.

Matt got up from the hammock and stretched. He'd forgotten how lethargic sitting in the sun made one. Running his fingers through his hair, he glanced around Tessa's yard. If he didn't find something to do, she'd come home from wherever it was she went to find him sacked out here.

He walked over to her garden and yanked at a weed only to have a tiny radish plant come out. Swell, first he criticized her life, then ruined her garden. He replanted the little plant, patting the dirt down around it.

Why did it bug him that she was devoting her life to Joe's memory? He knew lots of people who devoted themselves to different causes, from healing wounded wildlife to collecting lunchboxes. There was certainly nothing wrong with honoring the memory of a good man. So why did it annoy him so?

Matt found a genuine weed and pulled it out. Maybe because it seemed like such a waste. Tessa had had dreams and plans for her life when he'd known her back in high school. Now she seemed so willing to let those dreams falter.

"Matt?"

He spun at the sound of Tessa's voice and found her frowning at him from the corner of the house. He got to his feet, brushing off his knees. "I was just doing a little weeding," he said.

She came closer, frowning down at the garden. "The boys are supposed to take care of it."

Now did she think he was criticizing how the boys did their chores? "Hey, I was just looking for something to do to pass some time," he said quickly. "I got the pickup truck from Henry and was ready to head out to the farm once I got my stuff."

"The house isn't locked, is it?"

"No." He stood looking down at her, wanting nothing more than to wake up this Sleeping Beauty to the fact that life was for the living. Would a kiss be enough to do it, though, and shouldn't it be from her Prince Charming? He'd thought he was that once, but he'd been wrong. He looked away, toward the sound of a truck going down Route 12.

"No, the house isn't locked," he repeated. "I got my suitcase already. I just wanted to stay around to thank you for taking me in."

"It was no trouble."

He brought his eyes back to hers. "And to apologize for this morning. I didn't really mean to be telling you what to do with your life."

This time Tessa was the one who looked away. "That's all right. I flew off the handle, too."

"It's just that it seems—"

"Let's not start it all over again," she said quickly, her hand on his arm.

Her touch seemed to scorch, to awaken smoldering embers that should have died long ago. He reached down, covering her hand with his, and she didn't pull away.

"Tessa," he said, his voice hardly more than a whisper.

She came into his arms as if she belonged there, as if she were coming home. He took her lips in a rough kiss, and all of a sudden he was the one who was home. All the dark days of loneliness, all the long years of wondering, were forgotten. There was warmth and light and peace in Tessa's arms, plus a surety of what was right and good in the world.

He wanted to go on touching her forever. He wanted to stay here in her arms where the sun would always smile on him and he'd never feel alone. But then she was pulling away from him, taking the sunshine and the soft summer breezes with her. She pushed back her hair nervously, squinting up at him as the sun caressed her face.

"I don't want all this to start again," she said.

"All what?"

"You know what I mean. Us. Being friends is fine, but I can't handle any more."

"Friends is all I want," he said, though his heart wasn't sure it agreed.

There was a moment of silence, stretching out so that even the birds in the trees seemed to hush. He saw the past in Tessa's eyes, both the joy they used to share in each other's arms, and the other past, the time they were apart, which had left a sadness in her eyes and a shadow on his heart.

"Well, I guess I'd better get my stuff."

"I guess."

He turned and walked toward the house, where his suitcase sat on the steps.

"The electricity get turned on?"

He shrugged. "They promised it within twenty-four hours. That'll be up soon." He picked up his case and turned back to her. "I'm sure I'll see you around."

"You'd better. I don't want you leaving without saying goodbye."

"No chance of that. Maybe I can take you and the boys out to dinner one night to repay your hospitality."

"We'd like that."

"Right." This was an inane conversation. "Well, thanks again."

She smiled, perhaps deciding that silence was the best response, and there was nothing for him to do but leave. The sun seemed unbearably hot and stifling, and Henry's pickup was an oven. Hell, he thought, he'd be glad to be done with this place for good.

Chapter Seven

"There's Matt," Shawn said, pointing toward the post office.

Tessa had already seen Matt standing there talking to Bobby Owens, the realtor, so she didn't bother looking. Actually, her heart had seen him before her eyes had, but that seemed a point too petty to argue. She just put the rest of the groceries into the car.

"We've seen Matt around a lot of times since he got here," Shawn said.

"Edwardsburg's a small town," Tessa said, forcing a small laugh into her voice. "And we're not playing hide-and-seek, so you would expect to see people around a lot."

"How come Matt doesn't come around our house anymore?" Jason asked.

"He's only been in town a week, honey," Tessa replied. "And he's been busy getting the farmhouse cleaned before he can sell it."

Matt and Bobby Owens went into the town hall, and Tessa gave Shawn the cart to push back to the store. She wasn't really avoiding Matt. She just had a lot to do; that was why she had turned down his dinner invitation the last two times he'd called. She'd been working on the paper roses for the dance—Joe's dance—and didn't want to fall behind the schedule she'd set for herself.

Then the days were filled with the boys and work. She'd finished the soccer all-star uniforms last week, and Bruce was picking up a new order today—softball all-stars. She'd spend the rest of the month working on Edwardsburg High letter jackets. Then, early in August, she'd start getting orders from the schools in South Bend for their soccer season. Before she knew it, it would be fall and winter, basketball and volleyball seasons. She just didn't have time for Matt Anderson. She'd made him feel welcome when he came. Now it was up to someone else to keep him occupied.

"Why does Matt want to sell the farm?" Jason asked as he climbed into the back seat of the car. "Doesn't he like it?"

"He works all over the world," Tessa reminded him. "He would never be here to enjoy it. It's better to sell it to someone who can take care of it."

"I like it," Jason said. "I think it would be cool to live out there."

She smiled at her younger son. Maybe someday they could have a country place of their own. The uniform business was doing well. They could probably get a good price for the store. Matt thought they could.

Tessa gritted her teeth. Damn, damn, damn. Everywhere she turned, that man was pushing himself into her life. Trying to get her to move out of the ways that were comfortable and right for her family. But was there only one right way? And wasn't comfortable another word for rut?

"Hurry up," she said to Shawn, who was meandering back toward the car. "I have a lot to do this afternoon, and Mr. Moran is going to be over soon to pick up his order."

For once Shawn didn't give her an argument. Guilt began to gnaw at Tessa. There was no need to bite his head off. It wasn't Shawn's fault that she was mooning around like a lovesick teenager. She was old enough now to handle distractions. If one counted maturity by years, she certainly qualified. On the other hand—on the other hand, she'd better get back home and get to work.

And work she did, with a vengeance. She made the boys chili dogs for lunch, one of their favorite meals; then, while they were outside playing, she whipped up a batch of supergooey chocolate brownies. Afterward she tried to catch up on her bookkeeping. Her personal business checking accounts needed balancing, but the task turned out to be beyond her concentration. It was too nice a day to do paperwork.

What she needed was physical work, she decided. Her body was just too full of energy, and she needed physical exertion to burn it off. Tessa marched downstairs, her mind filled with useful tasks to be done in the store.

After filling a bucket with water, she attacked the shelves. She removed merchandise and then ran a damp rag over the empty space. By the time she reached the top of a shelf unit the bottom was dry, so she could restack the merchandise. Cleaning the shelves took most of the afternoon, generating a satisfactorily comfortable sweat and a relaxed tiredness.

The job did little to keep her mind off Matt, though. The man was haunting her thoughts; she wished he had never come back. Oh, really? a little voice mocked. She changed the water in her bucket and tackled the shelves on the other side of the room.

Matt didn't understand. The store and the house were one; she couldn't sell one and not the other. Suppose she sold off the uniform business; what would she put in the space downstairs? A floral shop? Edwardsburg wasn't big enough to support more than one florist; the one they already had was barely making it. What else had Matt suggested? A landscape architect? Country folk didn't need an architect to design their yards.

Besides, this whole place was a link to her life with Joe. They had bought the house once her youngest sister Jenny was in junior high and she and Joe could move out of her family's home. It had been run-down, but Joe had worked hard to fix it up.

By the time Bruce Moran arrived for his softball shirts late that afternoon, Tessa was thoroughly irritated with herself, but determined to remain in control.

"Hi, Bruce."

"Hi, Tess. Came for my order."

"Right here." She hefted the large clear plastic bag onto the counter.

Suddenly there was a sinking feeling in the pit of her stomach. Bruce was staring at the package, a bewildered look on his face.

"I don't know, Tess," he began slowly, as he opened his ever-present, brown file envelope. He pulled out a sheaf of papers and began thumbing through them.

"Is something wrong?" she asked.

He shook his head. "I was sure that I said light blue." He continued searching his records.

Oh, great. She glared at the pile of shirts, but there was no way that the navy blue would lighten any. Tessa pulled out her own records.

"You're right," she said with a sigh. The word light was written in just before a little above the color designation. Bruce must have decided at the last minute. But that didn't really matter because her records said light blue. She'd screwed up.

She could sell the shirts at her annual clearance sale, but cutting her losses wasn't the major problem. Bruce had been in a hurry for the shirts, and now time was even tighter.

"I have light blue in stock," she said. "I'll redo the shirts."

"I'm sorry to push you like this," Bruce said. "But I really need them tomorrow. That team's first game is the day after."

"I'm the one who should apologize," Tessa said. "I screwed up. You didn't."

"Can I get the shirts tomorrow?"

"First thing," Tessa promised him. "Come by as early as you like."

"Would seven o'clock be okay? I have to be at work by eight."

"I'll deliver them tonight if you like."

"No, we have to go out and won't be back until late. Seven is no problem for me."

"Fine, seven it is."

After trading more apologies with her, Bruce left. Tessa waited until she saw his car turn onto Route 12, then she slammed her fist on the counter. "Damn you, Matt Anderson. You're nothing but trouble." Since he walked back into her life, her mind had been unable to think of anything but him.

She threw the rejected shirts into a corner and began taking out light blue ones, checking them against the size list on her order. "All I need is to not have enough," she muttered to herself.

Lucky for Matt, she had the required number in the right sizes. This was going to be a long night. The team name and logo had to be silk-screened on the front, then a number and player name heat-applied to the back. She'd do better with the kids out of her hair. She went to the phone and called her sister, letting the telephone ring longer than usual. On a nice day like this, she was probably outside.

"Hello," Martha finally answered.

"I need to plant my kids with you tonight," Tessa said. "And I need them fed. I'll send a dish of brownies with them."

"Oh?"

Tessa didn't like the tone of her sister's voice, but beggars couldn't be choosers, so she held her tongue.

"Got something going tonight?" Martha asked.

"I have a big order that I have to finish by seven tomorrow morning."

"Oh."

The tone was filled with disappointment, and Tessa stuck her tongue out at the receiver. She knew she was the eldest, but she couldn't carry a load of maturity around every minute of the day.

"That's too bad," Martha said.

"It pays the mortgage."

"How is Matt doing?"

"Fine, I presume," Tess replied.

"I see him around a lot."

"I'm sure everyone does."

Martha giggled. "He sure is some hunk."

Tessa sighed. Almost thirty years old and her sister still acted like a teenager. "The boys will be over in a half hour."

After hanging up, Tessa called her sons in. "I have to work late tonight," she said. "Aunt Martha said you guys can come over and spend the night with her."

"Won't you need any help?" Jason asked.

"Yeah," Shawn said. "We can stay."

"You guys have helped enough," Tessa replied. "Here's some money. Ask Martha to rent a movie that you like. It's your summer vacation, so relax."

Shawn took the money. "Why don't you call Matt? He could come over and help you."

"I'm sure Mr. Anderson has work of his own," she said stiffly.

"I doubt it," her son muttered. "He's probably just sitting around and staring at the walls."

"I don't need anybody's help." Her words were sharper than she wanted, but they worked. Both boys scurried upstairs to pack.

Tessa turned to set up her equipment. She didn't need anybody's help. She was a strong capable woman. Most of all, she didn't need Matt Anderson back in her house. It was bad enough that he was always in her thoughts.

The croak of the bullfrog muscled in among the night sounds as Matt took a healthy pull on his bottle of beer.

"How the women treating you, old fella?" He directed his question down toward the pond in back of the old red barn, though it was too dark to see that far. "I imagine you don't have any trouble with that beautiful bass voice of yours."

The bullfrog replied that everything was cool.

"I thought so," Matt said. He finished his beer and set the empty bottle on the steps next to himself, then he leaned back against the porch pillar and sighed.

Sounded like the grotesque little amphibian was doing better than he was, but then he was probably satisfied with his pond. Most likely he had no desire to see what the ponds on the other side of the road were like. He'd spend the rest of his life in the mud and the weeds back there. He'd croak on a warm summer's night, love his ladies and watch his tadpoles grow.

Matt rubbed his eyes. Little beast didn't sound all that dumb. What did that make him?

He hunched forward and rested his elbows on his knees. What it made him was sick and tired of cleaning this stupid old house. If he could gather up all the dust he'd moved today, he could give Kansas a new layer of topsoil.

Why in the world was he bothering to clean the old place himself? He wasn't exactly poor. He could call in one of those cleaning services, and they would swoop through like a tornado, have the joint looking like a candidate for a *House Beautiful* cover.

Let strangers come in and paw through the rooms? Matt shook his head. No, he couldn't do that. That would be like sending your baby to the car wash for its bath. This old house had sheltered him for many a year and it deserved his consideration.

Matt wondered if his system was getting old and couldn't handle beer anymore. He'd only had two bottles after dinner, yet here he was getting maudlin.

No, it wasn't the beer. It was a serious case of nostalgia. He'd always remembered the bad parts about the farm, but now that he was here again, all he could see in his memory's eye were the good parts. Smelling the new-mown hay on a summer day. Pancakes and sausage on a winter morning before he went out to wait for the school bus. The new-life smell of a field plowed in the spring.

He sprang up, taking his two bottles to the garbage. If he kept this up, he might as well get a rocking chair and watch the Christmas trees grow. Since they averaged about a foot a year that should be real exciting.

Lightning flashed to the far west and the soft rumble of distant thunder followed. Matt sniffed the air. It was going to storm tonight. His colleagues who had grown up in the city always laughed when he said he could smell the rain. Once a country boy, always a country boy, he guessed.

Restless, but not knowing what to do with himself, Matt went upstairs to his room. Why the hell had he chosen to stay in this room, even to the point of calling it "his"? He shook his head. There was a bedroom on the first floor, but this was where his feet had automatically taken him that first night back. He'd come straight up here, dusted off the shelves and his old trophies and taken his field-and-stream quilt out of the cedar chest. Within minutes he'd been floating around in dreamland.

The room was in the southeast corner, and the old window shade was torn so that on a summer day, the early-morning sunlight was banging on his eyeballs at five o'clock. Of course, the four o'clock birds' chorus had already rendered him half-awake. Matt walked to the window and smiled out now into the darkness. He hadn't minded waking up early one little bit. It had given him a chance to see the land in the unspoiled innocence of a new day.

He took a deep breath of the pine-scented night air and looked up at the sky. Memories came pouring in, filling his mind like the incoming clouds were filling the sky. It was on summer nights like this that he used to sneak out and meet Tessa.

He'd go out the window onto the porch roof, drop to the ground and jog over to Winky Barrow's farm down the road. Besides being out of high school, Winky had big freckles all over his face, a job in the lumber yard over in Cassopolis and a beat-up old pickup that he let Matt use for a dollar and gas.

Matt took another deep breath and a smile broke his face. The old porch roof still looked sturdy and he had a beat-up old pickup right in his own backyard. Would Tessa be as glad to see him as she used to be?

The squeeze through the window was a tad tighter than Matt had remembered and the porch seemed to have grown some, but he got down okay without tearing his pants or breaking any bones. Within minutes he was roaring along the road toward town. Matt smiled. The pickup even had a noisy muffler, just like Winky's. For all he knew it might be the same one, the thing was old enough.

Lightning flashes were becoming bigger and more pronounced, and storm warnings hung heavy in the air. Matt figured he'd get to Tessa's before the rain, but not by much. There wasn't anything in the whole world like a Midwest summer storm to quiet a night. It was as if the earth relaxed, satisfying a powerful thirst with the drops pounding on its dry dirt.

Tessa's house was dark upstairs, but the lights were on in the store. Matt shook his head. Tessa was working again. But then, what could one expect? He was sure Joe hadn't left much money or insurance, and Tessa wasn't one to sponge off anybody.

Matt knocked at the front door. Through the window he saw her approach the door cautiously, but certainly without fear. Not like many women in the cities. Suddenly she hastened her steps. Matt was sure it was because she recognized him, and his heart warmed.

"Matt," she said, as she opened the door wide. "Is something wrong?"

"Just a powerful case of lonesome," he replied, stepping in.

The look that filled her face could hardly be called sympathetic. "Lute Connor's springer spaniel had a litter of puppies. I think they're about ready to leave their momma."

He tried a glare, but Tessa's face remained bland. "I was wondering how you were."

"I'm just fine, thank you," she replied.

"That's good to know. I can go home and sleep easy now." A bolt of lightning on the leading edge of the storm crackled in the dark sky. "Once it stops storming, that is. Thunder and lightning make a night real scary."

Tessa turned on her bare heel and marched toward the back of the store. "Shut the door behind you."

Her face hadn't been filled with acceptance, but at least she hadn't thrown him out. Sometimes a man had to take what a man was given. He followed her into the back room, where a sense of irritation seized him.

"You ought to get rid of this damn place before you work yourself to death."

"I screwed up an order and I have to redo it." She laid a shirt on the iron, applied numbers and letters for a name and lowered the cover. "Some days are hectic, but there are other times when I have little to do for weeks."

"Now that Joe is gone, you should sell the place and do something you like."

"I told you that Joe didn't have anything to do with this," Tessa said, a sharp edge to her voice. "I started the business."

"Yeah, I know. Because your husband wasn't making enough to support his family properly."

"Money isn't everything." She threw up the cover and put in another shirt, affixing a number and letters to it. "He gave a great deal to the community and all the kids that knew him in school."

Good old Saint Joe. Matt clamped his jaw tight before any insulting words could spill across his lips. He certainly hadn't come here to argue with Tessa.

Then why had he come here? Matt stared at her feminine frame. A solid countrywoman. Curves covering, but not really hiding, the strength she carried. A woman who came from generations like her who'd raised families and worked side by side with their husbands.

Standing behind her, looking at curves not at all concealed by short shorts and a tank top, however, wasn't exactly giving him a historical perspective. It was giving him a very basic viewpoint.

He turned to look out the window. The lightning was getting close enough to light up the street. "The boys sleeping or watching TV?"

"They're probably still up," she replied. "I sent them over to Martha's." She pulled out the shirt and inserted another. "They wanted to help, but I figured it was my mistake, not theirs."

"I can help."

"Nice timing." She laughed. "I have two more to do."

Matt returned to the dark, stormy scene outside. The initial raindrops were hitting the window. Tessa was right about his timing. It was just great.

Tessa had been his girl, but he had to go to college and then get jobs all around the world. No sooner was he out of sight, than she married Joe. Good old saintly Joe.

Another bolt of lightning danced on the earth, close enough to rattle the pane slightly. She had taken Joe's name and borne his children. They'd laughed together, cried together and shared dreams.

Matt shook his head, pondering the ironies of life. Joe was gone, but he still was a part of Tessa and this community. Matt was here and was part of neither.

"Well, that's it."

Matt knew Tessa was announcing the completion of her task, but he continued staring out at the street.

"Want me to turn out the light?" Tessa asked. "It'll make the show outside look more spectacular."

"Sure, why not?"

Much to his surprise, Tessa did turn out the lights. He felt, more than heard, her walk up to him. They stared out together at the show of the gods. Lightning danced like ballerinas on the far sky, to the drumming accompaniment of the thunder and the large intermittent drops spattering on the window.

She was so close.

His throat was dry and he couldn't think of anything to say. His arm moved out to take Tessa's waist. She slid in to him. He could feel their hearts beat in unison.

Tessa stood enclosed by Matt's arms, not wanting to move or even to breathe. All evening long a strange restlessness had been eating at her, building like the coming of a storm, until she felt ready to explode.

"Why does it seem like it's always storming when you're around?"

"It hasn't rained since the day I came," he pointed out.

"I didn't say rain, I said storm," she said, and pulled away from him to sit on the windowsill. Lightning flashed, turning the street to gold. "I feel like I've been walking on the edge of a storm since you came back."

"Is that why you've been avoiding me?"

"I haven't been avoiding you." But she made the mistake of looking at him as she spoke, of getting caught in his gaze, which seemed to scold her for stretching the truth. She looked out at the storm again. "I saw you downtown today and at the gas station yesterday and at the library the day before that.''

He sat next to her, too close for her ragged nerves. She edged away slightly.

''You've been turning down my dinner invitations,'' he said.

''It wasn't personal.''

''I see. Anyone who isn't Joe gets turned down.'' He took her hand, holding it lightly, but somehow she couldn't move. ''I think I'd rather it was personal.''

''Stop reading things into everything I say.''

She wanted to take her hand back, to keep all of herself safe in some little cocoon, but she didn't have the strength to pull her hand away. It was as if her whole being, the core of who she was centered in her right hand. She felt only the touch of his skin against hers, cool, yet fiery at the same time. She knew only that his thumb was rubbing the outside of her hand in gentle, rhythmic movements that hypnotized. She was certain only that she wanted this to go on forever.

''So if your turning me down wasn't personal, what was it?'' he asked.

She stared out the window. In the dim glow of the streetlights, she could see the rain pouring down. Sheets of it, like tears, trying to wash the earth clean.

''I'm not sure why you're here,'' she said finally.

''To sell the farm.''

She shook her head, dragging her eyes back to his. ''That's not what I mean. Why are you *here*? Why aren't you out at the farm right now, polishing silver or washing windows?''

''Didn't you ever learn not to wash windows in the rain?'' he teased, then slid his arm around her shoulder, pulling her closer. She didn't have the resistance to move away. ''I'm here because you're my friend and I wanted to be with you. Isn't that enough?''

"We were friends," she pointed out. "You don't know me now and I don't know you."

"Have we changed that much?"

"I have," she said, but even as she said the words she doubted them. Here she was, sitting in Matt's arms on a stormy evening. How was that different from the past? Hadn't she always sought refuge in his embrace?

"How are you different?" Matt whispered, his voice muffled as he buried his lips in her hair, leaving light kisses that made her hungry for more.

She tried to think, but his hands were sliding down her arms, pulling her closer to him, and her own hands seemed to have a life of their own. She held Matt, her arms around his waist, and laid her head against his chest. His heart was racing, just as hers was. His calm exterior was just a facade. She smiled, hugging the knowledge secretly into her heart.

"I'm more settled now," she said. "That's one way I'm different. And more sensible. I used to get upset at the silliest things."

"I always thought you were sensible," he said. "Your advice was always right."

Was it? she wondered silently. She'd told him to leave and never look back, advice that she'd questioned for the past fourteen years.

"You just needed a cool head to listen to," she said. "You always did just what you wanted."

"I guess." His hands pulled her closer, as if that were possible, and the night seemed to close in around them. It was still pouring, but the thunder and lightning had moved on.

"So," Matt said with a sigh. "This is getting us nowhere. You still haven't said why you've been avoiding me."

The night had always been a magic time when Matt's arms were around her, and that magic hadn't disappeared. She closed her eyes and let the spell surround her, sweeping her up into a world that no longer existed except in dreams.

"It's too easy," she said. "I was always able to talk to you about anything. You were my rock in high school, you were someone I could always lean on, and it would be so easy to lean on you again."

"What's wrong with that?" he asked.

She shook herself free of his spell, shook herself free of his arms and stood up. "Everything. I've got big responsibilities and you've got a job that takes you all over the world, but not to Edwardsburg. I can't forget how to stand on my own two feet."

He got to his feet and took her hand, bringing it up to his lips. "Is leaning just for a night so bad?" he asked. "You always made me feel whole. Maybe just for tonight, I want to feel whole again."

He took only her hand, but her heart, her whole body seemed to follow. Was leaning for a night so bad? she wondered. She didn't know, and stalled for time.

"Want to go upstairs?" she asked. "I've got a pitcher of iced tea and some freshly sliced lemon."

She took his hand and led him up to the apartment. It seemed quiet without the boys, and dangerous, too. Everywhere she looked was Matt, everything she heard was Matt. She got two glasses out of the cabinet and fiddled with the ice cube tray from the freezer. He took it from her hands and deftly emptied the ice into the deep bin.

"So you first," he said softly.

"What?"

He put ice cubes into each glass. "You go first. Lean on me. Tell me something that's been bothering you."

She sighed. "Shawn." The name had just come out; she hadn't thought or chosen. "He's so difficult since Joe's gone. I'm afraid I won't be able to handle him as he gets older."

"You handled me," Matt pointed out.

She shrugged and poured iced tea into the glasses. "I listened, that's all."

"So listen to Shawn, really listen. Let the rules be flexible when they need to be, otherwise stay tough. Just listen and really hear what he's saying."

"Sounds so easy."

"It'll be easier than you think." He picked up the glasses and carried them into the living room. They sat on the sofa, next to each other but not touching.

"Your turn," Tessa said.

"My turn's simple," he told her. "Just sitting here with you is enough to make me feel whole. I really miss having somebody around to talk to."

"Oh, come on," Tessa scoffed. "Finding somebody to talk to is easy."

"You've obviously never tried."

"Go to any bar and you'll find people to talk to. The world is filled with lonely people."

"That's not what I mean," he said. "Talking is one thing, listening is another. I never found someone who understood the way you did."

The space between them seemed to be getting smaller, but Tessa wasn't sure that was what she wanted. Her heart was ordering her to pull back, to retreat while there was still time. Did she want the closeness that was growing between them? Should she allow it to grow? She was a mature woman with two kids, not some giddy teenager who gave no thought to responsibility. Not some silly kid ruled by passions and feverish longings.

A little flame of annoyance began to flicker, and she did nothing to put it out. "It's taken you a long time to come back here then," she said. "You must not have had much you needed to talk over in the past fourteen years."

His eyes clouded briefly, as if in surprise. "Maybe I didn't realize how much I was missing."

She laughed, but the sound came out harshly. "That sounds like the kids. A toy can collect dust for years, and then when somebody else has it they suddenly want it back." Was that how he saw her? When the world was there to see, he gave her no thought, but now when life was tranquil—boring—then suddenly he needed her.

"This has nothing to do with Joe."

His interpretation of her words surprised her, for a moment knocking the anger aside. She put her glass down on the coffee table and turned to face him. "I never thought it had. I thought it was about leaving Edwardsburg to see the world and wishing you had stayed."

"Is that so bad?" he asked. "Wishing life wasn't an either/or proposition?"

She'd gone through those throes when she'd learned she was pregnant—how could she have Matt's support and help, yet let him escape from Edwardsburg? She'd learned from the struggle though, that you could either let your life be torn into bits, or use the pieces for your own quilt.

"It isn't either/or," she said. "You don't want both, you want everything. Want to leave and wish you'd stayed. Want to roam all over the world, but wish there was a home amid the roaming."

"Why are you so angry?"

"I'm not."

But she got to her feet and walked over to the window. Headlights swept Route 12 as a car sped out of town, illuminating bushes, trees and mailboxes for a brief moment before the darkness covered them again. Just as Matt had done—lit up things here for her briefly, then gone on his way. A county police car came into sight, moving slowly into town on its patrol. That was like her. The things that its lights lit up would be seen and remembered, a part of the pattern that made up her life.

"Do you regret not leaving?" Matt asked. He moved closer to her in the darkness. "Do you wish you'd made it out of here, too?"

The idea was so preposterous that she laughed, but she didn't turn around. "I did make it out," she told him. "And came right back because this was where I belonged."

"Then why are you mad at me for leaving? You told me to go, over and over again."

He was right behind her, his breath tickling the hairs on the back of her neck. Just his very nearness set her heart on edge, her empty arms longing for him. She crossed her arms in defiance.

"I'm not angry at you," she said slowly. "I'm mad at myself. I'm mad because I want to go back fourteen years and be wildly and madly in love. I want to pretend that morning will never come and that happiness can last forever."

She turned away from the window, away from her insane imaginings and found his arms open and waiting. She flew into them, holding him close and melting into his heart.

"You want everything," he teased gently. His hands were possessive, running in sweet rhythms over her back and shoulders.

She nodded, almost afraid to talk for fear of breaking this magic spell that let her be here with him.

"You have to relish the good times, to cherish them when they're here. Nothing lasts forever, but that's no reason not to take happiness when it comes by."

"That sounds like a smooth line," she whispered into his chest.

"No, it's the truth." He paused, his lips coming down to brush her hair. "I just learned it, as a matter of fact. Someone very wise told me I couldn't have everything, and I realized that was where I was going wrong. Wanting everything so much, that I wasn't seeing the good things that I had. I couldn't enjoy the moments of pleasure and magic that might never come my way again."

She pulled away then, just enough to look up into his eyes, to see the sadness and longing there, the hunger for the dreams they'd shared and the weariness left by life's disappointments.

"I'm afraid," she told him. "I'm afraid to let you too close again. My heart's always been a jellyfish where you're concerned."

"I'll go, if you want," he offered. But even as his hands loosened their hold on her, she knew it wasn't what she wanted.

"No." Her heart finally stopped its waffling. After all her anger, her indecision, she knew what she wanted with blinding clarity. "It's raining. You shouldn't drive in the rain."

"Tessa."

His voice made it sound like a prayer, like a breath upon the wind, and they came together. His hands made the years disappear, touching, caressing, delighting as she forgot about everything but him.

They were young and hungry for each other, clinging for strength against the storm. The distant rain on the roof was the rhythm of love, a curtain to hide behind as they fled back to the past. He was everything she needed and wanted. His touch made her come alive. Their lips met and the world receded. There was only the two of them, and forever stretched on ahead of them.

Tessa took him into the bedroom and, serenaded by the steady rain, they lay down together. Her hands touched him, tried to get to know his body once again. His skin was rougher, the muscles stronger than before, but the way her body soared was the same.

Matt pushed her T-shirt out of the way of his lips, then in impatience she pulled it off the rest of the way. His mouth tugged at the rosy tip of one breast, then kissed its way across the valley that lay between them to the other breast.

Tessa sighed, snuggling into the softness of the bed as she took more and more of his weight on her. She pushed his clothes aside and he shrugged out of them as she got rid of the rest of hers. Hot skin pressed against wild, desperate hungers, and she sighed, pressing deeper and deeper into the touch that was all things to her.

She was all fire, all storming desires, and knew nothing but Matt. Their bodies pressed together, his hands stroking lower and lower, as if willing the storm to consume her, to consume them both. Finally, they could wait no more and he entered her, and they moved together as the storm charged about them.

Suddenly they were in the vortex, in the center of the raging power. As one they breathed and moved, keeping each other safe and whole as they burst through the fury together. Then it was over, the storm was abating and a sweet, gentle languor took possession of her. She lay in Matt's arms, letting sleep wash over her.

Chapter Eight

"Good morning," Matt whispered as he wrapped his arms around her waist and his tight lips nibbled at the back of her neck.

Tessa's body began to melt into his, but she caught sight of the bag of paper roses in the closet. The paper roses for Joe's stadium dedication. The sun might have been shining outside, but none reached her heart. She pushed herself upright and sat on the edge of the bed.

"What do you want for breakfast?" she asked.

Tessa felt his body stiffen and edge away from her.

"You don't have to fix anything," Matt said.

He took her hand gently, but she pulled away as she pushed the hair back from her face. What had she been thinking of to let him stay?

"You ought to have breakfast," she said, forcing a softness back into her voice. "And I'm fixing some for me anyway. Making something for two isn't any more work than making it for one."

"We could go out," Matt said. "Didn't the Four Flags over in Niles always have a good strawberries and pancakes combo?"

"That's early in the summer when they have fresh strawberries."

Matt shrugged. "I'm sure they have other stuff just as good."

Tessa turned to face him then, looking into his soft brown eyes framed in a smiling face. It should have been wonderful this morning, waking up and looking into those eyes, except that she wasn't a kid anymore. She was a widow with responsibilities, debts to be paid.

"I don't know when the boys will be coming home. I'm sure it will be this morning, and I don't want them coming into an empty house."

"Call your sister," he said. "Find out when she's planning on bringing them over. I doubt if they'd mind staying a little longer."

There was no doubt of that in Tessa's mind. Martha spoiled those two rotten. They'd probably vote to live with her permanently if they had a chance. For a moment, her heart faltered. It would be nice to go out for breakfast. She couldn't remember the last time she'd been out on a date.

But then guilt came back to claim her soul. Joe had always liked to take her and the boys out to breakfast. After church on Sunday morning, they'd go over to the pancake house in Roseland. It had always been a wonderful way to start the week; the boys had enjoyed it as much as she and Joe. She couldn't go out to breakfast without Shawn and Jason.

Suddenly there was knocking on the door downstairs. "Tessa?" a voice called up the stairs.

"Good Lord! Bruce!" she muttered, flying out of bed. "I forgot all about him."

"Bruce?" Matt asked, suspicion in his voice.

"I'll be down in a second!" she called from the doorway, then grabbed a sweat suit from the closet. "Bruce Moran. He's come for those shirts I was doing last night."

"Oh."

She was out of the bedroom, combing her hair with her fingers as she hurried through the kitchen and down the stairs. Matt had better stay put. She didn't need him to make an appearance and let the whole town know he spent the night here.

"Sorry if I woke you," Bruce said. "You said seven wouldn't be too early."

"No, and it wasn't," she assured him and led him into the store. Actually, he'd rescued her from her own weaknesses. "I just forgot to set my alarm and the boys were at Martha's, so I didn't even have their banging around to wake me up."

Now why had she admitted the boys were gone? Her cheeks flushed with heat, but she hoped the room was too dimly lit for Bruce to notice.

"You get much damage from the storm?" Bruce asked.

Storm? The one outside had seemed pale in comparison to the one in her heart last night. "Not that I've seen. Why? Some places hard hit?"

"Some trees uprooted south of here. There was a report of a twister touching down near the airport in South Bend."

"Our lights were flickering for a while last night," she said, pulling his order from the shelf and putting it on the table. "Luckily it was after I finished your shirts." She patted the bag. "Here they are. Light blue."

"Hey, great, Tessa. Thanks so much."

"No problem. I'm just sorry about the mix-up." There hadn't been a sound from upstairs, and she was all smiles as she led Bruce over to the front door.

"Sorry about waking you up."

"Hey, we're even now." She walked out onto the porch with him, her smile weakening as she saw his car was parked right behind Henry's old pickup. No one needed to see Matt, that old truck just as loudly proclaimed his presence.

"So long, Bruce," she said feebly.

"Have yourself a good day now," Bruce said, then climbed into his car and pulled away.

With leaden steps, she climbed up to the apartment. Matt was dressed and waiting in the kitchen. His expression was somber, but he still looked so damn good. All she wanted to do was go over and rest in his arms again. To say, the hell with the town, the hell with tomorrow, let's just live for right now. She jerked open the refrigerator.

"I'm going to have a busy day." Sharpness had returned to Tessa's voice. "Why don't I just make some scrambled eggs and toast?"

"Sure." His voice was quiet. "What do you want me to do?"

"Just sit down and wait. There's not much to it and I'll be done in a few minutes."

She turned and got out a frying pan, then a carton of eggs.

"How about if I set the table?" Matt asked.

"Fine."

Tessa forced herself to concentrate on beating the eggs thoroughly. That was the secret to good scrambled eggs. Why wasn't there an easy secret to keeping her emotions and heart under control?

Joe had been a kind, wonderful, generous, easygoing man. And when he was with them, Tessa had been able to fill her mind and heart with him and their family. But that had all changed now that Matt Anderson was back in town. Of course, Joe wasn't here. But that thought didn't ease her concerns any. In fact, it just raised a most disturbing question. Would she still have loved Joe if he'd still been alive when Matt came home?

It hurt to admit it, but Tessa knew that she couldn't answer with an unequivocal no. Sure, she was grateful to Joe for everything he'd done for her and the boys, but she knew now that she'd always loved Matt. Matt Anderson, that footloose, rambling man, who'd held her heart captive years ago and was trying to do so again.

She turned to face Matt, who was standing at the table and smiling. "How do you like that?" he asked, indicating the neatly set table. There was a single red day lily in the water glass. Tessa had been so caught up in her self-analysis that she hadn't even heard him step outside.

She took a deep breath. "Do you want white or whole wheat toast?" she asked.

The intensity of his smile slowly dimmed and Tessa wanted to cry. "Whole wheat will be fine."

The eggs tasted like cardboard, and she would have liked to just chuck them out the window, but she forced herself to eat. Matt said nothing, either, and the silence got to be painful.

"Are you going out to the farm today?" she finally asked.

He took a while to answer. "Yeah. The guy who's been taking care of the trees is coming out to give me a tour."

"He did good work," Tessa said.

"Yeah."

They went back to pretending to eat. The sooner Matt Anderson was gone, the better off she'd be, Tessa told herself. Life wouldn't be as exciting but it certainly would be less of a strain.

* * *

"Last summer's drought didn't do you much harm," the man told Matt. "Some of the trees up here were hurt a bit, but most of this farm is good bottomland. Roots aren't that far from the water table."

Matt nodded and followed him up and down rows and rows of evergreens. The lean elderly man, face permanently tanned from a lifetime outside, walked with a sprightly step that belied his gray hair. His name was Al something, and he was part owner of a tree service and landscaping firm. He certainly knew his stuff and spoke with enthusiasm, but Matt had a hard time paying attention.

"They're almost all Colorado spruce," Al said, indicating the compact evergreens with short needles. "Those are the most popular ones for Christmas trees."

Matt nodded again. Over the years he'd almost forgotten what a Christmas tree looked like. During the Christmas season, he was usually out in some desert or tropical area where most of the people weren't Christians and didn't celebrate Western holidays like Christmas.

Christmas in Edwardsburg was always something special, with sleigh rides, midnight church services on Christmas Eve and visits of family and friends. Matt found himself picturing Tessa and the boys. Tessa would do things right for them. Christmas morning Shawn and Jason would probably be up early. They'd all have breakfast first, then sit around and open presents. Toys for the boys and slippers for Tessa.

Slippers. Matt almost snorted. He'd seen the pile in Tessa's closet this morning. Slippers were one thing she didn't need.

Matt forced his attention back to Paul What's-his-name. "There's a number of open fields in back of the pond,"

Matt said. "Was my uncle planning on putting in a stand of evergreens there?"

Paul shrugged. "Don't know. I was trying to get him to grow some other stock. You know, maples, crab apples. Landscaping stuff. But he was slow to take to new ideas."

"Tell me about it," Matt said with a laugh.

Maybe it was the water. It had produced his uncle, then someone like Joe, who must have bought his wife slippers for twelve Christmases in a row when she never even wore the damn things. Yes, it was probably the water that had made Matt so keen to get out of this dadburned town.

"Well, that's about it," Paul said as they drew near the house. "Find the right buyer and you should get a good price for it."

"Thanks for your time," Matt said.

"I'm a little strapped for cash," Paul said, "because I went out and bought a cherry picker and a backhoe. If it wasn't for that I'd buy the place myself. Good land. Can't go wrong with it."

Can't go wrong? Certainly not, if you wanted to tie yourself down for the rest of your natural life. *You don't hear the bullfrog complaining,* a little voice told Matt. That's because he's a stupid green frog, Matt replied. He clenched his teeth. Folks said that it was all right to talk to yourself, but you knew you had problems when you answered.

"Thanks again," he told Paul, and walked briskly into the house.

He opened the refrigerator and poured himself a glass of lemonade, then leaned back against a counter top and surveyed the kitchen. The place was starting to shape up. Sunshine poured in through the kitchen windows. The room could use new cabinets and appliances, but even without them it looked bright and cheerful. Tessa would probably like the big kitchen.

The lemonade suddenly tasted sour, and he poured the remainder into the sink. What was he thinking of? He was on his way out and she wasn't about to leave the shrine to Saint Joe she'd made over on Route 12.

Growing even angrier, Matt stomped outside and sat down on the porch. This was stupid. Joe had been his best friend, and here he was trying to paint him as every sort of scoundrel and jerk. It would have been better if Joe were still alive and they were competing for Tessa's affections. What he didn't like was competing with somebody who wasn't real. Somebody he couldn't match up to. Hell, even Joe, when he was alive, couldn't have matched up to his saintly persona now he was dead.

But Matt wasn't really competing for Tessa's affections, was he? he asked himself. There was no reason to win her over unless he was staying, which he wasn't. So what was all the fuss about?

Matt shook his head. It was Tessa's devotion to Joe, that was what Matt was fussing about. She was doing everything possible to keep Joe alive. His picture still hung on the wall. Even though she was a trained horticulturist, she was still keeping the sports store. And she was one of the major movers behind naming the high school stadium after Joe. When was she going to start living again?

The thought of the stadium should have increased his irritation, but instead he felt a dim glow of hope spread over him. There could be a very good and positive reason why Tessa was so involved in the stadium and its dedication ceremonies. Maybe she was ready to put Joe behind her and putting his name on a permanent structure was her way of keeping his memory alive for the community, while moving along in her own life.

He stood up and brushed at the seat of his pants. Joe was a good guy. With all that he had given the community and its kids, it was only right that the townspeople repay him in some way. Making the high school stadium a memorial to Joe was a good idea.

Matt walked down to the truck. The least he could do for his former best friend was to make sure that the ceremonies were the best ever. He thought that Tessa's bulletin board indicated there was a meeting in the Old Chicago Road School the day after tomorrow. As a property owner in the community, Matt had a duty to attend and see what he could do to help.

And, as a property owner, he should wear something a little more presentable than his light tan, almost uniform-like, construction outfit. With some time ahead of him, he should check out some men's stores in the malls in South Bend.

There were mostly women in the meeting room when Matt walked in, plus two young men and a man about his own age. Matt and his contemporary stared at each other.

"Matt? Matt Anderson?"

"Yeah," Matt replied.

The man stood up and walked over, hand extended. "Chuck, Chuck Webb. I was a grade behind you."

"Right." Matt quickly grabbed the outstretched hand, glad that the man had stated his name. He couldn't have remembered it to save his life; everybody used to call Chuck Webb "Frog," because he was so expert at snatching flies out of midair. "I understand you're the village president now."

"Right. And I'm sales manager for my family's farm implement dealership."

"Guess they won't fire you," Matt joked.

"Got a wife and three little ones to feed," Chuck said. "That drives me harder than any boss man."

Matt nodded and let go of Chuck's hand. Chuck had been pretty much of a goof-off when they were in high school. Now here he was, accepting the responsibilities of family and community. Matt wondered if carrying that burden had hampered Frog's fly-catching talents any.

"I understand you're in town to put the old homestead on the market," Chuck said, interrupting Matt's thoughts. "I've been away on vacation the past two weeks."

Homestead? Matt winced slightly. That wasn't quite the way he'd prefer to phrase it. "Uh, yeah." He shrugged. "Getting it cleaned up, shaped up. That kind of thing."

"It's a nice piece of property," Chuck said. "I imagine you won't be hanging around the old burg very long."

"Oh, I don't know," Matt replied. "I've got more than four months of accumulated leave time. I thought I'd take it easy for a while."

He hadn't really given the idea much thought until this moment, but it sounded like a good idea. He would really help Tessa put Joe behind her so she could start living again.

"Maybe you and I can do a little fishing," Chuck suggested. "Chew the fat about the good old days."

"Sure, why not?" Matt paused. "You on this stadium dedication committee, too?"

"I'm just helping out a little." Chuck put on a serious face and shook his head. "Ain't that something, what happened to Joe? Young, healthy guy like that and bang, he's gone. Goes to show, you can't tell a book by its cover."

"Yeah, that's true," Matt agreed.

Then Chuck Webb slapped him on the back and rushed toward the door. "Got another meeting," he said. "Give me a call one of these days. I hear the fish are so ornery they're spitting in people's boats."

Matt waved and was about to move toward one of the empty chairs when he realized a stern-faced elderly woman was marching down on him. Back when he was in school, Mabel Crenshaw had been an aging widow who taught high school English. Now she was much older, of course, but even if she was retired, Matt figured she was still finding some way to terrorize teenagers and pound verbs and syntax into their sluggish brains.

"Matt Anderson," she snapped. "When are you going to get that muffler fixed?"

"Muffler?"

"Yes, muffler. You roared around half the night all senior year, you roared around the few weeks before you went away to college, and now you're back doing the same nonsense. Keeping God-fearing folk up half the night."

Matt swallowed hard. Damn, he'd forgotten that Mrs. Crenshaw lived on Jefferson just north of Route 12. He'd passed by her house every time he'd gone to visit Tessa when she was in school and—since Tessa's present house was only a block from where she'd grown up—every time he'd gone to see Tessa since he got back.

"I'll get it fixed, ma'am," he mumbled.

"Good," the older woman said, turning on her heel.

Before anyone else could approach him, Tessa stepped through the door. Her mouth opened to respond to the greetings tossed her way, but her tongue froze as she caught sight of him. Obviously his presence surprised her, he thought, hopefully, for the good.

"Hi," he said, wishing they could have been the only people in the world.

Tessa looked around at what were now widely grinning faces. Her own face grew cautious and shuttered. "Hello," she said to him. "What are you doing here?"

He shrugged. "Just seeing if there's anything I can do to help with the stadium dedication ceremonies."

"It's not until the middle of September," she said. "Are you still going to be around by then?"

He shrugged again. "I might. You never can tell."

Blinking for a moment, Tessa appeared bewildered, but she quickly recovered and moved to the head of the table. It was obvious that she was in charge of the proceedings. That sounded like the same old Tessa he'd known.

"For those of you who don't remember or don't know him," she said, "this is Matt Anderson. He played football with Joe here at Edwardsburg High School."

Matt acknowledged the friendly greetings. After hearing the names of the women, he remembered most as classmates or related to classmates. Only two were new to the town and had never attended Edwardsburg High School. He shook hands with the two young men, who were teachers and coaches at the school.

Tessa proceeded briskly and efficiently through the meeting, guiding the group as they made decisions on the parade, the decorations, the homecoming dance and other items. Matt wondered how this competent young woman could also have been his lover of the other night, at the same time soft and yielding, demanding and fiery.

"Matt."

Blinking, he looked into a sea of faces staring at him. "What?"

"Steve was asking if there was any other coach special to you and Joe," Tessa said.

"Bart was like a father to us," Matt said. "He—"

"We were just talking about Bart Newman," Tessa said. Her voice had a note of suspicion to it, as if she were questioning his real motives for being at the meeting. "Bart's very ill and the doctors are advising him not to travel."

"Oh."

"That's why we're asking, were there any other coaches that were special to you and Joe?"

Well, why didn't you say so? he felt like snapping back, but didn't since they apparently had said so. Instead, he shook his head. "Most of them were fathers who helped out part-time. I don't really remember anyone in particular."

There was a silence and then Tessa spoke. "Maybe we'll have to have someone besides a former coach of Joe's for the main speaker."

"Why don't you get one of his college coaches?" Matt suggested.

"That's a good idea," Tessa replied. Others voiced their agreement. "Now, how do we go about finding one?"

"Alumni office, athletic director. There's any number of ways," Matt said.

"Would you like to take care of it?" Tessa was smiling sweetly. "I'm sure it shouldn't take more than a day or two."

He returned her smile. "Glad to." Anything to keep her smiling.

Tessa brought the meeting to a close and after the others directed a few more words of welcome at him, he and Tessa were left alone. Matt had been waiting for just this moment, wishing the others would disappear so he could be alone with Tessa, but now he wasn't sure what to say to her. He couldn't just ask if she was working on this dedication in order to put Joe behind her. And he couldn't say he was hoping to liberate her from the ghosts that haunted her. So, in silence, he helped Tessa close the windows, turn off the lights and secure the building for the night.

"Nice outfit," Tessa said as she locked the door behind them.

"Thanks," Matt said, looking down at his new slacks and shirt. "Thought I'd spend some of the spare change I had lying around."

Tessa laughed. "Must be nice. I've never had spare anything lying around."

His throwaway words had come out wrong. He didn't want her thinking he was loaded with money. "When you're on a big construction project, you usually work twelve hours a day, six days a week. The bank account builds up, but you don't have much time or energy to spend it."

"I guess nothing's free in this world," she said with a smile that Matt decided was one of understanding.

"That's true," he replied, as he looked around the parking lot. Theirs were the only two cars left in it.

"Mind if I walk you to your car?" he asked.

She laughed again. "Almost have to since they're parked next to each other."

Taking that as an enthusiastic yes, Matt took her hand and they walked in silence. He would have loved to take her home with him, to keep her with him all the night long, but she had the boys to care for. Actually the boys were easy to deal with. They could come along or be dropped off at Martha's. Joe's ghost was a lot harder. It seemed to ride Tessa's shoulders no matter where she went.

The walk to their cars was over all too quickly, and after sighing inwardly he gave her a light kiss on the lips. She clung a little longer than he'd hoped for, but a lot shorter than he wanted. When she pulled back, the streetlight above them flashed on her eyes, showing such pain that Matt almost cried out.

Chapter Nine

Small world, isn't it?'' Matt said with a laugh.

Tessa looked up from the tacos, stuffed cabbages and other frozen delicacies laid out in the freezer section of the grocery store. She didn't really want that easy smile to light up her heart, but if it did before she could forbid it, then she had no desire to hide it. Why not admit her joy was because of Matt's presence and not the culinary delights spread before her? Matt wouldn't be here forever. She should enjoy him while she could.

"I don't know about the world," she replied, "but Edwardsburg certainly is small. And getting smaller. It seems we run into each other every place we go."

"Maybe we just both go to the right places," he said. His smile was for her alone, reminding her of secrets hidden in the past and dreams they both shared.

Was Matt getting more relaxed? His laughter seemed easier and came much more quickly. Tessa would have sworn that being back home was doing him a world of good, but then, probably it was just taking a vacation that was helping him lighten up.

She hadn't been able to believe it at first when he told her about all the vacation days he'd accumulated over the years. If she had been in those faraway lands, she'd have wanted to spend all her vacations sight-seeing, but maybe when a person worked in foreign countries all the time, sight-seeing got rather old in a hurry.

She looked back in the freezer. "I don't know why I keep checking out this section," she said with a laugh. "I always decide everything's too expensive and I'm really not too tired to cook, after all."

"That's crazy," he said, for some reason sounding annoyed with her. "There's such a thing as being too careful with your money. You don't seem to value your time at all."

"I do, too. Besides, one of these dinners isn't really enough for a growing boy and they're loaded with salt." Her voice teetered on the verge of impatient snapping and she bit her tongue.

With a grandiose gesture, he dumped all his frozen dinners back into the freezer, but his eyes were dancing as he leaned closer to her. "Why do we always end up arguing?" he whispered.

"We don't always argue," she pointed out. People were watching them, smiling as if she and Matt were some sort of public property, like a team they were rooting for.

"That's true," Matt said suddenly with an ominous gleam in his eye. "We weren't arguing the night of the last storm."

Tessa might as well have hired a town crier, she thought, since her face got red enough for everyone in town to decide just what they'd been doing that wasn't arguing.

"Well, I'd better finish my shopping," she said. "I imagine I'll see you around."

"I imagine."

Actually, if the past several weeks were any indication, she'd be running into him two more times before dinner. In the two weeks since the night of the storm, she'd seen him at two stadium dedication meetings, twice at the post office, once at the town hall, a zillion times at the grocery store and three times at the library. It wasn't that she'd been looking for him, she told herself. Edwardsburg was a small town, and people were bound to run into one another. And if her heart turned somersaults each time she saw him, it wasn't anything that anyone needed to know about.

She turned her cart and headed down the canned goods aisle, only to find Matt right alongside her. She frowned at him in suspicion, but his smile was blandly innocent. He stopped to check out a can of peaches.

"Fresh fruit is better for you," she couldn't stop herself from saying.

"You're right." He put the can back with a look that bespoke intimacy. "I'm not used to having the choice."

She wanted to point out to him that the ultimate choice—of where and how to live—was his alone, but that veered too closely to personal territory.

"Well, I've spent enough money for today," Tessa said, then regretted her choice of words. She hated to make it sound as if she were barely making ends meet. "So I'm going on home."

He nodded. "I imagine the boys are waiting for you."

"Actually they're at a friend's house right now, but they'll bring home some big appetites."

"I don't doubt that," he said, nodding again. "I'm all loaded up, too, so I'm heading for the checkout myself."

They walked to the checkout counter, not exactly hand in hand, just pushing their carts side by side. Tessa sighed. There wasn't a thundercloud in the sky, so there was no reason for her to feel fluttery.

They said their farewells as they exited the checkout lane, then said more as they made their way into the small parking lot and loaded the groceries into their respective vehicles. Matt was still driving Henry's pickup truck, but he seemed to wear it as easily as his shorts and short-sleeved shirts.

Tessa sighed when she finally shut her car door. She was going to have to watch herself more carefully. She could only handle so many farewells before she forgot that one of them would ultimately be final. At the stoplight, she glanced at the gas gauge and decided she'd better fill up, so she took a right and pulled into Henry's service station.

She'd no sooner twisted off the cap of the tank when there was a rumble of a decaying muffler behind her. "Are you following me?" she asked Matt as he stepped down from his vehicle.

"There anything wrong with that?" he asked.

Only in the way it weakened her heart and made her forget all the truths she'd learned the hard way. "There are other service stations in Edwardsburg," she said.

"Henry told me that his truck won't eat anyone else's gas."

She inserted the hose in her tank. "And you believed him."

Matt uncapped his tank. "Folks claim Henry's an honest man," he said. "Are they wrong?"

Tessa just shrugged, concentrating her energies in filling the tank properly. She could hardly tell Matt not to frequent her brother-in-law's gas station.

"Say." Matt worked the pump to round off an even ten dollars before he replaced the nozzle and capped his tank. "I finally found a speaker for your dedication ceremonies. He's head football coach at Northern Illinois University now."

"Did he know Joe well?"

"Yeah, he was the backfield coach at Michigan State when Joe was there."

She nodded. "The school's just on the other side of Chicago. It won't cost much to bring him here."

He came over to stand close to her, very close. "Do I get a pat on the head for a job well done?"

"Two pats even," she said, as she patted him twice on his thick locks. Just that teasing touch was enough to send her heartbeat racing, and make her forget just what they were laughing about.

"My cup overfloweth."

Tessa just smiled tightly and hurried into the station, sensing Matt behind her. He actually wasn't following her, she scolded herself. After all, he had to pay for his gas, too. Billy was on duty and he took their money, then they made their way back outside.

"I should give you the speaker's name," Matt said.

"Yes," Tessa replied. "I should have it."

"I guess I could tell you at the next meeting."

"That would be fine."

They exchanged farewells again, only this time Matt didn't follow her. He turned right and went up M-62, while she hung a left and went into town.

Joe hadn't been anywhere in her thoughts until Matt brought up the speaker. In fact, it was Matt Anderson who'd staked out a big part of her mind lately. Guilt worked at her as she unloaded the car.

The house was so silent and still without the boys around. Too silent and still. She had too much chance to think and, as always these days, her thoughts revolved around Matt and Joe. Her husband and her former lover.

Former? Did the other night really classify as the past? Perhaps it was former and present lover.

She unpacked eggs and milk, stowing them in the refrigerator, but keeping her hands busy didn't keep her mind in tow. Her life had been so simple, so easy just a month ago. Joe had been her present, Matt had been her past. Now the past and present were all mixed up together, with only questions about the future.

She put down the stalk of celery in her hand and wandered into the living room, drawn to the picture on the end table of Joe with the two boys. It had been taken the Christmas before last, just a few weeks before he died. The boys were dressed in their new Edwardsburg High School sweat suits, but she barely noticed them as she stared into Joe's eyes.

"What should I do?" she asked him. "When I'm with Matt, it seems so simple. But then later I feel so guilty, as if I'd been cheating on you."

Joe didn't answer, of course, and she felt like a fool for the disappointed sinking in her stomach when the silence stretched out. What had she expected? A bolt of lightning and a voice booming out of the clouds?

His eyes just seemed to stare back at her, smiling slightly and filled with the gentleness that was Joe. He never seemed to know how to criticize. As a coach, as a father, as a friend, he always tried to coax people into doing their best. To do their best so they could be happy and proud.

When she told him she was pregnant, he'd never talked about blame, just how to resolve the problem. All he wanted was for everyone to be happy. Tessa stopped suddenly and put the picture down slowly.

Of course. All Joe had ever wanted was for everyone to be happy. And that was all he'd want now. He wouldn't want her mourning him forever, or feeling that she still owed him for the years of love he'd given her and the boys.

Tessa felt as if a weight had been lifted off her shoulders. She danced back into the kitchen to put away the rest of the groceries.

Matt took his large glass of lemonade and went out to the porch. The sun was moving over to the other side of the house and the back area was in the shade now.

He took a long swig from his glass, then stared down into the hollow where the old red barn stood with the pond behind it. Things were quiet back there now. The ugly old bullfrog was no doubt taking his siesta, sleeping with one of his ladies.

Sighing, Matt drained the glass, keeping one of the ice cubes in his mouth to munch on. He knew he should be getting back to shaping up the house. Shaking his head, he took another ice cube. To tell the truth, though, he didn't really know of anything else he should be doing. The house was clean and the yard looked neat. He should be putting the place on the market.

This time instead of sighing, he rubbed his eyes. He'd been spending a lot of time on the porch lately, looking out and watching the trees grow. All he needed was a beard and overalls, and he would be the perfect model for the American farmer, the last of the breed.

His hand went back to rub his neck and he noticed that the hair was getting a trifle long there. It was time to get the tips hacked off. He ought to get into town for a haircut—it was better than sitting on the porch all day.

But he didn't move right away. The old place was so peaceful, quiet and uncrowded. Matt wondered if he was getting old. *If he brought Tessa out here, he wouldn't feel old.* Groaning to himself, Matt quickly stood up and walked to the truck. He sure needed that haircut.

The afternoon was hot and muggy, but he was just as happy that the old truck had no air-conditioning. The warm air felt good blowing in his face. He crossed Route 12, remembering that Tessa had said a lot of the shops had moved out to the minimalls. He drove that way and spotted a sign that said Haircuts. It looked more like a beauty shop, but it was probably unisex. Matt shook his head. Even Edwardsburg wasn't immune to progress.

A couple of women were being worked on at one side of the shop, while an elderly man stood alone, staring out the window, on the other side.

"Can a man get a haircut around here?" Matt asked.

"Sure." The man slowly turned around, stared at Matt a moment and then burst into a broad smile. "Matt. Matt Anderson. Heard you were in town."

Blinking, Matt stammered. "Barney? What the hell are you doing still working for a living?" Barney had been old when Matt's aunt had brought him in for his regular haircuts as a kid.

"Can't relax and sit on my can all the time," Barney replied. "Then vacations wouldn't be any fun."

"Guess you have a point there." Matt got into the chair and Barney wrapped a shroud around him.

"I see you do ladies now," Matt said.

"Yeah," Barney said. "Me and Nell split the rent and answer the phone for each other. Sometimes we even talk to each other."

Barney started cutting Matt's hair, and they were silent for a long moment. "You've been here a long while," Matt said, during a pause in the barber's work.

"Yep," Barney replied. "Most all my life."

"Long time."

Barney shrugged. "The little woman still warms the bed at night, got grandkids to make me smile, enough to eat, and the roof don't leak. Man don't need no more."

This time it was Matt's turn to shrug. Put that way, he really didn't know what else a man needed. What was it *he* needed? "Some men need a challenge out of life," he replied.

"Got enough of that here. Pretty hard to make a decent living all your life and still have time for Momma and the kids. Then we need to grow the town enough to give our kids jobs, but not so much that we ruin the land and then got nothing to leave them and their kids."

Matt chose not to reply and they shared a long silence.

"Planning on staying long?" Barney asked, as he pulled the barber shroud off and shook loose the hairs.

"No. Just long enough to put my uncle's place up for sale."

"Don't be too quick to sell," Barney warned. "That's good land. Your uncle took care of it and the land took care of him. Got enough there for a man to take care of himself and raise a family."

Matt clenched his teeth momentarily. "Could be," he said. "But it's not for me."

"What do you do?"

"I'm in construction," Matt replied.

The barber shook his head. "That's real seasonal. Ain't sure from one day to the next whether you got a job."

Matt restrained a smile. "I work all over the world."

"Too bad." Barney folded up the shroud and placed it on the chair, then walked over to the cash register. "But if you kept the farm you wouldn't have to go halfway around the world just to find work. The land would take care of you and yours."

Matt was about to explain that he wasn't some unskilled laborer wandering around the world looking for work; he was a project manager, a highly paid on-site executive for his construction firm. But he just paid for his haircut. Barney wouldn't understand. He was the type that wanted his family and friends around him.

By the time Matt stepped outside, the heat felt oppressive and he was getting tired. It was this town and the Midwestern summer, although he thought he smelled a thunderstorm in the air. That was most likely the problem. A low pressure system always made a person tired.

He pulled out onto M-62, but this time when he hit Route 12 he turned a left. Matt wondered if Tessa was home. Maybe they could get a couple of Slurpies and go sit down by Pleasant Lake. It was the right kind of day for it.

No one answered either his knock or his yell, so Matt climbed back into the truck and made a U-turn in front of the store. Nuts. She'd probably taken the boys out someplace. School would be starting in another week or so, so they probably had a million errands to run. If he wanted anything, he should have thought of it one of the times he'd seen her in town over the past few days.

He slowed down as he neared the town hall. He knew that he should be setting things up to sell the farm, but he drove by the parking lot next to the real estate office. He'd go there tomorrow.

Suddenly he stopped and backed up. He thought he'd seen a good-looking country girl out of the corner of his eye.

A soft smile pulled at his lips. Tessa was in front of the post office, talking to a woman. Now the woman was crossing the street. Matt pulled into a side street and drove up to Tessa.

"Afternoon, ma'am," he called out.

"Why, good afternoon, sir."

Her smile did the craziest things to his heart. His eyes roamed from her lips to savor the rest of the view. The curves that were only barely hidden under her shorts and top seemed to argue the fact that she was fourteen years away from being a kid and was in fact the mother of two. She was still as beautiful as when she'd been a high school senior. Actually more beautiful. A lump rose in his throat, which he had to clear before he could speak.

"I'm sorely in need of help, ma'am."

"Oh, poor baby."

"I've been working on that old house," he said. "And I'm not sure if there's anything else I ought do to it before putting it on the market."

He thought a shadow passed across her eyes, and Matt wondered for a moment if he was going to get another lecture about keeping the farm and not wandering around the world looking for a job.

But Tessa just smiled. "The boys have football practice at the high school this evening. I could come by after I drop them off. It would be near to seven."

"I'll be waiting."

They waved to each other, and Matt put the truck in gear. If he bought a little wine and put it in the refrigerator, it would be just right by the time Tessa arrived.

"Okay, guys," Tessa said, as the four boys—her own two and a friend for each—tumbled out of the car into the high school parking lot. "Lennie's mother is picking you up at eight-thirty, and I'll come get you at his house by nine-thirty at the latest.''

Jason was already running up the walk, and Shawn just threw a "yeah, Mom" over his shoulder. Rather than being dismayed at their offhand reaction to her instructions, Tessa was relieved. She'd been more than a little worried that one of the boys would comment on the fact that she had showered and curled her hair before dinner, an unheard-of time for her. Or the fact that she was wearing her good shorts and the new shirt Martha had given her for her birthday last month. School must be weighing on their minds—there was nothing like having only a few more days of freedom to distract you from your mother's appearance.

Tessa stopped at the stop sign at Route 12, then turned right, a smile bursting out on her lips. She'd always loved the farm with its big old house high on the hill, overlooking acres and acres of Christmas trees. Even as an adult she still believed that Christmas was a time of magic, so the Christmas tree farm had to be a magical place.

A warmth spread through her body and her stomach quivered ever so slightly and deliciously. Of course, Matt's being there didn't hurt her anticipation any.

She turned onto M-62 with a sigh. As a kid, she'd always believed Matt was lucky to live on the farm, but when she'd gotten to know him better and learned how desperate he was to leave, to run away and see the world, she'd felt a sadness about the farm. If even the magic of Christmas trees couldn't hold him, what could? She'd never tried, and wouldn't this time, either.

The farm came in view and the pine scent drove away any gloomy thoughts. She stopped by the windmill and left her sandals in the car. The first thing she did, after closing the car door, was take a deep breath. Lungfuls of Christmas and childlike joy.

"Hello, there." Matt came down off the porch toward her. "Welcome to Anderson Manor."

"I've always loved it here," she said.

Matt looked around. "I appreciate it more now than I used to." He shrugged. "Or maybe I'm just more willing to admit it."

Was he thinking of staying? Tessa roughly pushed that thought away. One heartbreak in a lifetime was enough. "What is it you want me to see? I've got a kit bag packed full of advice."

He took her hand, leading her into the house. "I've sort of got the place cleaned up."

His touch was nondemanding, just friendly, but smiles bubbled up from her heart. She felt like a teenager again, just a wee bit wiser in her expectations. "Looks like you've done a reasonable job with the house," she replied. "I'd never have guessed it was closed up for so long."

"I don't know." He shrugged. "What should I do with the furniture?"

The furniture was obviously comfortable over the years to the people who'd owned it, but it was not old enough to qualify as antique. The upholstered furniture in particular was frayed and sagging, and tended to make the rest of the house seem run-down. Not the impression Matt would want to give to someone looking at the house.

"I'd hold a garage sale and sell it."

"How about the rugs?"

"Pull them up, then sand and wax the floors. They're oak."

"Paint the walls?"

"Good idea. Something neutral, like a light beige."

"How about the kitchen?" he asked, taking her arm.

Tessa swallowed hard, a delightful tension building in her stomach. If he stayed this close, she'd have trouble telling a kitchen from a dining room. She'd be able to think more clearly if she moved away from him, but that would probably require a powerful effort. And she wasn't sure she was up to it. She wasn't certain she wanted to be.

"Well?" he prodded.

She forced herself to look around at the big, cheerful room. It was full of old cabinets and appliances that had a certain charm, but only if you didn't have to live with them.

"I don't know," she said. "The house would certainly be more attractive with a new kitchen, but I'm not sure the buyers of this kind of property are really concerned about things like that."

"You mean, they might not be interested in the house at all."

Tessa nodded. "They might just be interested in the farm's commercial potential."

Matt was quiet as he gazed around the kitchen, and Tessa wondered what he was thinking about. Was he concerned about the people who might buy the house he grew up in? Or did he just have some other questions about fixing up the house? She knew she'd feel sad to think about the house standing empty, devoid of love and laughter.

"Want a little drink while I think of any other advice I need?"

"Sure."

He pulled out a small wine tapper and filled two glasses with a pale pink wine. "You want me to drag some chairs outside?" he asked, as she held the door open for him.

"No," she replied, taking a glass from him. "The steps will be fine."

The wine tasted cool and light, and she concentrated on it and the trees as Matt sat down next to her. Tessa sipped and breathed slowly and deeply fighting to slow her heartbeat. She came nowhere close, but it was part of the game to try.

"So what happened when you left Edwardsburg?" Matt asked. "How'd you decide to come back here?"

Tessa looked at the broad skies stretching out beyond the edge of the Christmas trees and laughed. "I went away the summer after I graduated. Mom was sick, but seemed to be managing all right, and money was real tight, so I planned to work for a year in Chicago to help her and Dad out. Everyone thought I was being so wonderful, but I couldn't believe my luck. I was getting to see the world, to live in a big city! It seemed like cheating whenever somebody said how generous I was to help out the family."

Tessa sipped at her wine. That was a touchy, painful time for her to go back to. "Anyway, our neighbor's oldest daughter was already working at a big insurance company, and she got me a job at the same place."

"Did you share an apartment with her?"

"No." Tessa laughed. "She was living with a boyfriend at the time, so I got a little place by myself, on the west edge of New Town. It was sort of a singles' area."

He was silent, and Tessa took a moment to gather her thoughts, so she could explain things to Matt. It suddenly seemed so monumentally important that she be precise, that he really understand who she was.

"You know how we always complained that there was no privacy in this town?" she asked. "How everyone was so nosy and knew everyone else's business?"

"Yeah."

"Well, that's what I missed in the big city." She took a gulp of wine and sat silent for a moment, shaking her head. "I mean, nobody cared about anybody there. They all lived in their own little cubbyholes. No one asked how you were, how things were going. And the reason they didn't was because deep down they just didn't care.''

He was silent again, and Tessa worried that she wasn't communicating well.

''And the weekends were the worst. I used to walk the beaches. From Oak Street to Rogers Park and back again.'' She sipped her wine. ''I wasn't into singles bars or any of those kinds of things.''

She remembered how lost and out of place she'd felt. How she laughed too loud, was too pushy, didn't dress right, wasn't slender and glamorous. She just plain didn't fit.

''Then one day my purse was snatched, right out in broad daylight, with people all over the place. I kicked my high heels off and ran the kid down, but I couldn't hold him.'' She shook her head at the memory. ''No one stopped to help me. No one even called the police.''

He put an arm around her shoulder. Maybe he did understand.

''So I decided there was no use staying someplace I wasn't happy. I came home for a weekend and found out Mom was a lot sicker than she let on. They needed my help more than they needed my money, so I moved my stuff back here.''

And came back to learn she was pregnant, something that would have brought her back anyway. The big city was no place to have a baby by yourself. All in all, she'd known Edwardsburg was where she belonged. She took a deep breath.

''I guess I had my try at life away from here,'' she said. ''It wasn't me. I came back because this was where I would be happiest.'' She lay back against him, her heart at peace.

''You were lucky,'' he said, his arms closing around her more tightly.

''Oh?''

"I used to think you had a guardian angel looking out for you."

"You did?" She felt his lips brush her hair, and a sweet contentment washed over her. "It must have taken naps occasionally."

"No, I don't think so. You wandered away but it brought you back home again."

If that was having a guardian angel, maybe he had one, too. He was home now. But she said nothing.

"Nothing was ever so straightforward for me," he said. "I had drudgery sometimes, but I also had excitement. I was lonely at times, but then I made friends all over the world."

And you had nothing here to pull you back, she silently added. Nothing and no one, because she'd refused to use their love as a bait to lure him back to her. Had she been a grand and brave heroine, sacrificing herself so that he could find happiness? Or had she been just terribly wise, knowing that he wouldn't be happy here in Edwardsburg and would grow to resent whatever was chaining him there?

"Do you know," he asked, in a voice that was hushed as a whisper, "that I've never found anyone quite like you?"

She turned in his arms, wanting and needing this moment to treasure in times to come. "You don't have to look anymore. You know where I am."

His lips came down to touch hers in a welcome that set fire to her thoughts. She was all woman, melting hot liquid that wanted to mold to his form, to take nourishment and life from his being. Their lips danced and backed away, tasting of their hungers before clinging again. What words were needed when their hearts spoke as one?

Off in the distance, a gentle rumble broke through their passions. Locked in each other's embrace, they looked off to where storm clouds were gathering on the horizon. A flash of lightning split the darkness, and Tessa snuggled closer into Matt's arms.

"Notice how it's always storming since you came back?" she asked.

"The gods are angry that I'm here?"

She didn't like that theory. "Maybe they're angry you left."

"Are you?"

She turned back into his embrace, sliding her arms around his chest to pull him closer. His heart raced beneath her breasts, sending currents of excitement into every corner of her being.

"I was," she admitted, taking his lips for the briefest of kisses. "I thought life would be perfect if it went on like it was when we were in school."

He slid his hands up under her shirt. His touch felt cool and ever so soothing, yet wherever he touched seemed to burn. "Maybe I should have stayed."

His lips left hers, blazing a path along the neck, finding every sensitive spot that increased the heat of her fire. "No," she whispered. "You had to go. The world was waiting for you."

"Maybe it wasn't what I really wanted," he said.

She shook her head and tightened her hold on him. "It was. Edwardsburg could never have made you happy."

Another clap of thunder jolted the air; tremors seemed to shake the foundation of the house.

"Maybe we should go inside," Matt said.

She nodded, letting him draw her to her feet. "My grandmother said widow women always get horny when it's storming."

He just smiled as he pulled her into the safe darkness of his home. "I'd better keep a close eye on the weather forecasts for this area then."

* * *

"You're going to get soaked," Matt said.

It was storming in earnest now. Intermittent bursts of thunder and lightning encouraged the raindrops. Tessa stood naked in his bedroom, solid and womanly, staring down at the small heap that was her clothes.

"When this shirt gets wet," Tessa said with a laugh, "I might as well be naked."

Matt patted the bed by his side. "You can wait until it lets up."

"No." Tessa shook her head. "I told the boys I'd be picking them up about now. Besides, it's nearly their bedtime."

"I doubt they'd mind staying up."

"I'm their mother," she replied. "Some things I don't put up for a vote."

She pulled on her clothes as he watched, every movement filled with grace and serenity. He could watch her forever.

"You don't seem so uptight this time," he said.

She shrugged, but kept her eyes on the clothes she was putting on.

"I guess it's hard having another lover after being married for fourteen years."

She shrugged again. "I've just been thinking things over," she said. "I doubt Joe minds my being happy."

A lump rose in Matt's throat. Was she finally letting Joe go? He didn't know what to say. Maybe silence was best.

"You got some extra towels?" she asked.

A frown crept onto his face. "Yeah."

"Give me two."

"What for?"

She laughed and came to him, putting her arms around him and drawing his head to her breasts as she kissed him on the forehead. "I'm going to wrap myself in them so I stay dry running for my car. That way when I pick up my boys, I'll be all dry and proper."

He gave her a farewell kiss. It wasn't quite dry, but it certainly was proper.

Chapter Ten

So, am I making my fortune?" Matt asked, settling down in a lawn chair next to Tessa.

"Uh, yard sales aren't usually the key to a fortune," she said. "You'd better not send in your resignation yet."

"Shucks." He lay back in the chair and closed his eyes, soaking up the sun.

Tessa just smiled his way, then gazed out at the crowd of people milling around Matt's yard, inspecting all the junk he'd cleared out of the house to sell. She couldn't believe it was the Labor Day weekend already. The kids were back in school, business was in its usual early September lull, and she and Matt were no longer the object of everyone's attention. He'd been back for more than six weeks now and she was getting used to seeing him, used to her heart racing whenever he was near, and used to the emptiness when she was alone.

"Hi, Sis," Martha said as she plunked herself down on the grass next to Tessa. "How's Sleeping Beauty's sale going? Got any bargains for me?"

Matt opened one eye just enough to glare Martha's way. "I'm not sleeping, I'll have you know. Just resting. Running a garage sale is hard work."

"Why is it then that all the price tags are in Tessa's handwriting?"

"I let her help," he noted, then closed his eyes again.

Martha just grinned and turned back to Tessa, but Tessa barely noticed. Her eyes were on the crowd, but her heart was reliving bits and pieces of the past month and a half. Nothing major, just little moments when she and Matt had seemed to achieve real closeness.

There was that time that Matt was playing catch with the boys and he dropped a pass, much to the boys' delight. They'd teased Matt unmercifully all evening, their play dissolving into a wrestling match on the living room floor. Then there was the afternoon when the four of them had gone shopping for the boys' new school clothes, and Shawn and Jason had listened so carefully to all of Matt's suggestions. Or the time he came over for dinner and spent the whole evening fixing the leak under the kitchen sink. Time and time again, just as now, they all seemed a family, as if they belonged to one another and would forever.

"So anyway," Martha said, prodding Tessa with her foot, "where's that clothes rack you thought I might be interested in?"

Tessa called Shawn over and asked him to take Martha into the kitchen where some things had been set aside. Her son gave her a mock salute and ushered his aunt up to the house.

"He seems to be settling down," Matt said. "Don't you think?"

"He stopped snarling at you a while ago," Tessa pointed out with a smile.

"I don't figure it's over," Matt said. "Teenage boys snarl all the time."

Tessa shrugged. "I'll snarl back."

Matt laughed and stared out at the lawn, covered with furniture and knickknacks from the house. A young couple carrying an old wooden step stool came toward them.

"We live in an apartment complex over on Hickory Road," the woman explained as her husband paid for the item. "This piece will make the place a little less bland. You know, more like a home."

Nodding, Matt counted out their change. "That's at least fifty years old. My uncle made it."

"Golly," the woman exclaimed. "I'd never sell it if it were mine."

But then you have a home you're building, a place to store memories, Tessa thought and watched them depart. "I envy them," she said after a moment. "Just starting out, the whole world stretched before them."

Matt reached over to take her hand, a frown on his face. "That makes you sound ancient. I don't know how you feel, but you look pretty damn good to me."

"Thank you, kind sir," she said with a laugh that didn't reach all the way down to her heart.

"Hey, Matt!" Shawn came rushing over, football in hand. "Things are slowing down some. Want to play some catch?"

Matt looked over at Tessa. "Go ahead," she said. "I can handle the crowds. Besides, Martha's coming back here. I'll make her my assistant."

Matt bent to brush her lips with his, and the warmth that blossomed inside her was as much from love as it was from familiarity. It was as if they'd always been together and always would be, it was—

Her breath stopped as she shot her thought process into reverse. Love. That was what she'd thought and that was what it was. Not a leftover love from years ago, a love born of whispered secrets and holding fast against the storms. No, this was a love of now and today, of the present's hopes and needs. It had nothing to do with yesterday's heartaches or tomorrow's fevered dreams.

"That old clothes rack is great," Martha said, sitting down in the chair Matt had just vacated. "You can't buy them like that anymore."

"No?"

This love wasn't planned, that was for sure, but was it bad? How did she feel about falling in love with Matt Anderson, the world traveler, again?

"So, is it good to get the boys back to school?" Martha asked.

"I guess."

Tessa didn't know what to think. She felt whole when she was with Matt, whole and at peace, as if the world had finally fallen into place. That was well and good as long as it lasted. Once he was gone, the heartaches would be back.

"What's the matter, Sis?" Martha asked. "You got something heavy weighing on your mind?"

"Not hardly," Tessa assured her, clearing her mind of all shadows. "Just thinking how fast the summer went."

Martha snickered. "They say time flies when you're having fun."

Tessa preferred not to read anything into her sister's tone, but just gazed off at Matt and the boys tossing a football around. "The boys and I are usually active during the summer," she said. "We go swimming at the lake often, and this year we went horseback riding a few times."

"Horseback riding, huh? Was that your only new activity this summer?"

Tessa could feel her face grow warm. Her most dangerous activity of the summer hadn't been spending the night in Matt's arms, but letting her heart off its leash.

Martha's gaze followed Tessa's. "How long is he going to be here?" Martha asked.

A tightness took Tessa's stomach and slowly squeezed. "He said he had a lot of vacation due him." She paused and forced herself to breathe. "But I imagine he'll be leaving soon after the stadium dedication ceremonies."

Nothing was forever, Tessa reminded herself. Momma had always said to savor the view when you were on top of the mountain so that you had something good to remember when you were stumbling about in the valleys. And she would have lots of good to remember.

"There you go, Matt," the Realtor said, pushing some papers at him. "Signature at the X's, there, there and there."

Matt stared at the forms in front of him, then forced his hand to move and affix his signature in the appointed blanks. When he came into town, he'd been all anxious to sell the old place. Clean it up a little, turn it over to a Realtor and split. Now, here it was September and until now he hadn't made a move to finish things up here.

"Farmland is back on the upswing." The realtor tore out Matt's copies of the forms, folded them to put in an envelope. "We've registered a seven-percent price increase over last year at this time."

"Think it would move any faster if I fixed up the house?" Matt asked. "You know, like maybe put in a new kitchen?"

"Don't waste your money. No one is going to buy that property for the house."

Tessa had said that, too, and Matt felt the same uncomfortable twinge now as when she had said it. That didn't make any sense. Hell, the place had never meant anything to him.

"You mean, it'll go for its commercial value alone."

"Absolutely." The man nodded vigorously. "And a Christmas tree farm will do better than most. Low maintenance. Not like a dairy farm or even a grain farm. A buyer can hire a tree service to drop in once in a while, trim and clean things up. The new owner will pull money out of that place for years without putting hardly anything in."

Just taking and not putting anything in the land. His uncle would never have stood for that. Uncle George had believed you took care of your land because it took care of you.

"In fact, you could do that yourself," the Realtor said. "That is, unless you need the capital the sale will bring in."

"I don't need the capital," Matt replied, standing up. "I just . . . don't want the responsibility."

"Either way, you'll get a good collar out of that property." The man shook Matt's hand. "See you at the dedication next weekend?"

"Sure," Matt said and hurried out the door. By the time he walked the few steps necessary to reach the old pickup, he had a good case of irritation started. The truck had been parked in the sun, and the hot interior didn't help cool him any.

"Damn." The word came low and under his breath. Matt stared down the little street, now showing few signs of life. Kids were in school and many mothers had returned to work. But the town had a pulse, an ebbing and flowing of life. It wasn't the dead old burg he'd always thought as a kid.

He headed up M-62, but at the crossroads with Route 12, the truck made a left turn. Damn thing was always doing that. He'd have to mention that to Henry one of these days. If he didn't fix it soon, the old truck wouldn't be able to navigate a straight line to save a life.

Still, as long as he was going in that direction, he might as well drop in on Tessa. The kids would be in school and she might be lonely. Actually, Matt couldn't imagine a woman like Tessa ever being lonely, but what the heck. He didn't have anything better to do that afternoon.

He pulled up in front of the store and mopped his brow with a handkerchief before getting out. The bell on the door tinkled its combination warning and greeting as he stepped inside the store.

Tessa looked over her shoulder from where she was working and smiled. "Hi," she said.

She was working at the iron again. "Isn't it a little hot for that kind of thing?" he asked.

She slammed the iron shut and laughed. "I don't think I'd have much business if I made my customers check the weather before they gave me an order."

"It would be better to do that kind of stuff at night," he said. "Gets nice and cool in the evening this time of the year."

Shrugging, she pulled out a finished shirt and replaced it with another, adding numbers and letters. "I have to have this order finished by tomorrow, and Shawn has a football game tonight, which I have to go see. It's an easy team and the coach said Shawn would most likely play. He plays tight end and the eighth-grader ahead of him is pretty good. He's faster than Shawn."

Matt stared at the heat application iron. It was that or stare at Tessa in her shorts and T-shirt. And that wasn't the prescription for a clear head.

"Besides," Tessa said. "I don't mind the heat at all. It means another day I can go without shoes."

He smiled, more to hide the pain that need gave him. It didn't matter what Tessa wore or didn't wear. She was all woman and nothing in the world could hide that. He was going to miss her.

"Here," he said, stepping forward. "Let me do that."

"Why? I'm not helpless. I can handle my own business."

"Would you stop arguing?" He stepped into her place, taking out the shirt. He put in a new one and picked up the numbers and letters that Tessa had already laid out.

"Boy," she exclaimed. "Why don't you be a big bully and just push me aside?"

"That's what I thought I did." He spelled out the name as it was written on the order form, laid in the number twenty and pushed the iron down.

"What am I supposed to do now?" Tessa asked.

"Sit down and be a lady of leisure," he growled.

"You're certainly a cheerful little fellow."

"That's me," he replied.

"How about if I make some iced tea?" she asked.

"Yeah, fine."

He didn't look up, concentrating on his work. Tessa's soft footsteps moved away and then stopped.

"You put the old place on the market today?" she asked.

"Yeah."

He was thankful she didn't press the issue; she just left him alone to finish the shirt. He had another one in the iron when she came back with two glasses of tea.

"It's not like I'm selling the family pet," he burst out. "People sell houses and land every day. Some sell places they were born and grew up in. I only spent part of my life out at that old farm, and it wasn't that big a part of me.

Sure, my uncle made me do chores, but hired hands don't get any feelings of attachment to their places of employment. Do they?''

"You were more than just a hired hand," Tessa pointed out gently.

"I know." He ran his fingers through his hair, slightly ashamed of his outburst. "They tried, but we just weren't close. It wasn't anybody's fault. We just couldn't work things out. Aunt Hilda and Uncle George were older when I came, and at best I was just a nuisance in their lives. An angry nuisance. Angry at life for having taken my mother and father. I was really a first-class teenage punk."

"It sounds like you're still angry," Tessa said.

He looked over at her in surprise. There was such a gentleness about her, such a softness that he wanted to rest in, yet at the same time she was strong enough to weather any storm. He took a shirt out of the iron and set up another one.

"I don't blame them for my unhappiness," he said.

She took a long sip of her tea and then laid the glass on the worktable. "But you blame yourself," she pointed out. "You haven't really accepted the fact that wanting to leave here was all right. You know you couldn't have stayed here and filled your uncle's shoes, but you haven't forgiven yourself for being who you are."

He stared at her for a long moment, seeing—or maybe feeling—the truth in her words. So much of the anger had been on his side in the past, and he'd never really rid himself of the feeling that he'd abandoned his aunt and uncle, that he'd turned his back on all they'd tried to do for him.

"I guess I never felt as if I was needed here," he said slowly. "If it had been more of a general farm, with some livestock, maybe then I would have felt I had to stay. Felt like I was needed. But Aunt Hilda and Uncle George handled things before I came, and I knew they'd handle them after I left. I felt like an intruder in so many ways."

Tessa just sighed and waited while he took a shirt out of the iron. Once he had the next one in and the iron clamped down on it, she went on. "There're all sorts of needs," she pointed out. "Just because the farm chores had already been worked out efficiently didn't mean they didn't want and need you in their lives. Every time I saw one of them in town, they would tell me what you were doing. They were so proud of you and of the gifts you sent them."

His heart had been shadowed when he came here, and now it was moving into total darkness. "That doesn't exactly make me feel better," he said.

"Well, it should," Tessa said. Her voice was impatient, her eyes flashed at him. "You brought a real joy to their lives, especially as they got older. You were someone that belonged to them, a part of them that would live on even after they were gone."

"And so I'm selling their farm. A great way to repay them," he muttered. The timer went off and he released the clamp on the iron, but there were no more shirts to do. He frowned into his iced tea.

"Matt, they knew you would sell the farm," Tessa said. "They might have dreamed that you'd come back and run it, but in their hearts they knew you wouldn't. And that was okay with them. Whether they gave you the farm as a home or the money from selling it, they were giving you something to remember them by. Something that hopefully would make your life better, whether that life was lived here or off in Australia, working on that dam."

Matt grimaced. "Australia's not on my agenda anymore," he said. "When I called the company to arrange to take some of my vacation time, they assigned someone else the project. Just reached back into middle management, pulled out another name and packed him off to Australia.''

"Is that a problem?''

He didn't answer for a moment, but looked around the storeroom as if searching for wisdom among the shelves of T-shirts, boxes of socks and baseball hats. But these were just uniforms, just the components to outfit everyone to march to the same drummer. That was what he'd left here to avoid, following along like everyone else in a life that was a carbon copy of everyone else's.

"No, it's not a problem. I don't care about Australia, per se,'' he said. "It's just a bit of a shock to find out that I wasn't as indispensable as I thought.''

"Indispensability can get to be a burden,'' she said. "You can get to feeling trapped by it.''

"I guess.'' Matt reached over and started folding the shirts that he'd imprinted, now that they were cool. He was just getting stagnant, that was all. Sure, lots of what Tessa said made sense. She was right about most of it. Maybe all of it, but the real problem was that the town was getting to him, nagging at him and making him feel the outsider again. Not by anything anyone said or did, but just because he had no real place here.

Well, he'd be gone soon. The stadium dedication was coming up next weekend, so things would be winding down. He'd give the corporate offices a call in a day or two so that they could find him a project.

"Shawn's going to play tonight,'' Jason said, as the three of them settled down on the bleachers of the high school football stadium.

"He thought he was going to play tonight,'' Tessa corrected him.

"No," Jason said. "He really is. Alex Giles got a bad bruise on his leg. Coach Borden wants him to rest it so he'll be ready next week, when Edwardsburg plays Dowagiac." Jason turned to Matt. "Dowagiac is just awesome. They win all the time."

"I heard our junior high has a strong team this year," Matt said.

Jason made a face. "Yeah, but Dowagiac is still awesome."

Tessa and Matt shared a smile over her youngest's head. He was so patient with the two kids. It would be so great if—

No, she wasn't going to dream those dreams or even entertain those thoughts. The farm was for sale now and he would be gone. Probably for good.

The Edwardsburg junior high school team came trotting onto the field, and Tessa pushed all thoughts of Matt's departure out of her mind. Matt Anderson was hers for only brief moments in time, not forever. She had to be glad for the sunshine he gave her. She, Jason and Matt stood up and clapped for the team.

"Great seats," Matt said as they sat down again. "Near the fifty-yard line and not too far up. Must have paid a fortune for them."

Smiling, she looked around at the partially filled stadium. "It's a good crowd for a junior high game," she said. "It gets full when the high school teams play. Tonight a lot of people who would be here are over at Niles watching the older kids play."

"It looks like the school games are still a big deal around here," Matt said.

"Yup," Tessa replied. "About the only thing that's changed is girls' sports are bigger. They're getting good crowds for basketball and softball games."

"That's small-town mid-America for you," Matt said.

He had a smile on his face, but Tessa felt irritation grow within her. "What's wrong with that?" she asked. "It's made good people out of a lot of kids."

His face turned serious. "I wasn't criticizing," he said. "Honest."

Irritation fell back before the onslaught of guilt. That was stupid, she thought. He'd made an innocent comment and she'd jumped down his throat. He could not want to live here, but still say things that weren't critical. It was just that since she'd heard he put the farm on the market, everything seemed different. She felt as if she were walking a tightrope, trying to balance between depression and a giddy pretense that everything was fine. She was finding out how lousy she would have been as a circus performer.

"They're kicking off," Jason said.

The three of them rose with the rest of the crowd to watch the ball spiral up into the air. It came down at the ten-yard line, and the Edwardsburg player carried it out nearly to the thirty. The crowd clapped and cheered. Just watch the game, she ordered herself. Just watch and don't think.

"See, Mom." Jason was pointing toward the field. "I told you Shawn was starting."

Tessa looked down to see her older son lining up with other first-stringers. The standard mix of maternal emotions—pride, fear and hope—churned in her heart. She was certainly happy to see him start, but she hoped he wouldn't get hurt or embarrass himself by a boneheaded play.

"Looks like he's playing tight end," Matt said.

"He mostly blocks," Jason said. "Shawn doesn't catch too good."

"Jason," Tessa protested. "Your brother can catch the ball as well as a lot of people on the team."

She gave Jason a sharp look and was happy that the boy chose not to argue with her. Shawn was so determined and worked hard, but Jason was the more talented. Would Shawn eventually come to resent his younger brother for being able to perform at a higher level with less effort?

There was a groan of disappointment from the crowd, and Tessa bit her lips as her heart sank. Shawn had just dropped one of the few passes thrown his way.

"Hard hands," Jason said matter-of-factly.

"He wasn't quite under it, either," Matt added.

Jason nodded sagely. "That's Shawn all right. Hard hands, slow feet."

Tessa didn't know whether to laugh or cry. Should she laugh at the easy relationship that had developed between Matt and her sons, or cry because she knew he would be gone soon? Or she could laugh at herself for being so irresponsible as to fall in love with Matt again, but that, too, seemed more like a cause for tears.

"Hard hands, slow feet." Matt repeated Jason's words. "That reminds me of another kid who used to play for Edwardsburg."

"Oh, yeah?" Jason said. "Who?"

"You know him," Matt said with a laugh.

Jason just shook his head.

"He was an outstanding lineman who played with your father. In fact, if it wasn't for this guy, your father wouldn't have had any holes to run through."

"You!" Jason shouted, pointing a finger at Matt.

"Absolutely," Matt answered.

Cry. That was what the situation called for, Tessa was sure now. It was best that Matt would be leaving soon. As Shawn grew, he would look more and more like Matt, not just in his football skills, but physically. Then what would happen? Would Matt finally notice the resemblance?

She should have told Matt she was pregnant years ago. He certainly had a right to at least know about his own child.

Matt and Jason had a continuous and animated conversation throughout the entire game. Tessa had thought Shawn would miss Matt the most; now it was obvious that Jason, too, had become attached to him. Oh, Lord. Why did Matt have to come back home?

The game ended with Edwardsburg winning easily. "Can we go to get ice cream?" Jason asked as they waited for Shawn to exit.

"I'm sure Shawn will be sore and tired," she said. "He played most of the game."

"He's tough, Mom," Jason said.

If the truth were known, it was Tessa who was tired. In fact, she was totally exhausted. She didn't want to go anyplace. She didn't want to talk to anybody, especially Matt.

"Hey, Shawn," Jason shouted as his brother came toward them. "You want to go get ice cream?"

"We're not going," Tessa said sharply, before Shawn had a chance to answer. A quick glance told her that Matt's questioning, concerned eyes were not something she wanted to look at. She softened her voice as she addressed Shawn. "You had a good game, honey."

"I dropped two dumb passes," Shawn grumbled.

"Catching ain't your thing," Jason assured him.

"Sure," Matt added. "They'll probably move you to tackle next year, after you bulk up a little."

"Yeah," Jason said. "You didn't blow a single block. I mean, I didn't see anybody get past you."

Shawn glowed and walked straighter under the praise that Matt and Jason heaped on him. Tessa hung back behind the three of them and carried her load of gloom alone. When they reached her car, she crawled into the back seat while

Matt and the boys squeezed up front. It would be good when Matt was gone. Then life could return to normal.

The boys were tired and the ride home was quiet.

"I guess it's been a hectic day for everyone," Matt said.

Tessa nodded. "Yes, I think we should hit the sack."

He nodded. "See you tomorrow?"

"I'll be around," Tessa answered.

Tessa forced herself to concentrate on her boys, and she didn't turn around at all, not even when the faulty muffler roared in their ears. Should she tell Matt about his son or shouldn't she? How would she explain keeping the secret all these years? Oh, God. It was going to be a long night.

Chapter Eleven

I told you guys you should have hurried," Tessa scolded. "Now I'm going to have to drive you to school."

"I don't like bran flakes," Jason muttered.

"We can walk, Mom," Shawn assured her.

"No," Tessa said. "If you walk, you'll be late for class."

"We won't miss anything," Shawn replied. "It takes everybody a while to get started in the morning."

"Just get your books, please, and let's go," Tessa said.

The boys got their backpacks, stuffed in their lunches and they all trooped out to the car. Silence shared the ride to school. What with the homecoming weekend and the stadium dedication at the end of the week, she'd been preoccupied and the boys must have caught her mood. It was impossible to get them to do anything that required even a hint of organization.

If the truth were known, she hadn't been any Sally Sunshine herself lately. This dedication had been the whole focus of her life for months, yet she was feeling so listless and growing more depressed as the day came closer. And it was all due to Matt. With him around she couldn't concentrate.

Oh, it wasn't that he was always coming to see her, keeping her from her work, but she saw him at Henry's service station and at the convenience store. She saw him in her thoughts and in her dreams, but they hadn't actually run into each other that much. Their last real conversation was two days ago, when they went to Shawn's football game. Since then there were just a few accidental meetings here and there around town.

No, she couldn't blame Matt for her lack of concentration. She just had to discipline herself more, keep her heart and her mind on track. And she was going to, right from this very moment. She pulled into the junior high school parking lot and turned off the engine.

"I can handle it," Shawn said, as he and Jason hurried from the car.

Tessa opened her door and got out. "You're late," she pointed out. "And I'm sure they'd like an excuse from a parent. Unless, of course, you'd rather get a detention?"

She took her son's sour face as a negative and went with them into the school. The school secretary filled out late excuse passes for the boys. Tessa watched as they took them and trudged down the hall toward their rooms.

"It's certainly a joy to see them hurry to class," Tessa said.

The secretary laughed. "Don't worry. They'll make it by lunch."

"Right," Tessa said. "Why worry? They won't miss what's important." She turned to leave.

"Has Matt sold the farm yet?" Dot asked.

Tessa stopped at the office doorway, partially turning back. It was all right; her resolve was not in danger. People were bound to ask her about Matt, but that didn't mean that once she'd answered their questions he had to linger in her mind.

"I haven't heard that he sold it," Tessa said. "I imagine it'll take a bit of time to get it done."

"I hear farm prices have been going up," Dot said.

Tessa nodded. "Yes, I heard that, too."

"Do you think he'll hang around until it's sold?"

Tessa shook her head. "He doesn't have to. If he gives someone power of attorney, he's free to leave."

"Yeah." The secretary sighed. "It'll be a sad day when Matt Anderson goes. This town can use some handsome hunks around. Livens the place up a bit."

Maybe too much, but Tessa just smiled and opened the office door. "Thanks again, Dot." Tessa waved and hurried out into the hall before the secretary could think up any more questions about Matt.

Tessa hurried across the parking lot to her car. There was a sharpness in the air. Winter was down the road a bit, but the barefoot season was coming to a close. Autumn was a touch of heaven in Michiana, though. Sunshiny warm days, clear skies and cool nights for sleeping.

Unfortunately, Indian summer was not a good time for working inside. It was too beautiful to stay cooped up inside when winter promised long enough for that. A restless urge took over Tessa's foot. Instead of hitting the brake and turning into her driveway, she hit the gas pedal and pointed the car's nose toward M-62. Once through town, she opened the window next to her and breathed deeply of the cool morning air.

The sky was a deep blue, a few trees were tinted with just a hint of gold, and the air surged life into her soul. She felt free, felt that only sunshine lay ahead for her. Then over the hill she drove, and the first thing she saw on the other side was the red, white and blue For Sale sign. The air leaked out of the balloon of joy that the beautiful fall day had been building for her.

She let the car roll to a stop in front of Matt's property, left her shoes inside and stepped out on the side of the road. The earth still held the coolness of a September night and felt good on her feet. She walked along the grassy strip and looked up the winding lane at the old white house on the hill. It was a solid old farmhouse, made to shelter families. Yet some investor from Detroit or Chicago would probably buy the farm and let the house fall into disrepair.

Sighing, Tessa went over to a big rock by the turnoff from the highway into the lane and sat down. It hurt to see Matt throwing the old place aside as if it were a worn-out shoe, but what did she expect? It was a family home, and he didn't have a family, not one that he knew of. And that had been by her choice.

Tessa bent her knees, bringing her feet up onto the rock so that she could wrap her arms around her legs, resting her face on her knees. Why couldn't Matt have just stayed away? Shawn considered Joe his father, and no one would have said otherwise. Sure, it was a challenge to raise the boys without a father, but things had been relatively straightforward so far. Get up in the morning, take the boys to school, run the store, do chores, haul the boys around after school, go to sleep at night. Sometimes the nights dragged into forever, but everybody had their good times and bad times. It all balanced out.

Now everything was messed up. People were getting reacquainted with Matt and would remember his looks. Sooner or later somebody was bound to see the resemblance in Shawn. Questions would arise in people's minds.

The biggest question boiled in her own mind. Why hadn't she ever told Matt about his son? She had known where he was, and if she hadn't had the exact address, his aunt and uncle had it. She could have written him.

But then what would Matt have done? Probably come running back home to marry her. He would have gotten a job, helped care for her brothers and sisters and gone to school part-time. Other children would have come, and he would have been stuck in Edwardsburg, the place he hated from the bottom of his heart. By now he probably would be hating her, too.

Joe hadn't minded at all. In fact, he had seemed to like everything about their community. He'd been happy as a teacher and, even when they went on vacations, he'd considered coming home the best part. She sighed. If only Joe hadn't died. If only Matt hadn't come back.

She could tell him now, of course, but would his reaction be any different? Maybe he wouldn't feel duty-bound to marry her, but he probably would feel he had to stay around for Shawn's sake. Matt was older now, had seen more of the world, so maybe his need to escape wasn't as strong. Or it could be worse. Now that he'd seen the world, maybe Edwardsburg would be even more intolerable.

But in either case, it was Shawn she was most concerned about. What would the truth do to him? Shawn had adored Joe. Finding out Matt was really his father would mean Shawn would lose Joe twice. Once in death and once if the truth got out. And could she expect that the truth wouldn't get out once Matt knew? Not that he would blurt out the secret to any and all, but he'd be around. That in itself would cause questions. Then, too, his attitude toward Shawn would change. Damn. What was she to do?

The roar of a decrepit muffler startled Tessa out of her reverie. Nuts, it had to be Matt. Why had she come out here to do her thinking? It was too late to run away, so she stayed on the rock.

Surprise registered on his face as he turned into the drive and stopped. "What are you doing way out in the country, little girl?"

His smile was wide, but Tessa didn't feel any sunshine from it. The shadows were too deep in her heart. She just shrugged. "It was too nice a day to stay inside, so I took a drive."

"Nice of you to come by this way," he said.

"I always thought this was the prettiest area around Edwardsburg," Tessa said, wanting to make sure he knew she hadn't come out for his company. "These rolling hills, woods and meadows are just beautiful."

Matt looked out over his farm for a moment, apparently trying to find the beauty she saw. His sunglasses hid his reaction as he turned back to her. "Care for any coffee?" he asked.

"No, I should be getting back to work."

"I just got myself a cheese coffee cake for breakfast."

"You're going to get fat," Tessa said.

"I'll have that much less to eat if you share it with me."

She nodded her reluctant agreement and stood up, brushing off her fanny.

"Hop in. I'll give you a ride up to the house."

"I'll bring my own car," she said.

Matt shrugged but he kept his smile and put the truck in gear, roaring up to the house. Tessa followed at a slower pace. Even her car seemed to be pulling back, telling her to go home.

Tessa put her shoes on before she left the car, a small reminder to herself to keep her heart in line, then walked onto the back porch and into the kitchen. Matt was already pouring coffee at the little table he had kept from the yard sale, apparently having started the coffee before he went to pick up his cake. After cutting a healthy piece of coffee cake for each of them, he sat down across from her.

"So is everything in shape for the dedication ceremonies?" he asked.

He couldn't have chosen a better topic. "Pretty much so. The only thing that's really left is decorating the gym, and we're doing that on Wednesday and Thursday."

"I'm available if you need any help."

She forced a shrug. "We can use all the hands we can get."

The silence stretched out, broken only by the sounds of their eating.

"Want some more cake or coffee?" Matt asked.

Tessa had barely finished what she had. "No, thanks. I'm really full. I already had breakfast with the boys."

"Oh."

She ought to go. She had a million things to do in these last few days before the dedication. Last few days before Matt left? Her body seemed unwilling to move, though.

"I guess you must be really excited," Matt said. "After working all this time for the dedication, and now it's finally here."

Tessa stared into her empty coffee cup, turning it slightly so that the remains in the bottom ran to one side then another. "I'm not sure excited is the word for it."

He watched her for a long moment, then turned away. He got up and rinsed out his cup, then turned it upside down in the dish drainer. "No, excited probably isn't the word is it? I guess I was pretty dense not to see it. You must really be missing Joe now. All this stuff done in his honor must really bring home the fact that he's gone."

"In a way." She turned away from Matt, from the sympathy in his eyes that could be her undoing, and stared out the window next to her. The Christmas trees swayed gently in the breeze. "It's more that once this is done, I'll be losing a link with him." She wouldn't feel that Joe was there to protect her, a reason to keep her dreams focused away from Matt.

"But not your last one."

She turned toward him, a question in her eyes.

"You still have the boys," he said. "They've got to be the best link you could ask for to Joe. You'll always have part of him with you as long as you have the boys."

And a part of Matt, too.

The sun was at the right angle to spill into the kitchen and into her eyes, causing them to tear from the brightness. She got to her feet, blinking away the sudden wetness. "I'd really better be going. I've got some work at the store to get out of the way."

He walked out the door with her and down toward her car. "Want to go out to dinner tonight?" he asked. "All four of us. I still owe you one."

Loving him was one thing, being reckless with her heart was another. "No, not tonight," she said. "We try to keep weekday evenings quiet once school starts."

"Sure. Hadn't thought of that."

He opened the car door for her and she climbed inside. "Well, thanks for the breakfast."

"Thanks for the company."

There seemed to be nothing else to say, so she started the car, pulling away with a bright smile and a wave. And a rapidly breaking heart.

Wednesday morning, after a quick breakfast, Matt drove to the high school. He wasn't sure that his plan to stay for the stadium dedication had been a good one, but he would see it through. He'd thought that Tessa would be letting go of Joe by this time, but she still seemed as attached to him as ever. Oh, she made love with Matt a few times and he'd felt she was growing closer to him, but lately she seemed to be retreating. She'd been clinging to Joe with even greater determination.

What was the point of it all? Matt asked himself as he walked into the high school. Supposedly he was going to liberate Tessa from her feelings for Joe and reintroduce her to life. What a laugh! All he'd done was confuse himself about what he wanted from life and where he belonged. Tessa was exactly the same as she'd been when he came— beautiful, exciting and in love with her dead husband. She'd probably only turned to Matt because of what they'd meant to each other in the past.

Matt found a handful of other workers already in the gym. Claire and Peggy were cutting crepe paper streamers, Mabel Crenshaw and some others were stapling the program booklets, while Tessa was laying out bunches of paper roses. He went over to join her.

"Howdy, boss ma'am. Private Anderson reporting for duty, ma'am." He tried a snappy salute, but her eyes seemed clouded.

"Hi, Matt" was all she said, and went on counting out the stupid paper flowers. This had all the earmarks of a funeral.

"What are we going to do with these?" he asked. "Are they for wearing in our teeth?" He picked one up to demonstrate, but Tessa wasn't even looking at him.

"Want to bring that ladder over here?" she asked. "We need to start hanging these."

"Sure thing." He got the ladder and set it up where Tessa indicated, but he stopped her as she was about to climb. "Let me go up. You hold the ladder."

Tessa looked from him to the top of the wall. "Considering your size and strength relative to mine," she said, "I think it would be a better idea for me to go up and you to hold the ladder.''

"It gets high up there."

"I've been climbing trees ever since I could walk," she said with the first laugh he'd seen on her lips in days. "Or don't you think you're strong enough to hold the ladder?"

She'd always known how to get a rise out of him, in more ways than one. He stepped aside. "Ladies first."

Shucking her sandals, Tessa grabbed some of the paper roses and scampered up the ladder like a young squirrel. Matt watched her ascent, just to make sure she made it safely, then resolutely forced himself to look out over the gym.

Gritting his teeth, he let the air out of his lungs. Lordy, Lordy. Why had he stayed here as long as he had? Okay, so the town wasn't as bad as he'd remembered. It sure wasn't Edwardsburg that had held him here, though. It was a certain lovely lady whom he never should have let go in the first place.

"Have you had any lookers for the farm?" she called down to him.

His eyes went up and stopped on a pair of well-rounded legs. Not as many lookers as those legs have had, he thought. He forced his eyes back out over the gym.

"Just one," he replied.

"It's still early."

"Oh, yeah," Matt said. "I'm not in any hurry."

He let his eyes wander around the gym, but he saw back into yesterday, not the workers there now. He'd brought Tessa to the homecoming dance his senior year in high school. She'd been a sophomore, a kid really, but she'd outshone all the girls there. Her dress was some sort of silvery blue. She was kind of embarrassed because her mother had made it, but it suited her perfectly. She'd seemed like an angel just floating through the world, bestowing blessings on a lucky few.

He had been one of the lucky ones, only he hadn't known it then. He'd thought he was cursed and hadn't recognized what a treasure he held until he lost her.

Be honest, he scolded himself. He hadn't recognized his loss until he came back here this summer. He'd known something was missing in his life, something wasn't quite right, but he hadn't put a name to his emptiness until he came around the corner of that house in the storm and saw her there, taking down clothes from a clothesline. And he was too damn late.

He shifted his hold on the ladder. He'd be leaving next week, he guessed. He really had to call the home office, set up a date when he was coming back, give the personnel honchos time to find him an assignment. He knew he had to get back to work. His spirit wasn't geared to this kind of inactivity. If he stayed in Edwardsburg, he'd be joining the living dead. Things were bad enough already with his mood swings and general, all-around grumpiness.

He'd stay around for a few days after the homecoming and the dedication ceremonies, then he'd split and head back to his world, the big wide world of large-scale construction projects around the globe. That was why he had become a civil engineer, and that was the only place he could be happy.

"Okay. Want to move the ladder down a bit?" Tessa asked.

Matt moved it where she indicated and then got into position to hold it. "The boys all excited about the weekend?" he asked.

"Are they ever!" Tessa glanced down at him. "They are so proud, I'm surprised their buttons haven't burst off their swelling chests."

"Joe must have been some dad," Matt said.

The silence seemed thick enough to slice. "Yeah, he was," she finally said. "There was nothing he wouldn't do for them."

How could anyone compete with that? Matt asked himself. His eyes wanted to drift up again, but he held firm. Lately, he'd been having a lot of trouble being realistic, and at times like this, when he really wasn't that busy, a stray, idiotic thought would wander into his mind. Would Tessa be willing to come away with him?

Then reality would come crashing down on him in the form of a simple statement like the one Tessa had just made. Joe had been everything to them, and this was where his memory lived. Tessa loved this little town. Her family was here and so was Joe, still alive in everyone who had ever known him.

Fool, Matt berated himself. You know darn well she'd never want to leave. But he had to, before his sanity totally escaped him.

"Hey."

He looked up and found those legs almost on top of him. In fact, one bare foot was tapping him lightly on the shoulder. A broad smile lit his face.

"I'm all done here," she said. "Let me get down so we can move the ladder."

"Oh, sure." He let his hand slide up her leg, over her buttocks and around her waist as she came down.

"My goodness." She laughed. "This is such attentive service."

"I don't want you to get hurt," he said.

"I'm not exactly fragile," she scoffed. "Many's the time I fell out of a tree and just bounced."

He stood there and looked into her eyes. Cool blue ponds of tranquility. Did he really have to travel around the world?

Couldn't he just settle here with this lady and watch some tadpoles grow? Suddenly his jaw tightened. It sounded nice, but he wasn't a frog.

Matt cleared his throat and took his hands off Tessa. "I'd better move your ladder."

For the next few hours, that was all he did. Moved the ladder, handed her paper roses and kept his mind empty.

"Well, I think we've just about reached the end," Tessa said as she hung the last streamer of roses.

Unfortunately, she was right. He had just about reached the end.

Chapter Twelve

Jason stared at the clock on the kitchen wall. "Shouldn't Matt be here by now?" the boy asked. "I mean, he couldn't be lost."

"No, he's not lost, honey," Tessa said. "But Mr. Harmons's plane could have been late."

"Maybe they stopped for a couple of snorts," Shawn suggested.

"Shawn!" Tessa exclaimed. "Mr. Anderson knows we're waiting. He wouldn't be so rude."

Her elder son just shrugged, but he edged out of range of her glare. Tessa sighed. Shawn had been up and down since Matt came back, surly at first that Matt was somehow threatening Joe's place in their home, then lightening up when Matt told them stories of Joe and played catch with them. Lately, though, Shawn was going back to surly. Tessa wasn't sure it had anything to do with Matt; this whole dedication weekend could just be awakening painful memories for them all.

The grumble of a muffler burst in on Tessa's consciousness and she gratefully accepted the interruption. She stood up, watching the old pickup stop in front of the store. Tessa had offered Matt the use of her car, but Matt had said he didn't know a football coach in the world who wouldn't prefer riding in a pickup truck.

"Sorry we're late," Matt said, as she walked out onto the porch. "The plane was behind schedule."

"Late coming out of Chicago." Matt's passenger came toward her, holding out this hand. "O'Hare is a real zoo."

"Tessa," Matt said, "this is Bud Harmons, head coach at Northern Illinois and Joe's backfield coach at Michigan State."

"Pleased to meet you, Mrs. Barrett." Bud was a wiry man in his late forties with snow-white hair in a crew cut. He had the easy, down-home style that probably served him well with the parents of the muscular young scholars he recruited for his team.

"We'd better head on to the restaurant," Matt said.

"My car is a little on the small side," Tessa said. "But the boys and I can squeeze into the back."

"The three of us can fit in front in the pickup," Matt said. "The boys can ride in back."

"Oh, boy!" Jason exclaimed.

"I don't know," Tessa said.

"I grew up riding in a pickup in Iowa," Bud said with a wide smile. "My daddy always said any boy that fell out of the back was too dumb to keep anyway."

"We're not dumb," Shawn assured everyone.

"All you guys've got me outnumbered," Tessa grumbled, but she made her way to the pickup as the boys tumbled into the bed in back.

"We're going to the Dock," Matt said, as they soared over the railroad tracks. "Reasonable food and a little bit of atmosphere."

"Does it have linen tablecloths?" Bud asked.

Tessa shook her head. "No."

"Good," Bud replied. "It's been my experience that good tablecloths drive the price up and the quality down."

Tessa just laughed and relaxed. Shawn wasn't the only one who had been getting more and more tense as this day approached. Without really being aware of it, she'd been getting nervous, too. Part of the cause was the ritualistic saying goodbye to Joe, but another part was knowing she'd also be saying goodbye to Matt soon.

Well, saying goodbye was just as natural a part of life as saying hello, so she'd just better get used to it.

They went into the restaurant, and the bartender pointed them toward the dining room. There was an empty table next to the windows overlooking Eagle Lake, and they sat down.

"Mighty relaxing place," Bud said, gazing out at the sailboats gliding over the surface of the lake. "I can see why Joe was so fond of it."

Tessa glanced at Matt, searching his eyes. Would he agree or disagree with Bud's comment?

"There's something about watching sailboats that erases tension," Matt said.

The perfect host, Tessa thought. His remark was bland enough to seem in agreement, but actually told her nothing except that he was well mannered. A waitress came and took their orders.

"And if I remember rightly," Matt went on, "watching the corn grow has about the same effect."

"Oh, no," Bud corrected with a laugh. "I see a whole lot of cornfields out where I'm from, and there ain't nothing relaxing about them. There's one out beyond my practice field, and I can tell you some of them cornstalks move faster than my backfield. That's enough to give a man ulcers.''

They all laughed and greeted the arrival of their drinks and salads with smiles. Tessa found she was hungry, much to her surprise. She'd thought her stomach was too tied up in knots for her to be able to eat much.

"Did you really know our dad?" Shawn asked Bud suddenly.

"Sure did." The man smiled, as if looking back into the past at people and places they couldn't see. He returned to the present with a shake of his head. "He was a fine man, someone to be proud of."

Both boys seemed to grow inches taller, and Tessa felt her eyes mist over.

"Matt's been telling us stories about when they played together in high school," Jason said.

"Yeah, but I wish it was like now, with all the videotaping of games, so we could've really seen him play," Shawn finished.

Bud's tanned face crinkled up around the eyes as he stared off into the distance. "I'm afraid we didn't videotape, either, when he was there, though some of the games might be on tape in the archives. I'll make a few calls when I get back next week and see if I can get some copies made for you."

"Would you?" both Shawn and Jason cried together.

Matt found Tessa's hand and squeezed it. He knew how much that would mean to the boys and, in turn, to her. How she was going to miss his understanding!

"Your dad was one of the best boys I've ever coached," Bud was saying. "Could have made it in the pros. No doubt about it in my mind. He could have made it big."

Shawn nodded. "If it hadn't been for his knee."

Bud stared at the boy, then at Tessa, appearing perplexed. "Huh?"

"He injured his knee," Tessa reminded him, feeling a bit perplexed herself. The man said he'd known Joe very well. How could he have forgotten about his knee injury? "He tore up his knee just before the season in his junior year."

"Oh, that." Smiling, Bud shook his head. "He banged it up a tad, but it wasn't anything serious. Didn't need surgery or anything. The doctors said some ice, a few days' rest, and he'd be as good as new. Joe said he was bored hanging around the dorm so we let him come home. He rarely needed supervision in his training."

This time it was Tessa's turn to stare. Matt's hand closed more tightly on hers, as if he sensed impending disaster.

"In retrospect, letting him go home turned out to be a mistake," Bud said. "He came back when it was time, but only to pick up his stuff and tell us he was finished with the game."

Bud shook his head, but Tessa barely saw it. Even though Matt's hand still held hers, she was sinking fast, going back to a time when Joe was the rock she had clung to. He'd said his knee was gone, that the doctor he was seeing in Lansing said his playing days were over. And after that, he always wore a knee brace when he went running or participated in any athletics.

"He said the college game was a business, that it wasn't fun anymore." Bud shrugged. "Probably didn't matter that we let him rest at home. If he was tired of the game, he was tired. Once you lose your love for the game, you should quit. Without desire, all that work and practice is too big a price to pay for playing."

"I don't understand," Shawn said. His voice was trembling and Tessa knew she should reach out to him, but she couldn't. The darkness that surrounded her was too deep.

"Takes a big man to know when to quit," Matt said gently. "Lots of people would have just gone on because that was what was expected."

That weekend Joe came home, that was when she'd told him she was pregnant, those days when he was home resting his knee.

"But Dad had talent," Shawn said. "And Mom always says you're supposed to use your talent."

"Football's just a game," Bud told the boy.

"And your dad had lots of talents," Matt said. "He took care of you guys, coached lots of kids and helped them grow. Maybe those talents are more important."

Joe hadn't grown tired of the game, Tessa knew. He'd given up everything—the money and glory of a professional career—just for her. Just so she could have a father for her child and the respect of the community. Tessa wanted to cry, but forced herself to stare out the window at Eagle Lake and breathe.

"Matt's right," she was finally able to say to the boys. "The talents Daddy used were the important ones. Those are the reasons he'd want to be remembered and why we're going to remember him tonight."

Their dinner came then, much to Tessa's great relief. Not that she was hungry, but the others were distracted. She glanced over at the boys; both were eating with their normal appetites. When her eyes reached Matt, though, she found that he was watching her. He knew, just as he always seemed to know, that the foundations she was resting on had been shaken.

She would have loved to rest in Matt's arms, to tell him what Joe had done for her and why she owed him even more than she had thought. But the very reasons why she owed Joe much more than she could ever repay were the very reasons why she couldn't tell Matt the whole story. Matt was part of it, and to reveal all that Joe had given up for her was to reveal the truth about Shawn, something she couldn't do, now more than ever.

"Are you okay, Tessa?"

Matt's eyes were searching her face and she forced herself to smile. "I'm fine," she said quietly. "I guess it's just the excitement." She picked at her food. "The fish is great, isn't it?"

"Yeah." Matt wasn't fooled by her change of subject, but he let it pass and began to eat.

"Did your dad ever tell you how he won the Illinois game for us that sent us to the Rose Bowl?" Bud was asking the boys.

"He won it for you?" Jason whispered with awe in his voice

"Sure," Bud said. "We were down by three with two minutes left in the game and . . ."

There was a huge crowd assembled in the fields behind the high school for the bonfire when Matt pulled into the parking lot. During dinner Tessa had barely said two words—two spontaneous words, that is—that didn't sound forced and wooden. He hadn't had a chance to talk to her after dinner, but he was hoping to pull her aside before the ceremonies started.

"Tessa, there you are," Chuck "the Frog" Webb called out and hurried over to welcome her and the boys into the crowd of well-wishers.

There went his chance to talk to her alone, Matt thought, watching as she was pulled farther and farther from him.

"Uh, Matt?"

Matt turned to find Bud still at his side. "Hey, Bud, I'm sorry," Matt said. "I guess Chuck didn't know you were our guest of honor. Hang on, we'll catch up to him."

Matt was about to take the coach's arm when Bud stopped him. "No, that's okay. I was hoping to talk to you alone."

Matt looked at the man more closely. Though Bud's face seemed to fall naturally into laugh lines, his eyes were quiet.

"Joe never told anybody he was quitting, did he?" Bud asked. "I mean, it didn't take a brick wall to fall on me to let me know that his wife had no idea. And if he didn't tell her he was tired of the game, I'm betting he didn't tell anybody."

"Not as far as I can tell," Matt admitted. "I wasn't here then. I'd just gotten out of the Army and was starting school in Colorado."

"So he let everybody think his knee had gone out, rather than admitting the truth."

Matt shrugged. It was so easy to believe. Once he really looked back, he realized that Joe had never been the one touting his chances in the pros; it had been everyone else. Joe had been laid-back, not really pushing.

"I guess it would have been hard to make people understand," Matt said. "He was such a hero around here."

"Local boy who was going to make good?" Budd nodded. "Don't worry. The way I see it, he *was* a local boy who made good. One of the few who had his priorities straight."

Chuck Webb was heading back, looking around him as if he'd lost his date, and Matt waved him over. A few minutes later, the bonfire was lit, and the school cheerleaders were leading everyone in a few rousing cheers for their team. Then Bud was being led up on the podium and the real festivities began.

Matt found a spot saved for him next to Tessa and the boys. He sat down and gave her a reassuring smile. She looked like a tight rein was holding her in control and even the squeeze he gave her hand seemed to have no effect.

Worry ate at his insides, though he fought to keep it from showing. Sure, it had to have been a shock for Tessa to learn that Joe hadn't liked the game anymore, but it wasn't the end of the world. And it didn't negate the whole ceremony, as her look seemed to be telling him. Joe was a hero to everyone here whether he had quit the game of his own accord or had been forced out by injury. They were honoring him for who he was and what he'd done for them. How could Matt make Tessa see that when he couldn't get to talk to her alone?

Bud began to speak. He told tales of Joe's first practices that made everyone laugh, talked about Joe's talent, the reason he'd been so highly recruited, and ended up with references to how much good he'd done once he returned to his hometown. Harmons was a natural storyteller, and the audience took to his down-home style as if it were biscuits and gravy. But Tessa's reactions all seemed a bit off. She laughed and clapped, but it was as if the crowd's reaction set her off, not Bud's words.

Matt wished he knew what to do. He'd been taken aback himself at the news that Joe had just walked away from the game, but a man had to do what a man had to do. It had been Joe's life, and if the game hadn't been fun anymore, then he had every right to walk away from it. Life was too short to stay in something just because you were good at it and people expected you to.

There were times when Matt felt that way about his own job. At first, everything had been exciting. New experiences, exotic locales, the whole nine yards. Now there were days on end when he would finish his twelve-hour shift, then hide in his quarters with a good mystery or espionage thriller. Of course, these past weeks of vacation had put him in a much better mood. He could now face his job with a renewed interest and vigor.

People were standing and cheering, and Matt snapped awake as Bud stepped back from the podium. Matt joined in the cheers at about the same time Tessa did. Why was Joe's quitting such a big deal to her? It wasn't as if Joe had committed some kind of heinous crime. Or was Tessa's own identity so tied up in the heroic Joe that she couldn't stand the fact that he was a man, plain and ordinary, like everybody else around him?

Chuck whispered something to Bud, who smiled broadly as Chuck turned back to the microphone. "Ladies and gentlemen," Chuck said. "Please be seated and join us in a very special ceremony." He cleared his throat and shuffled some papers in front of him. "Joe left us much sooner than any of us would have wanted, but he didn't leave us empty handed. He left a lot of kids better off for the knowing of him, but he also left a bit of himself behind."

Tessa closed her eyes as if in pain, and Matt took her hand. It was cold as ice.

"And, in Joe's honor, and because they're damn fine boys," Chuck said, "we want Shawn and Jason Barrett to be honorary members of the Edwardsburg High School football team. That is, until they can become members in their own right. Shawn, Jason, come on up here."

As the crowd roared its approval, the two boys shuffled up onto the stage, cloaked in that weird mixture of pride and embarrassment so peculiar to a boy in his early teens. Their shoulders were straight, but they hung their heads slightly.

Chuck Webb held up two football jerseys. "As honorary members of the Edwardsburg team, we want you boys to have these jerseys. Both have your father's old number— 35—but each has your own name."

The boys were beaming as they each took a jersey. They turned them around to show the crowd the big white block letters spelling their first names.

Chuck waited for the clapping to die down, then leaned forward into the microphone. "In addition to the jerseys, you boys get to sit on the bench for all home games."

"Until they get too pesty," Matt said with a laugh, but Tessa didn't respond.

Once the speeches were made and the boys given their jerseys, there wasn't much left to be done. Joe's name was up on the stadium sign for all to see, and Chuck said the best christening the new stadium could have was for the team to win their football game tomorrow. Then the homecoming queen and her court led the crowd in the school song, after which everyone started drifting away. The bonfire was dying out and the fire seemed to have gone out of the evening.

Matt stood up to greet those who came over to him and Tessa. Bud didn't need a ride, a high school coach from Elkhart who wanted him to look at a couple of prospects who were playing tonight would take him to the airport later. Tessa shook hands and wished Bud a good trip, but her voice was lifeless, drained of enthusiasm and energy.

"Hey, Mom," Shawn shouted as he and Jason finally came running over. "Aren't these jerseys neat?"

Tessa nodded.

"They're just like the real players wear," Jason added.

"Yes, they're very nice."

They had to get away from here, Matt thought. They had to get away from all these people, so he could talk to her and find out what was wrong.

"Mom," Shawn said. "Everybody's going over to the minimall for pizza. Can we go?"

Tessa just stared at her son.

"We'll keep an eye on them, Tessa," Martha said, appearing from somewhere behind the boys, "if you don't want to join us."

"Can we, Mom?"

"Sure," Matt answered, not waiting for Tessa to say no. "You guys go on. I'll take care of your mother."

Wearing huge smiles, Shawn and Jason danced off with their friends. Matt had reacted spontaneously to the boys' request, but now he wondered if Tessa would be angry with him for usurping her authority. But no, her face wore the same wooden expression it had all evening. Matt would have preferred her being angry. Anything besides this dead spirit.

"Crowd's thinning out," Matt said, taking her arm and leading her toward the pickup. But his feet slowed as he saw how crowded the parking lot was. Everyone might have left the bonfire, but they hadn't left for home yet.

"Let's wait for them to clear out, shall we?" Matt said. Without waiting for an answer, or maybe not expecting to get one, Matt led her over to the benches that had been placed around the smoldering bonfire. It was warm near it, but not unpleasantly so, and it was quiet.

Tessa sat down while he remained standing, resting one foot on the bench as he looked toward the parking lot to make sure they remained undisturbed. She said nothing, but stared into the fire with an intensity that frightened him.

"What are you so upset about?" Matt asked.

She shrugged. "A lot of things."

Matt took a deep breath, feeling as if Joe was watching over his shoulder, urging him to make her understand. "Come on, Tessa leaving football was Joe's idea. Hell, if it wasn't any fun, then there was no use going through all the pain and agony of practice, getting hurt and everything else connected with the sport. And the higher up you go, the worse it all gets."

Tessa shook her head. "That's not the way it was."

"According to Bud, that's the way Joe said it was."

"It doesn't matter what Joe said." Her voice was a whisper, quiet and deadly. "I know the real reason why Joe quit."

Matt let the silence play a while before asking, "And what was the real reason?"

"He did it for me." This time he could barely hear the words.

"People rarely make that kind of life-changing decision for someone else."

"Well, he did," Tessa insisted. "I needed help."

Matt sat down next to her. "I'm sure you could have managed your brothers and sisters without Joe's help. You were doing a lot of the work when your mother was still alive. I'm sure you could have handled it all after she was gone."

"You don't understand," she murmured.

Her eyes appeared to be glistening in the glow of the bonfire, and Matt sat quietly, waiting. He couldn't lead their discussion anymore because he had no idea where they were going. If there was anything he should know, she'd tell him.

"Joe came back because I was pregnant."

Matt's stomach twisted slightly, but he just stared off into the bonfire. The idea hurt, ached inside him.

"I was scared. It was like everybody knew about my shame. But where could I go? This was my home. This was where I belonged. I knew I didn't belong in a place like Chicago."

He stood up again, kicking at a piece of wood that was smoldering on the edge of the fire. A deep, dark depression settled in him. Tessa had been his girl, not Joe's. He knew it was stupid to be jealous. He'd been in the Army for three years, and though they'd been writing, it wasn't the same as if he'd been there. Tessa had been young, and Joe had been her friend, too. It was only natural that she turn to him.

"Your pregnancy couldn't have been that big a deal," Matt grumbled. "I haven't heard anyone mention you being pregnant before you were married in all the weeks I've been here."

Tessa stretched her legs out in front of her. "We got married. Don't you remember how folks around here are? The first baby comes anytime. All the others take nine months."

Matt nodded. That wasn't just an Edwardsburg philosophy. Raging hormones were understood the world over.

"Everybody felt we did the right thing, so they forgot about it," Tessa said.

Matt stared over at the parking lot. The crowd had thinned to almost nothing. He was sorry they'd stayed here to talk. This wasn't anything he'd wanted to hear. "I still don't see what the big deal was," he said. "He had family here, too. I bet if he'd asked them, they would have helped with your brothers and sisters and he still could have played college ball. He wouldn't have been the only married player on the team."

Tessa was staring at him now; he could feel the hardness in her eyes and he turned to face her as she said, "It was a real big deal, Matt."

Why? Because she'd been Matt's girl and found somebody else once he'd left? He'd spent the whole evening, the whole past month and a half hearing how wonderful Joe was, and he didn't want to hear it anymore. He was tired. He should never have come back; he never should have stayed. This had never been his home and never would be.

"Joe was the second man that had ever made love to me."

As if he'd forgotten. Why was Tessa stating the obvious?

Tessa got to her feet and stared him right in the face. "Joe gave up his football career for me. Because I was in trouble and he wanted to help me. He became my baby's father before he'd ever lain in my bed."

Chapter Thirteen

Matt couldn't believe what he'd heard. Somehow the sounds must have gotten muddled up and come out wrong inside his head.

"What are you saying?" he asked.

She looked at him briefly, then turned away. The fact that she wouldn't look at him seemed to send a chill through the evening air.

"Joe wasn't Shawn's father," she said quietly.

The silence stretched out to painful tightness; a claw was twisting his insides, turning him inside out. He took a deep breath, but the air burned.

"I am," Matt said.

The certainty of it surprised and stunned him, taking the breath from his lungs. He felt as if he'd been pummeled into immobility. He was numb. Frozen. But he knew.

"Yes," Tessa whispered.

Matt sank onto the bench and stared into the fire as if it were from another world, another lifetime. He had a son. For thirteen years, he'd had a son and had never known it. Had never seen him learning to walk, never tucked him into bed, never helped him with homework.

"You never told me," he said. "Why not?"

He could see the faint glow of the fire glittering in the wetness on her cheeks, but he felt nothing. Not for her, not for himself. All there was was a vast emptiness inside him.

"You didn't want to stay here," she pointed out.

"I didn't think I had anything to stay for."

"All you ever talked about was leaving," she said, her voice a quiet wail. "About how you were going to blow this old burg and see the world."

"I was a kid."

He went back to that time, to the pain and anger and loneliness he'd felt back then. How he'd always felt an outsider no matter what he'd done. How the only time he'd felt whole had been with Tessa. She'd been the one who had the secret, the key to making him belong, yet she'd kept him from it. The numbness started to burn away under the fire of anger.

"I was dumped on my aunt and uncle and never had anything or anybody that belonged to me," he said. "And I never belonged to anybody. What the hell did you expect me to say? That this would be home forever?"

"All you ever talked about was leaving," she repeated.

The anger grew with a fierceness that defied reason, consuming everything in its path. "I just told you. I didn't think anybody needed me. Damn it, I was a kid, a stupid punk kid."

"What do you think I was?" Her voice was rising to match his. "I was only nineteen years old. My body was full grown but I still had a ways to go in emotional maturity. And you were only twenty-one, finished with the Army and ready to go to college. It wasn't just the travel. If you'd stayed here, you would have given up your education, your career, everything.''

Her eyes were on him, pleading with him, but he had no forgiveness left inside. Tessa was trying to make it seem that she had done a favor, that Joe had done him a favor, but no one had asked if he wanted those favors done.

Now everyone was worshiping at the shrine of the great Saint Joe. Joe, the real man. Responsible and caring. He cared for his community, he took care of Tessa, and he took care of the kids. It didn't matter whether they were his or not.

Damn it. Matt's anger grew. He could have been responsible and caring, too. He would have taken care of Tessa and Shawn, loved them completely. If he'd just been given the chance.

''Matt, Joe was here.''

''Right. And I was in Colorado, on the other side of the world where the mail and telephone don't reach.''

''I'm not trying to make excuses, I'm just trying to explain how things were then.''

''Yeah, I know.'' His voice was tight as he tried to hold back the hurt and anger, but he didn't really care what showed. He was being eaten alive with pain, pain Tessa had caused, and he didn't care if she knew.

''It's hard to talk about it,'' Tessa said after a moment. ''I've been carrying this secret for a long time.''

Was he supposed to feel sad for her? What about feeling for him, for all the years he'd lost with his son? He took a deep breath and got to his feet. ''Well,'' he said coldly, ''then I guess it's best we don't push it.''

Matt turned away from her eyes, wide open and dark with hurt. There was no reason to push it. She'd made the choices years ago, decided that he shouldn't be a father to his son, shouldn't even know that he had a son and certainly shouldn't be called back to live in Edwardsburg. So nothing had really changed, had it? He still wasn't really wanted back here.

"I need to get home," he said. "Time for me to be on my way. I have to start getting things together."

Tessa got to her feet, also, and they started walking toward the parking lot. Their hands almost touched as they swung close, but it seemed as if miles were between them.

"I'll drop you off at your place," Matt said.

"You don't need to. I can walk."

"For God's sake, Tessa, just get in the truck."

She chose not to argue any further and got into the truck in silence. Its small confines seemed to accentuate his anger and her sorrow. He started the engine with a roar and pulled out of the lot. The ride to her house was short, and the churning emotions in his heart didn't have time to sort themselves out. He pulled into her driveway and stopped.

"Matt." Her voice was barely audible. "I—"

"It's late," he replied. "I've got to get home."

She climbed out of the pickup and walked slowly up the front steps of her house. With a quick glance at her sloping shoulders, he restarted the engine and pulled away. What kind of person did she think he was? What kind of person was she? Nothing seemed to be right anymore, nothing certain.

Tessa's lips were quivering by the time her feet hit the stairs and the dam broke as she burst into her kitchen. Stumbling to the table, she fell into a chair and let the pain in her heart pour out in gut-wrenching sobs. She cried and cried, until there were no more tears left and all that remained was the pain.

It had all seemed so right back then. Matt was gone just as he'd wanted and Joe was there, just as he'd wanted. Sure, there hadn't been the same excitement with Joe that she'd had with Matt, but a marriage needed more than passion. A marriage was commitment. It was respect and affection. It was caring and being there when the other person needed you. And she had had all of that and more from Joe.

Now she had nothing. Tessa's lips twisted into a grimace as she swiped at her eyes. No, that was wrong. She had a whole lot more than nothing. She had a pile of trouble.

Matt was so angry with her that he couldn't see straight, and on top of her guilt over that, she had to deal with Joe's having quit football to take care of her and the baby. In trying to do the best for everybody, she'd messed up a lot of lives. In trying to let everybody be happy, she brought the people she cared most about nothing but pain.

The clock in the living room signaled ten o'clock. Tessa wearily pushed herself up, and went to wash her face in cold water. She had to go get the boys; everybody would be wondering where she was.

Her keys were on the table where she'd left them, her purse right next to them. Everything seemed so normal, yet nothing was. The house looked and felt the same, the soap smelled the same and the faint noises of traffic in the distance were the same. Yet everything was different.

She got into her car and turned onto Route 12, recognizing the numbness setting in for what it was, shock. Unable to cope with the pain, she'd turned off all feeling. It was just as well, she told herself. She'd never get through the next half hour at the pizza parlor otherwise.

"Hi, Tessa," the hostess said with a broad smile. "We were wondering when you'd get here. I think they saved you some pizza."

Tessa chose not to tell her that food was the last thing she wanted. "Where are the boys?" Tessa raised her voice to match the din of Edwardsburg's past and present jocks. "Have they been behaving?"

The hostess laughed. "They've been holding their own."

Tessa grimaced slightly. "Noisy in here."

"Yeah." The woman nodded. "Most of that is due to the old-timers. You know how it is with the guys. The older they get the better they were. By the time time they hit their fifties, they were a combination of Babe Ruth, Jim Thorpe and Superman."

Forcing a smile to her face, Tessa nodded. "I'd better go join my crew, or they're going to send out a search party."

It was slow going through the crowd, but Tessa finally reached the table where her boys were sitting with Martha and Henry.

"Hi, everybody," she said, putting her arms around Shawn from the back and smiling down at him. "You guys ready to go?"

"I got some pop left," Jason said.

"I haven't finished my pizza," Shawn announced.

"It's late," Tessa pointed out.

"Tomorrow's Saturday, Sis," Martha said as she slid over to make room for Tessa on the bench. "They can sleep in."

Tessa gave her sister a sideways glance, then sat down in an empty seat. Martha was right. The kids could sleep late tomorrow. And the only reason she wanted to go home was to cry alone in her bed. That certainly wasn't anything to make a scene over. Besides, she didn't have any tears left in her.

Henry slid the pizza toward her while Martha filled a glass with beer from the pitcher at the other end of the table.

"So where's Matt?" Martha asked. "Leave him at your place?"

The joys of a small town. Someone had seen Matt taking her home, and now everybody knew about it and was quickly drawing erroneous conclusions. Tessa sipped her beer, then nibbled at a piece of pizza.

"No, he had to go home," she finally got the strength to say. "He's leaving soon and has to get his things together."

"Another construction job in some godforsaken spot in the world?" Martha asked.

"Hey, a man's gotta take work where he can find it," Henry pointed out.

Tessa said nothing. Shawn had joined some other kids at a video game, and the way he held his head, the way he laughed, all reminded her of Matt. Matt, who was alone and hurting.

"Hey, Mom, where's Matt?" Jason came over to ask her. "We were telling some of the guys how he used to play with Dad, and they wanted to hear about that big game their senior year."

"He didn't come, honey," Tessa said, fighting not to see the disappointment in his eyes. "But you know that story well enough to tell."

"It's not the same," Jason said.

No, it wasn't. Nothing was the same. Matt had brought something special into their lives, and now it was gone. A sunshine that was hidden behind the clouds, except that the clouds always went away eventually. But in this case, the sun would be the one leaving.

"Hey, Tess, where're you hiding Matt?" Chuck Webb asked her.

She just shrugged, pretending to be busy with her pizza, but Chuck waited for her to answer. "He didn't feel like coming," she finally said.

"Glad you did," Chuck said, patting her on the back as he went by. "This weekend is really going to be something to remember."

That was true enough. She doubted that she or Matt would ever forget it.

"Boy, we're gonna whomp on Cassopolis today," Jason said, excitement spilling the words from his mouth like overflowing water.

"I hope so," Tessa replied as she parked the car. The lot was practically filled, with cars already parked along the road. She didn't see Matt's pickup, though. Her heart was uncertain if that was good or bad, so she stayed lost in gloom.

"We gotta win, Mom," Shawn said. "I mean, it's our homecoming. We're celebrating naming the stadium after Dad and everything."

"I'm sure the team will do their best," Tessa said.

They got out of the car and followed the crowd into the stadium. The boys were wearing their Edwardsburg Bronco jerseys and talking about how they got to sit on the bench with the team. She didn't know how they were managing to keep their feet on the ground and walk next to her, but she was glad they were. Their excitement was contagious, and for a time she could forget—

"Hey!" Jason exclaimed. "There's Matt."

Feeling a tremor in her hands, Tessa jammed them into her pockets and stood waiting as the boys ran back to greet him. Practically pulling him from the truck, they chattered at him nonstop. She wasn't sure what she should say to him; she hadn't really planned on being forced together like this, but maybe it was best. Maybe this way they would sit together and reestablish some rapport, then talk things out. There were issues they needed to cover, not here certainly, but they needed to reopen the lines of communication.

"Hi, Matt," Tessa said as he and the boys reached her.

Matt nodded to her, then kept listening to some involved story Shawn was telling. Fear shook her heart. Would he listen that intently to a story of Jason's, or would Matt only pay attention to Shawn from now on?

A bunch of young boys caught up to them, pushing and pulling at Shawn and Jason as they all entered the stadium. It gave her the chance to talk to Matt, to greet him again and share some innocuous remark about the game or the weather, but her tongue seemed tied in knots.

"The boys were afraid you weren't going to make it," she finally said.

He looked at her then, his eyes cold and withdrawn. He was shutting her out, refusing to forgive or understand.

"When I go, I'll say goodbye to them," he told her.

And what about to her? Would he say goodbye to her, or slip out of town without a word?

"Of course," she muttered.

Then the boys were heading off toward the players' bench and she and Matt were alone, without a cushion of kids to protect her from his anger. She watched the boys run off, somehow feeling as though they were leaving forever, that nothing would be the same again, which was ridiculous. They were only going to watch the football game.

"They are so excited about sitting on the bench," Tessa told Matt, then tried for humor. "Much more so than you and Joe ever were."

His eyes stayed dead and lifeless. "It's a day they'll always remember," he said, then, with a little nod at her, moved down with the rest of the crowd finding seats on the bleachers.

She tried not to mind his leaving her. After all, they had hardly parted as the best of friends last night, and what was there of consequence that they could discuss in the middle of the game? And what could they say until those items of consequence were discussed?

Nevertheless, her heart sank as she turned and found an empty seat a little off from the main body of the crowd and midfield. The band was lining up, ready to march onto the field, so she forced herself to watch the festivities. Claire and Peggy arrived, finally free of dedication committee duties, and joined her.

"Isn't it great weather?"

"Boy, we're going to kick butt today."

"I think everybody and his brother's here."

Tessa smiled when she was supposed to, nodded at the right moments and even made appropriate comments at the right times, but she was more than relieved when the game started. No one would expect conversation, and she could just stare down at the field and pretend she was watching. What caught her eyes most, though, was her older son, sitting there on the bench, wanting to be another Joe.

What were they going to do? Before Matt had come back, when he'd only been a part of her life in dreams, everything had been simple. Joe was Shawn's father, if not by genes, then by all the love he had given him. It was only right that Shawn idolize him. But now Matt knew he had a son. Could they all go on playing that same old game?

A cheer arose from the crowd and Tessa clapped, too.

"Wow, can you believe it?" Claire cried, hugging Tessa. "No one's ever scored that fast against Cassopolis."

Tessa looked at the scoreboard and realized they were winning. "They're really hot today," she said, as they kicked the extra point. Shawn and Jason were beside themselves, rushing over with the other players to congratulate the kicker. At the other bench, the Cassopolis team huddled, ready to regroup.

No, it was impossible to go back, Tessa knew. Cassopolis couldn't go back and erase that touchdown, and neither could she go back and erase her words to Matt. And she didn't really want to. Too many people had been hurt in the past by the things they didn't share. She should have shared her pregnancy with Matt; Joe should have shared his real reasons for quitting football with her. All she had to do now was to go on, and the only question was to where?

Would Matt want Shawn to know the truth, or would he be willing to wait a while before telling him? Her decisions had been the pits lately, but could she leave the decision of when to tell Shawn entirely up to Matt? She knew Shawn better, she knew how devastated he would be to lose Joe again.

Suddenly it was halftime and the crowd got to its feet, milling around. She slowly walked down the steps of the bleachers, where she found Jason searching for her. "Matt's buying us ice cream," Jason shouted, then skipped by.

Tessa watched as Matt rounded up not just Shawn and Jason, but their friends, too, and herded them all over toward the concession stand. How the boys loved him; but then, how he loved the boys, also. They all swarmed around him like moths to a flame. He got as much from them as he gave.

The boys were drifting back now, in twos and threes, walking slowly and enjoying their ice cream bars. She put a smile on her face for all of them, but it faltered slightly as she saw Shawn coming back with Matt. The look on the boy's face was one of adoration. Not quite as he had looked at Joe, but close.

All of Shawn's dreams seemed to be centered around following in Joe's footsteps. He wanted to play football for Michigan State, then become a high school teacher. A burning sensation stung Tessa's eyelids and she rubbed at them. What if he knew that Matt was his father? Would he want to leave Edwardsburg as quickly as possible? Would he want to build bridges and dams? Travel all over the world, footloose and fancy-free?

Genes or environment? Which was stronger? Psychologists had been arguing that point for ages, and here she was with her own little minilab.

Tessa closed her eyes. *Tell Shawn. Don't tell Shawn.* She felt herself running in circles, and getting nothing from it but dizzy.

"Tired?"

Tessa's eyes flew open as a hand dropped around her shoulder, but she relaxed again as she looked into Martha's sympathetic eyes.

"Getting old, Sis? Those late nights too much for you?"

"Yeah, I guess," Tessa replied.

They both watched as the pom-pom squad began a routine in the middle of the field. Nothing was ever different, Tessa thought, as she watched the young girls perform. People could be aching, falling apart, but life would go on around them. Maybe it was good this way. She could pretend to be alive, pretend to care about everything.

"It's a good game," Martha finally said. Her arm stayed around Tessa's shoulders.

"Yeah, it is."

Martha seemed in the mood for chattering, and Tessa was glad. That meant her sister wouldn't push at her for anything, nor would she let anyone else. Maybe, Tessa thought, she could just hold on until Matt left; then she could fall apart privately.

"Now you boys behave yourself tonight," Tessa ordered as they spilled out of the car.

"We'll have to," Shawn muttered.

"Yeah," Jason agreed. "Lennie's grandmother is one tough lady."

"Jason."

But both boys were already running toward the house, giggling all the way. The tiny Mrs. Duran, Lennie's grandmother, was in the doorway, waving to Tessa. She waved back, and pulled out of the drive.

Tessa smiled to herself as she turned onto Route 12. Mrs. Duran was such a little thing, and spoke in a gentle voice, yet the children listened to her as if she were Attila the Hun. Actually Lennie and her own kids were respectful types, and they all loved the old lady. Joe's mother lived in Florida and

Tessa's own mother was dead, so Mrs. Duran was the nearest thing to a grandmother that Shawn and Jason had.

"You have fun at the dance," Mrs. Duran called. "Stay up all night dancing if you want."

Tessa waved again, then pulled away. The boys were staying overnight, so she could kick up her heels and party until dawn if she chose to. Her smile turned into a grimace of pain. Partying all alone wasn't usually much fun.

Though the naming of the stadium was the most lasting activity of the homecoming weekend, most of the committee's energies had gone into the dance preparations. It was to be the best homecoming dance they'd ever had in Edwardsburg. Before Matt came home, she'd been looking forward to it. Once he was back and she'd discovered the ecstasy of his arms, she'd thought the dance would be heaven. Now it would be pure torture.

Oh well, she could sit around and jaw with the ladies, exchange recipes and talk about the mischief the boys got into. Maybe she could take a few extra turns serving punch or refilling the plates of cookies.

Tessa parked her car and stood for a moment, looking up at the evening sky and sniffing the air. The weather forecast had mentioned the possibility of thunderstorms, but the sky was clear and there wasn't a hint of moisture hanging in the air. It was a good thing, Tessa told herself as she marched into the high school gym. She really didn't think she could stand the pressure of a thunderstorm tonight.

Martha was already at the door as she stepped in.

"Hi, Sis," she greeted her.

"Hi," Tessa replied as she turned in her ticket and stood for a moment, looking around the wide expanse of the gym. It had the magic that every homecoming dance had—a high school gym that someone had tried to transform into paradise. The basketball backboards were still there, and so were the bleachers pushed into the wall, but there was something special in the air that made you see only the paper roses and crepe paper streamers. Everything here was done with love. Tessa sighed and stepped farther inside.

"Matt's here," Martha said.

"Oh, that's nice." She forced a smile to her lips. "It'll give him a chance to talk to everybody before he leaves on one of his projects."

Martha stared at her a long moment. "Right," she said softly.

They watched the couples dancing. Some were teenagers, students at the school, but a lot were former students who had come home for one special weekend. Actually, for most of them this was home; the occasion was just an excuse to return to the old school and pretend they were young.

Tessa had never felt so old.

"Is Henry coming?" she asked.

"Oh, yeah," Martha replied. "He just has to get things settled at the station." She looked at her watch. "He'll be along in another half hour or so."

Tessa nodded absently, still looking out over the dance floor, when suddenly she stiffened. Matt was dancing with a young woman.

"That's Polly Peters's friend," Martha said. "You know Jenny, don't you? She's Bud Schuyler's niece."

The young blonde laughed at some witticism of Matt's, and Tessa just nodded. She hadn't expected to spend time with him tonight, and was glad he'd found someone else to talk to. Really she was. That ache in her heart was because she hadn't eaten.

"Jenny works in Chicago, and I guess the blonde is her roommate," Martha went on, as if it mattered. "Things must be a little slow in Chicago this weekend."

The dryness in Martha's tone reminded Tessa that she was thirsty. "Can I get you a drink?" she asked Martha.

"You can walk me to the bar," Martha said, "and I'll get myself one."

They walked in silence, then sipped their vodka gimlets in more silence. Matt was dancing with someone else now. Tessa thought it was the Saylors' youngest daughter, who was working on her Ph.D. at Ann Arbor.

"Hi," Henry said as he joined them.

"Hi, Henry," Tessa replied, a smile easily coming to her face. Her sister's husband was a nice man, she thought.

"Hi, hon," Martha said, placing a light kiss on his lips. "You're early."

"Things were quiet at the station," he replied, "so I got an early start on my cleanup."

They stood in silence for a moment, and Tessa watched Matt swing by again.

"Want to dance, honey?" Henry asked Martha.

"I have to go to the little girls' room," she replied. "Why don't you get your toes warmed up on Tessa?"

"Sure," he replied and led Tessa onto the floor. They danced properly, as one would expect of a woman and her brother-in-law.

"Are the boys looking forward to their game tomorrow?" Henry asked after several minutes of dancing.

"Yes, they are," Tessa replied. "They like to watch football games, but love to play them."

Then they danced silently until the music ended. Tessa returned Henry to Martha, but before she could sit down, John Hore asked her for a dance.

"Nice crowd," John said.

"Yes, it is," Tessa agreed. "We should meet all our expenses."

When John brought her back to Martha and Henry, Chuck Webb was waiting for her. "Great band," he said as they made their way around the floor.

The same band was hired for every occasion in Edwardsburg that required one, but the group was good. "It must be good," Tessa said. "Everyone's dancing." Matt was with a redhead who had to have graduated from high school recently.

"Nice how everyone's mingling," Chuck said. "You know, the committee's making everyone feel welcome."

"Yes, it's great."

Don Walsh came after Chuck, then Dave Foley and Johnny Walinski. They exhausted the topics of the weather, the football game and the gym decorations about ten times over by then, and all Tessa wanted to do was sit down and relax, but her brother Dan was waiting when Johnny's dance was over.

"Dan, this is getting too much," she finally moaned.

"What? Can't I dance with my favorite sister?"

"Your favorite sister wants a break. Buy me a drink and I'll never tell anyone how you tried to fly off the barn roof."

He looked astonished. "That wasn't me," he cried. "That was Paul."

"Sure it was."

But regardless of who had tried to play Superman, Dan got a drink for her and led her outside to sit on the steps. She leaned back and stared up at the stars, feeling almost like a high school girl again, leaving a dance because her beau had quarreled with her. Except that Matt had always been her beau and their arguments had never lasted long enough to generate into silence. Until now.

"I love you all, Danny, but it's too much," she said after a minute.

"What's too much?"

She just shook her head, too tired to play games. "You know who was heading my way? Amos Delaney. And he's eighty-five, if he's a day. I'd be afraid to dance with him—he'd have a heart attack or something."

Danny stared at his own drink. "They care about you, Tess. That's all. They hate to see you hurting."

"And who says I am?" she asked, even though she knew it was a stupid question.

"Come on, Sis. Everybody in town knows you and Matt have had an argument," Dan said. "What was it about? He leaving soon?"

"I guess," she said with a shrug. Everybody knew? Well, what had she expected? Everybody here knew everything.

"So make him stay," Dan said.

"Sure, just like that." She watched as a car slowed down and turned into the parking lot. It drove around without finding a space to park and finally pulled onto the practice field behind the school.

"Tell him about Shawn."

Tessa stopped breathing and slowly turned to face her brother, the car forgotten. "Tell him what?" she whispered.

Dan shrugged and took his turn at staring at the stars. "You know what I mean," he said uneasily. "If you want him to stay, you know, you could tell him about Shawn."

The late-arriving couple had reached the parking lot. Tessa could hear the sound of their shoes on the pavement, so she held her words, and her breath, until they went inside. "How long have you known?" she finally asked.

Dan shifted his position. "I don't know. Forever. You never went out with Joe. You'd always been Matt's girl."

Tessa sipped her drink only to find the glass was empty. "I see," she said carefully, and set the glass on the edge of the planter. "And who else figured it out besides you?"

He just looked at her, and her heart sank into her shoes. "No," she whispered. What was that she'd just thought? *Everybody here knew everything.* "Everybody knows?"

"Well, I don't know about everybody," Dan said slowly.

"Which means you aren't sure of Amos Delaney."

Tessa sat in silence for the longest time, wondering what it took for the earth to stand still and time to stop moving. "He knows," she finally admitted. "I told him last night. That's what all this is about."

"Oh."

Tessa had to laugh in spite of her pain. "My thoughts exactly." She got to her feet and reached down to pull Dan to his. "No, little brother, there aren't any easy answers when you screw up royally."

"Hey, you didn't mean to," he protested.

No, she hadn't, but that didn't mean that a lot of people weren't still hurting. She took Dan's arm and walked back into the gym with him. She had learned one thing over the past twenty-four hours, and that was that she still loved Matt just as much as ever. And that he still had the power to break her heart.

Chapter Fourteen

Sunday morning dawned cloudy and cool, just like Tessa's mood, but the sky managed to change before the boy's football games. Tessa's mood did not.

"We both gotta win today," Jason said.

"You bet," Shawn said. "Edwardsburg's gotta sweep the weekend."

Tessa turned the car into the parking lot behind the junior high, and both boys looked off toward the high school stadium down the road.

"Two more years and I'm going to be playing there," Shawn said. "Just like Dad."

Tessa didn't point out that Joe had never played in that stadium, that when he played, the high school had used the field back here, where the boys were actually playing this afternoon. It seemed she was doing nothing but jeopardizing her sons' dreams these days, so she just stayed quiet.

She parked the car and walked toward the playing field, Jason and Shawn slightly ahead of her. Suddenly, as the boys talked, they disappeared and Tessa saw instead Joe and Matt. She saw Joe in the way Jason held his shoulders, and Matt in the way Shawn tossed his head when he laughed. Joe was there in the way Jason moved, his darting quick movements as he tried to avoid his brother's playful cuff. Matt was there in Shawn's roughhousing.

Tessa hurried to catch up to them, her heart aching and ready to break. She had lost them both, Joe and Matt. Joe was dead and gone forever; Matt was lost to anger and her silence over the years. All she had left was the boys. She caught up to them, coming between the two and putting an arm around each.

"Now you guys be careful," she admonished them.

"Mom," Shawn grumbled as he furtively looked around at his teammates, who were standing in full football regalia, waiting for the coach. "How are we supposed to play football and be careful at the same time?"

"Yeah, Mom," Jason added. "You want us to be wimps?"

"I don't mean that," she said, though she wasn't sure just what she had meant. She playfully mussed their hair, wishing she could keep them close always. "I mean, get yourself warmed up, stretch, and when you're on the field, concentrate."

"Yeah, yeah," Shawn said, and Jason nodded.

"Hello, Shawn. Hello, Jason," a male voice said near her.

"Hi, Matt," they chorused.

Her heart had tried to skip a beat, but settled down to a mere race. She turned slowly, hoping to find his sunshine had returned, but the shadows still clouded his eyes. She forced the smile to stay on her lips and in her voice. "Hi, Matt," she said.

His nod was quick, his "hi" as brief as possible before he turned back to the boys.

"Going to be tough games today?" he asked.

"Probably," Jason replied.

"Most likely," Shawn said. "The Blue Devils are always tough."

"Yeah," Matt agreed. "They always were back in my day, too. So who plays first?"

"Me," Shawn said.

"Well, good luck." He patted each of the boys on the shoulder, before nodding toward the stands. "I'm going up to the top so I can watch you guys better when you play. Better not mess up any of those catches we've been practicing."

"No, sir."

"No way."

The three of them watched as he marched up the stadium steps, then Tessa found the boys were staring at her.

"Are you guys mad at each other?" Jason asked.

"No. Of course not," Tessa lied. "Why would you think that?"

"Because you act like it," Shawn said.

"You don't really talk to each other anymore," Jason said.

"Mom talked to him," Shawn said. "Matt isn't talking to Mom."

"Yeah," Jason agreed.

"He said 'hi,'" Tessa pointed out. "Just not much else. I think he has a lot on his mind lately."

Shawn just grunted while Jason stared at her.

"He's trying to sell his farm," she explained. "And he's trying to get a job lined up so he'll know where to go from here."

"Why doesn't Matt like it here?" Shawn asked.

Tessa clenched her jaw tight for a moment. Why indeed? "His job takes him all over the world," she replied.

"Couldn't he get a job around here?" Jason asked.

"Shawn, your coach is here," Tessa said, breathing a sigh of relief. "You'd better get over by your team."

She grabbed Shawn for a hug before he hurried off to join the others, and Tessa bit back a smile as he shook his head. Poor guy, burdened with a mother who fussed over him. Her eyes wanted to wander up to the last row in the stadium where Matt sat staring out onto the field, but she just watched Shawn's team huddle around their coach. It would be nice for the boys to have a father, someone to balance off her excessive mothering. But then, they'd had a father and the fates had taken him away. And as for Matt, she didn't know what he wanted, but he didn't seem ready to forgive her.

She and Jason chose some seats in the bleachers. "I'm going to miss him when he goes," Jason said.

Tessa had been watching the boys on the field do their stretching exercises, hardly an engrossing bit of action, so she let her eyes move over Jason slowly. "Miss who, honey?"

"Matt." His voice was impatient, as if she ought to have known whom he was talking about.

And of course, she had. Who else dominated her thoughts, both waking and sleeping? She loved Matt, but she wasn't certain her heart had finished with Joe. The only thing she was certain of was that she'd hurt people she loved.

At the farmhouse that evening, Matt held a cup of coffee in his hand and leaned against the doorjamb between the kitchen and the dining room. Most of the furniture had been sold or given away, and the place was almost empty. He'd thought that emptying the house would take the spirits out, too, leaving nothing but a shell that needed a coat of paint, but the spirits of the old house were tougher than he'd expected. They still hung around, giving life to the memories that lived there. The smell of newly baked break, a red-hot stove on a winter's day, the clutching grasp of an August thunderstorm and his aunt humming a Christmas carol during the holidays. They were all there, floating like dust motes in the air.

Suddenly Matt's eyes burned and he strode over to the sink and dumped his coffee. He didn't remember his aunt doing anything with Christmas carols, humming them or singing them. It must be some illusion.

He hurried back upstairs. He'd better finish his packing quickly, or he'd burn the damn place down. Maybe if the memories had no home they'd have to go someplace else.

Grimacing a little, Matt forced himself into his room. Damn. He had to get out of this place and soon. This wasn't his room anymore. He was selling the old place. For all he knew, the new owners might wreck the house, to give them space to plant more trees. The old red barn would probably go, too.

He went to the shelves where he'd been packing that morning before he stopped to go to Shawn's and Jason's games, and stared down at the trophies lying in the box. There were two of them, side by side like soldiers fallen in battle. One was for taking the championship when he and Joe were in eighth grade. The second was for first place in the shot put in the junior varsity track tournament his sophomore year. Joe had already been on the varsity team, capturing trophies in the hundred-yard dash and the hurdles.

Matt had never made the varsity track team. Instead he became catcher for the varsity baseball team. And every ribbon Joe won in track, Matt matched with one in wrestling. He wondered if Shawn or Jason would want any of them.

For a moment he stood there, staring down into the box of trophies, then shoved it aside with his foot. Whom was he kidding? The boys had Joe's trophies and ribbons; why would they want his? He was nobody to them, nothing. A stranger who'd wandered in with a few good stories, and who'd wander back out again soon enough.

But was that what he wanted?

The sound of a car on the gravel lane caught his attention, and he went to the window just in time to catch a glimpse of Tessa's car before it pulled around to the side of the house. Why was she here? he wondered, but didn't move to go see. What did they have to say to each other anymore?

A few moments later he heard her footsteps on the porch. The doorbell rang, then she knocked. He didn't move until she opened the front door and called out his name. Slowly, he walked down the stairs. She was waiting just inside the door.

"Hi," she said. "I wasn't sure you were here."

"I was upstairs," he said with a shrug.

She looked beautiful in her jeans and shirt, with her hair loose and windblown. More beautiful than she had in high school. That angered him somehow, as if she were deliberately more beautiful now than when she was his.

"What can I do for you?" he asked, coming all the way down. He didn't ask her in, didn't offer her something to drink. He was being a lousy host. He knew it, but he didn't care.

"I thought we ought to talk," she said.

"About what?"

Her eyes flashed at him. A fire that was smoldering deep inside flared up for a moment, but then died down again.

"About Shawn," she said. "I have to know what you want to do."

"What I want to do?" he repeated with a laugh. His eyes followed her gentle curves, and his body remembered the feel of her beneath him, awaiting his love. But the memory didn't soften him, it made him strong, made him more determined that he wouldn't let her close enough to hurt him again.

"Since when did you start caring what I wanted to do?" he asked.

That hurt her. He saw her eyes flinch in surprise before she looked away. Rather than feel pleased, he felt disgusted with himself and turned away. She followed him into the kitchen, where he took two bottles of beer from the refrigerator and, after opening them both, led her out onto the back porch.

He handed her a bottle, then sat on the steps, staring out into the wooded acres of the farm. The trees swayed gently in the evening's breeze, while he tried to will peace and serenity into his soul. It was too tough a job.

After a moment, she sat next to him. Not close enough to touch, but near the other railing. He thought of the last time she had been here, sitting on the porch on a summer's evening, but he slammed the door on yesterday. Summer was just about over and raking up old memories did no good.

"So what do you want to know?" he asked, his voice quieter this time. He didn't allow himself the luxury of watching her, just glanced her way from the corner of his eye.

"What you want to do about Shawn," she repeated.

He looked at her then. "What's there to do about him?" he asked. "You afraid I'm going to sue for custody?"

"Matt."

He laughed as he looked away. The evening sounds of the farm seemed to mock his bitterness. "That would be pretty hard to do, though, wouldn't it? I mean, who'd believe me when I said he was my son? Everybody knows Saint Joe was his father."

She put her hand on his arm. "Don't, Matt," she said. "Be angry at me. Blame me, but don't take it out on Joe."

"I doubt that anyone will notice his halo tarnishing." He turned away and took a long drink of his beer. It cooled his anger somewhat.

"I didn't mean to keep you from Shawn," Tessa said. "I just never thought you would care."

He looked at her, bitterness about to flow from his lips, but she just held up her hand.

"Okay, I was wrong," she snapped. "I admit that, but if we're going to spend every time we're together heaping more guilt on my shoulders, we'll never resolve anything."

She was right, he knew she was, but it was an effort to still his tongue. More beer helped. After a moment he said, "What do you want to resolve?"

She took a deep breath and clung to her beer bottle. It didn't look as if she had drunk any of it. "What do you want to do about telling Shawn the truth? Do you want to establish some sort of relationship with him? What about Jason?" She ran one hand up the side of the bottle, sliding over the condensation that had formed there. "I want Shawn to get to know you and care about you, but I don't want either of them hurt in the process."

"I don't, either," he said carefully. Somehow he hadn't expected her to ask all this. "But all the rest." He shrugged. "I guess I hadn't gotten to the point of thinking everything through."

She put her beer bottle down and turned to face him. "What are your plans about your job?"

He shook his head. "I don't know when I'm going back. Soon. Probably this week."

She nodded, looking down at her hands as if for strength. She must have found it because her eyes were cool when she faced him again. "Do you think we could wait to tell Shawn?" she asked. "I'm not saying never tell him, but he's only thirteen and he really idolized—"

"Joe," he finished for her. "I know. But is that ever going to change? Will he never be willing to have a regular schmuck for a father?"

"You're not a schmuck!"

"I know that, but I'm not Joe. I never was and I never will be." He got to his feet, running his hands through his hair as he stared off toward the old barn. "Ah, hell. I don't want the kid hurt. Of course, we shouldn't tell him now."

"I'm sure he'd like to hear from you sometimes. Jason, too. They're very fond of you." She'd gotten to her feet, also.

He could hear that old bullfrog down in the pond, singing some evening song. "Yeah, sure. I'll write to them. Send them something now and then."

"They'll be bragging about you instead of Joe soon enough." There was a smile in her voice, but it didn't touch him.

"I doubt it." He turned back. "What about money?"

Her eyes grew shuttered. "We're doing fine," she said. "I know the house may not be the best, but—"

"I'm not criticizing," he said with a sigh. He took her hand and gently pulled her back down to the porch floor. "Look, I've got nothing but me to spend my money on. I may not be the world's best father—I haven't the foggiest idea even how to be one—but I would like to feel I was doing something for him. For them. I don't want to put up a wall between the boys."

"I'm glad you feel that way," she said.

"I've got some savings and a bunch invested in stocks and bonds. It could be for their college." He smiled just slightly. "In case they don't get football scholarships."

She nodded, her lips tight. To keep in refusals or gratitude, he wondered.

"Then I'd like to send a little extra besides that," he went on, since she hadn't refused. "Maybe you can save it and send the boys to camp next summer."

"Michigan State has a good football camp for junior high boys," she said. "I can look into it."

He shook his head. "No, a regular camp where they go swimming and fishing and make bracelets for you out of nylon thread. They have to learn that there's more to life than football, and that if they aren't good enough or get tired of it, it's okay. Everybody pushed Joe, and he had to lie in order to get away from the pressure."

"He did it for me," Tessa corrected.

"He did it because he wanted to," Matt said. "If he had wanted to play football still, he would have found a way. He quit because he wanted to." Matt took a deep breath, waiting for her to contradict him. When she didn't, he went on. "I want the boys to learn there's a lot of ways and places you can be happy. They should be themselves and not follow in anybody's footsteps too closely."

"Okay. I hadn't thought about it before, but you're right."

There was a long silence, too long after a time to breach. She must have felt it, too, because she finally got to her feet and walked down the few steps to the sidewalk. "Thank you for everything," she said. "I'm glad we got all this settled."

"No problem." He fell in beside her as she walked around the house to her car.

"You've been understanding about everything," she said.

"Hey, I'm a hell of a nice guy," he said.

She stopped and turned to face him. "You are, Matt Anderson. You are a hell of a nice guy." She leaned over to kiss him gently, as the dew kisses the grass, then she stepped into her car.

Was that it? Was she just going to leave like that? Did he want to let her?

"Tessa!" he called out.

She stopped and leaned out the window. He had no idea what he wanted to say and swallowed hard.

"If you ever need money, or something happens to you or one of the boys, I want you to call me," he said.

She nodded.

"I mean it," he repeated. "Promise you'll call me the next time you need help."

A shadow crossed her face, but she nodded again. "I promise. We'll stay in touch."

She started the car then, and he didn't stop her as she drove away, down the lane and then out onto M-62. Then she was gone from sight. The evening sounds came back full force, but he barely heard them. This place wasn't for him; there was nothing here asking him to say. Not the farm, not the town, not Tessa. She hadn't once asked him to stay.

Tessa held her breath a moment, then let it out in a sigh of disappointment as she rounded the corner of the supermarket aisle. For a while there, she'd never known where she'd find Matt. In the grocery store, at the library, at the gas station. Anytime she turned around, he'd be there.

But those days were gone. More than likely he was back at the old farmhouse packing and making phone calls. He'd said he was leaving this week. He must have things to arrange before he left Edwardsburg.

In a way, she'd be relieved once he was gone. This not speaking was getting awkward and attracting attention. The boys had wanted to invite him out for hamburgers after

Sunday's game, but luckily he'd left by the time they had showered and come out. They had told her to keep an eye on him, so she'd caught the blame, but that was better than letting the boys know just how deep the rift between them had become.

He had been reasonable when she went to see him Sunday night, though. She hadn't known what to expect, but he'd been understanding and assured her that he wouldn't exclude Jason from his attention. She guessed she'd have to arrange a meeting before he left, though, so he could say goodbye to the boys. Surely he wouldn't be planning to slip away without a word again. Her heart plunged at the thought, but she grabbed a few bags of frozen vegetables and told herself that he wouldn't do that again. Not to the boys. Feeling more and more tired, Tessa pushed the cart up to the checkout counter.

"Hi, Jane," Tessa said, trying unsuccessfully to keep the weariness out of her voice.

"Did last weekend wear you out?" the checkout clerk asked as she rang up a box of spaghetti.

"Yeah," Tessa said. "I guess all the work leading up to it and everything else just plumb tuckered me out."

"You all did a nice job," Jane said, as she picked up a can of corn. "I know I had a ball."

Tessa smiled. She'd thought it was torture. "Thanks."

"Fourteen dollars and eighty-three cents," Jane said.

Tessa gave her a ten and a five.

"Has Matt sold the farm yet?" Jane asked as she gave her the seventeen cents change.

"I don't think so," Tessa replied.

"Doesn't really matter, though," Jane went on. "I imagine he could just leave it with the Realtor."

"I would think so."

Tessa walked out to her car, irritation nipping at her heels. Why ask her if Matt had sold the farm yet? She wasn't his agent or confidante. In fact, she wasn't anything to him. That thought didn't soothe her any, and she found herself slamming the car door extra hard.

Tessa decided to do some other chores before heading for home. After all, the boys were in school and there was nobody else waiting for her anyplace. She needed some light bulbs, so she pulled into the hardware store parking lot.

"Hi, Ted," Tessa said as she walked into the hardware store.

The elderly clerk nodded to her as she walked by him. She picked up a couple of boxes of indoor bulbs and one 150-watt outdoor bulb for over the garage door.

"Bobby was in just this morning," Ted said as he rang up her purchases. "Said he's getting some solid nibbles on Matt's farm."

"That's nice," Tessa mumbled, digging in her purse for money. She thought Realtors were supposed to be a little more circumspect about the property they were showing. They probably were, but not in Edwardsburg.

"Guess that means Matt will be hitting the road soon."

"I would guess so," Tessa replied sharply. "His job does take him all around the world."

"Matt's getting a little long in the tooth." Ted dropped the change in her hand. "You'd think he'd be getting tired of living out of hotel rooms and construction trailers."

"He's only in his mid-thirties.

The clerk shook his head solemnly. "Man ain't given but three score and ten. Old Matt's halfway there. It's all downhill for him now.

"Well," Tessa said, forcing a cheerful note into her voice, "that should make the trip that much more exciting then, shouldn't it?"

She bustled out of the store before Ted could reply. She would have thought that a man with ten grandchildren would have enough in his own life to keep him busy without concerning himself about others.

Tessa slammed the door again after she got in the car. It was a good thing that her last stop was at the drugstore. Mabel Jenkins clerked there, and she didn't say but two words a month. If Tessa had to slam that car door one more time, the fool thing would fall off.

The old-fashioned bell tinkled its welcome as she stepped into the drugstore, but Tessa kept her head down and hurried back to where the first-aid supplies were shelved. She picked up a box of adhesive bandages, and added a roll of tape in case she was getting low.

Mabel Jenkins scowled at the price and rang up the sale. The cash register flashed the total and Tessa counted out even change for Mabel, who accepted it and silently bagged the items.

"I hear Matt's almost got the farm sold," Mabel said.

Tessa blinked in surprise at the extended conversation.

"Just as well," Mabel added. "The boy never seemed to fit in here anyway. Best for everybody he be on his way."

"Thank you," Tessa said curtly and hurried out the door.

She threw the package in the back seat and shut the door softly, careful not to slam it. It didn't close all the way, just as Tessa's breath couldn't seem to come, so she popped it open, then slammed the heck out of it. She started the engine and pulled out from the parking spot. Spinning the steering wheel sharp, Tessa let the rear wheels throw some gravel for exercise. Who in the heck did everyone think she was? Matt's mother? His sister? She'd been Joe's wife and the mother of his children. Her heart wanted to contradict that, but she refused to let it.

She knew that she was no more to Matt than anyone else in town was. It would be a good idea for them to realize that. She had two young boys to take care of, and she didn't need another.

With a few judicious turns, her route home took Tessa by the high school. Debris from Saturday's dance was overflowing a Dumpster by the side of the school and seemed to call to her. She turned into the drive and parked by the leftover streamers, broken balloons and plastic garbage bags filled with the paper roses she had made.

With a soft sigh, Tessa got out of the car and walked slowly over to where all the refuse lay. For a moment, she didn't want to touch it, or didn't dare. It was as if she were one of those fragile balloons, ready to crumple up at the slightest touch.

Finally Tessa pulled out several roses and looked at them. They were crumpled and stained but still pretty. Like an old lady who'd lived a good and useful life.

Tessa sank down onto the concrete car stop nearby, staring at the flower in her hands, willing it to come to life. But it stayed paper, stayed a weak imitation of the real thing.

The flowers had been her gift to Joe, made with love and wrapped with guilt. She hadn't loved him as she had Matt, but he had given her so much. He'd given her children a father, and he'd given her respect and affection. He'd given her acceptance in the community that was her home. She'd come to realize years ago that Edwardsburg, this tiny little bulge clustering around Route 12, was the only place in the world for her. Was her love for Joe just a weak imitation of the real thing?

Tessa twirled a rose in her fingers, her eyes blurring. Her and Joe's relationship hadn't been all that one-sided. She'd given him a great deal. She'd given him a second son, a good home, the respect of a good woman and gentle affection every day of her life. She hadn't pressed him for money and had encouraged him to do the job that he enjoyed.

And she'd also given him love. Not the same exciting passion she'd given Matt, but love had many faces, like a beautiful diamond.

Matt was right. There was no reason for Joe to have quit football on her account. If he'd wanted to, he could have played for Western Michigan and stayed closer to home. No, Joe had quit because he wanted to. Probably, as his former coach said, because it hadn't been fun for him anymore.

And if college ball hadn't been fun, then the pros would have been even less so. Maybe Joe hadn't wanted to be bought and sold like a side of beef. He'd always marched to his own drummer, unaffected by money or the opinion of the crowd. A strong sense of self was the biggest gift he had given the boys.

Tessa looked at the crumpled flower in her hand. She felt closer to Joe at this moment than she had for ages, felt his wisdom in the air and his love all around her. Whatever Joe had been, whatever decisions he had made, it was all in the past. This was today, now, and he was gone.

The flowers had served their purpose, and it was time for them to be put aside and let other things take their place. The same was true in her life. There were pieces that were meant to be put aside, and she had to move on.

Chapter Fifteen

Matt walked slowly through the trees, row after row of spruces and firs towering over his head, their needles filling the air with their tangy smell. These trees had been planted before he left for good. In fact, he'd helped plant them the summer he came back from the Army. They were getting almost too tall, though, and would be among those harvested for this Christmas. Then, next spring, a new crop would be planted here, little seedlings that would fight the elements to survive and grow. Just as he had survived and grown.

When he was a little kid, maybe four or five at most, and heard that his aunt and uncle lived on a Christmas tree farm, he'd thought the trees were all decorated for Christmas. He'd imagined row after row of brightly lit trees with ribbons and bells hanging all over them. He'd begged his parents to take him to see it, but once he got here, years later, the magic he expected hadn't been there.

Now he walked slowly up the slope to the house. When he was out of the trees, he turned to look back. All he saw was green, waving below him in the gentle breeze. Here and there a bird flew up, singing in delight at the day's brightness. Tessa would say he was wrong, that there was magic here. She'd say that he'd never tried to see it, that he'd come with an idea of what magic should be like, and hadn't seen it in other forms. And maybe she was right. But maybe, too, the magic wasn't here for him. Maybe you needed to be somebody special to see the magic in a place, and he just didn't have the right eyes to find it here in Edwardsburg.

Matt walked into the house to find the telephone ringing. He hurried to answer it, grateful for the reprieve from his heavy thoughts.

"Hey, Matt," Bobby Owens bellowed in a hearty fashion. "I got you a buyer for the farm."

"Oh? That's good," he said listlessly. If this wasn't a sign that it was time to be on his way, he didn't know what was.

"It's not a straight-out purchase," Bobby said. "But I think it could be a good deal."

"Oh." Matt didn't really care.

"The buyer doesn't have enough funds up front, so she'd like a lease, with option-to-buy agreement."

"I'll rely on your judgment," Matt told him. "Whatever you advise is fine with me."

The realtor cleared his throat. "There's something else."

What now? He just wanted to be done with the place. "You take care of it," Matt said through clenched teeth.

"The buyer is Tessa."

Tessa? Matt closed his eyes against the sudden shock. Why was Tessa buying the house? How could she afford it? And mainly, what did it mean? Matt's eyes blurred. Would she put Shawn in his old room? Was she trying to force some kind of connection between them, maybe bring his son just a little bit closer to him, to his memories?

"She wants to meet with you. Talk some things over."

There was a lump in Matt's throat now, and it hurt. "No."

"No?"

"I . . . I have too many things to do," Matt said. "I'm leaving in a day or two. Most likely tomorrow."

"Oh."

"I want you to take care of everything, Bobby. Just do whatever's right and fair."

Matt hung up before Bobby could say anything else. He walked to the kitchen window to look out over the big red barn. Knowing Tessa, she wouldn't change much around the place. Maybe fix up the kitchen, do some repairs, but she probably wouldn't drain the old pond in back.

"You're safe, you ugly old croaker," Matt muttered. "Safe to raise another zillion tadpoles."

Taking a deep breath, Matt pushed himself away from the window and fought back the pain that wanted to wash over him. He marched briskly to the phone and dialed his company's office in San Francisco.

"John Pedersen in personnel, please."

After several moments, the brisk voice came on the line. "Pedersen."

"Hey, John. Matt Anderson here. I'm ready to go back to work. Where're you sending me?"

"Matt. We were just talking about you this morning."

"Oh. Is that good or bad?"

The personnel manager laughed. "Good. Real good."

"Yeah?"

"There aren't any project openings right now. So we want you to come to San Francisco, spend some time on the corporate staff."

Work inside? Play corporate politics? "That's nice," Matt said. "Now, what's the good news?"

"Always the joker, aren't you, old buddy? The assignment will do you good. It'll look nice on your record when you're considered for top management."

Matt felt a heavy load moving in on his shoulders. "When do you want me in?"

"Two or three weeks will be okay."

Two or three weeks? He'd be climbing the walls by then. Or buying himself his overalls. "Get me a ticket for tomorrow."

"Sure, Matt. I'll have my secretary take care of it. Does she have your number?"

"Yeah."

"We'll put you up at the Mark. First class."

"Thanks."

Matt walked slowly back to the kitchen window and stared out. Damn. Why hadn't he been born a frog?

"It's for you, Mom," Jason said, holding the telephone receiver out to her.

Tessa finished chopping the mound of onions, then put the knife down on the counter. "Thank you, honey." Jason snatched a cookie and went back into the living room.

"Hi, Tessa. Bobby here."

A sudden attack of nervousness choked off her reply, and Tessa bit her lower lip instead.

"It's all systems go," the realtor said, enthusiasm giving each word an extra bounce.

"When are we going to get together?" Tessa asked.

"He said we should just work it out among ourselves."

Tessa made a face at the mouthpiece. "But we have a lot of things to work out. I don't have enough for a good downpayment, and I don't know how long the lease should run before I lose my purchase option. I also need to check with the man who's been taking care of things for the bank to see what kind of tree inventory I have."

"Matt said just work it out and don't bother him."

"But there are decisions he should be making," Tessa protested.

"He doesn't want to get involved, Tessa. You know him. That's the way he's always been."

She didn't reply. Now that Matt was leaving, folks were awfully negative about him. It was as if they considered his moving a rejection and wanted to punish him for it.

"I'm just following the wishes of my client," Bobby said. "And he said whatever we work out is fine with him. So we'll fix it so it's most advantageous for you."

"Well, I certainly don't want to cheat him."

"No one's cheating anybody. Everything will be on the up-and-up. I mean, contracts have to be signed. Matt just doesn't want to be bothered with the nitty-gritty."

"How about if I give him a call myself?" Tessa asked.

"No problem by me," Bobby replied. "But don't aggravate him. I see you coming out with a good deal on this transaction."

Tessa promised she would be cool, and hung up. Then she added the onions and seasoning to the spaghetti sauce while convincing herself that she should call Matt. They had parted on good terms, she reminded herself. Or at least they hadn't been arguing any longer. She could call him as a friend, as a client interested in buying a home, as the mother of his son.

She dialed his number before she did much more thinking. It rang several times before he answered, sounding out of breath.

"I thought for a while you were out," she said. There was a long moment of silence, and Tessa worried that he'd hang up on her.

"I just had one phone put in," he said. "And I was upstairs packing some stuff away."

Nervousness dashed in again, and this time it twisted Tessa's tongue. She took a deep breath, letting it out slowly. "There're a lot of things we need to talk over."

"Cover them with Bobby," Matt said. "I've given him full power of attorney."

"But it's your place, Matt. And I'm going to be living there, hoping to buy. I thought it would be better if the two of us worked things out."

"I'm not into contracts and that kind of stuff," he said. "So I don't see what purpose the two of us talking would serve."

"I . . . I don't want to cheat you."

He continued as though she hadn't spoken. "Just as I don't see what purpose your taking over the farm is going to serve."

He seemed not to have heard her, and irritation rose at his words. "I have a degree in horticulture, and I seem to remember someone advising me to sell the store and go into something that I was trained for."

Matt was silent and Tessa felt a momentary flash of triumph at having used his own words to put him in his place.

"Like I said, Tess, I don't know too much about real estate. Bobby and the bank will take care of everything. I'm sure they'll work out something fair to both of us."

"Matt—" But the dial tone was buzzing in her ear and Tessa slowly dropped the receiver in its cradle. Mindlessly she went back to the stove and stirred the spaghetti sauce. She wanted the farm, she really did. It was the type of work she wanted to do. It was a good place to raise the boys, with a lot more space but still in town, so they wouldn't be leaving their friends. And then there was the magic. Christmas was a special time, and any place that dealt with one of the important symbols of Christmas had to be special, too. Magical, even.

"We're going out, Mom," Shawn called from the living room.

Tessa could only nod, and soon heard their footsteps clattering down the stairs. Moments later, they appeared in the yard, tossing a football back and forth. Not everybody saw the magic, though, she knew. Would the boys see it, or would they see only that they were farther away from their friends?

The phone rang and she eagerly raced to answer. Maybe Matt had changed his mind. "Hello." The quiver in her voice invaded the hand holding the receiver.

"Hi, Tess. This is Julie."

Julie? Julie Coffman. Her father's Aunt Ada's granddaughter. "Yes, Julie," she said, trying to keep the disappointment out of her voice. "What can I do for you?"

"I don't know if you know," the girl replied, "but I work for the travel agency after school."

"Oh," Tessa said. "That's nice."

"Yeah, I work a little in the office, and I deliver plane tickets and reservations to people who order them."

Tessa was not sure what the purpose of this conversation was. "Sounds interesting."

"Sometimes. At least I don't have to sit in a stuffy old office all the time."

"That's good."

"Anyway, the reason I called you is that I have to make a delivery out to Matt Anderson at his farm."

"Oh." Tessa felt her stomach sink. Now she knew what the purpose was, but wasn't certain she wanted that knowledge.

"He's going to San Francisco tomorrow," Julie said. "He's got tickets on a flight out of South Bend late in the morning and a connecting flight out of Chicago O'Hare at two o'clock."

"I see." Tessa could feel herself growing tired.

"He'll get into Frisco late in the afternoon and will stay at the Mark Hopkins Hotel. It's one of those expensive ones."

Tessa took a deep breath to steady her nerves. "He's been planning on getting back for a while now. I guess he's used up as much of his vacation time as he wanted."

"Yeah," Julie said. "Well, I just thought you should know."

"Yes, well, thank you."

"I'm sorry."

"About what?"

"Well, I—" There was an embarrassed pause. "I mean, we—" Another strained silence. "A lot of people thought things were going to work out. You know, like between the two of you."

Tessa forced a laugh through her tight lips. "Things don't always work out the way folks think they should."

"Ain't that the truth," Julie said, her words solidly based on the worldly wisdom of a junior in high school. "Well, gotta go. Good luck on your farm."

Tessa sighed. There wasn't anything more efficient for transmitting information than a small town's word-of-mouth telegraph.

The spaghetti sauce needed only so much stirring, so Tessa went to the window again to watch the boys pass the football. Matt was leaving. No great surprise. She'd known for weeks, months even, that he wasn't going to stay. So why then did it hurt? Why then did it hurt worse than it had the first time he left? She wasn't pregnant this time, wasn't anything but hopelessly in love with a man with wandering feet.

Or were his feet wandering? There'd been no reason for him to stay before, wasn't that what he'd said? That he'd never felt that he was needed here?

No, that idea fell through even before Tessa's mind could formulate it, and her heart seemed to fall through with it. He knew about his son, but was still leaving. If that knowledge wouldn't keep him, then certainly her love for him wouldn't be enough. But what about for her? Could she live with herself if she just sat back and let him leave like that?

The last time, she hadn't tried to keep him. Maybe this time, she should try to do things a little differently. Besides, hadn't Joe always told his teams that the game wasn't over until it was over? Her back might be against the wall, but she had time for one more play.

Matt woke up to sunshine, but felt as if clouds were covering the sky—would always be covering the sky, as far as he was concerned. He dressed in jeans and an old shirt, since he still had chores to do before he left later this morning. Chores to do or shrines to visit? he asked himself, then slammed his shaving equipment into the bag.

He hadn't said goodbye to Shawn and Jason. He'd thought about it last night, but hadn't come up with the courage to face his son. How do you say goodbye to someone who was a reason to keep living? Now it was too late. No, he'd stop by the school. He couldn't leave without saying goodbye. Not to them.

But what about Tessa? a little voice asked. Tessa knew he was leaving, knew why he was leaving, and why goodbyes weren't possible, he told himself and hurried down the stairs. She understood. But somehow his heart didn't.

Damn it all. He was leaving none too soon.

He started to run water into the coffeepot, but then stared out the window in amazement. The trees had stuff hanging all over them. It looked almost like Christmas decorations. What the hell—

He turned off the water, which had run over the top of the pot and all over his hand, then went to the kitchen door.

Sure enough, the Christmas trees near the house all had ornaments on them, glistening in the early-morning sun. He stepped out onto the porch and around to the front of the house. The trees out here had bows on them, and bells, and Tessa was teetering on a step stool trying to affix a star on the top of one.

His eyes burning and his stomach rapidly tying itself up in knots, Matt walked carefully down to where Tessa was. He reached her just as she got off her stool.

"Hi," he said.

She jumped, unaware that he'd been there. "Oh, hi. Good morning." She tried to smile, but it came out weak and lopsided.

"What are you doing?" he asked, nodding toward the trees. He was almost afraid to ask, almost afraid that it had nothing to do with him and everything to do with her buying the farm. "Is this some Edwardsburg ritual for new owners of Christmas tree farms?"

She looked back over her handiwork, glittering in the morning sun. "Sort of," she said. "Actually, it's sort of a ritual for new Edwardsburgians."

"New Edwardsburgians?"

"You know, people new to Edwardsburg. Small towns have their own sort of charm that's sometimes lost on newcomers. Just like the magic of Christmas tree farms is sometimes lost on newcomers to the farms."

"I see." Though he didn't. Or didn't think he did. Pipe cleaner candy canes swayed on the branches.

"And just who is this for then?" he asked.

She shrugged. "I know it's a little late—twenty-six years to be exact—but isn't late better than never?"

"For me?" He just looked around him, at the trees so absurdly decorated in the September morning. Even the birds seemed confused; their twittering seemed louder than ever.

"You told me ages ago that this is what you thought a Christmas tree farm was when you were little—rows and rows of decorated Christmas trees. So I got out all our decorations and borrowed Martha and Henry's and Jenny's and Dan's and Louise's and the Widow Crenshaw's—"

"Not hers."

Tessa nodded. "Everybody's who I could reach last night." She came a step closer to him, bringing him a step closer to an impossible dream. "There's always been magic here. I used to think you just didn't want to see it, but then I thought maybe you were looking for the wrong kind."

"I knew it was here."

"See, I thought that if we could make things here a little more like you had expected, then maybe it wouldn't seem so bad here."

"It hasn't seemed bad here for a long time," he admitted.

"But you were leaving."

He wasn't sure what to say; opening his heart wasn't the easiest thing to do, so he stared at the trees. Only the fronts had been decorated, the sides facing the house. He watched a squirrel eye a glass icicle with suspicion, then turned back to Tessa.

"Nobody asked me to stay," he said simply.

She stared at him, her mouth literally open in astonishment, then the light of anger grew in her eyes. "You mean, all this time, you've just been waiting—"

What he chose not to wait for was the explosion that was sure to follow, because it wasn't that easy. "I've never felt like I belonged," he said. "You know that better than anyone."

She nodded carefully.

"I had to leave that first time," he admitted. An absurdly smiling snowman peeked over Tessa's head to grin at him, giving him the courage and the words to speak. "I was sure the world was better and more exciting than anything around here. And it was. I didn't give this old place much thought at all until Aunt Hilda and Uncle George died. When I came back here, none of my notions about the place seemed to hold water."

There was a box of ornaments at her feet. He picked up a silver ball decorated with a strand of holly and hung it on the tree. "All of my ideas about life and what I wanted seemed full of holes. I didn't know what I wanted anymore, just that when I was with you everything seemed so easy, so straightforward."

"But you never talked about staying," she pointed out.

He shrugged, managing a halfhearted grin. "Hey, just because I got a degree and a good job didn't mean I had any sense." His smile disappeared as he sobered. "It wasn't until I found out about Shawn that everything really fell into place. I thought I was fighting Joe's ghost and wanting to set you free, but when I found out about Shawn, I suddenly had a stake in how things turned out. I suddenly realized that I wanted to set you free for me, not for some vague humanitarian reason. I wanted you for myself. I wanted you and the boys to belong to me."

"Matt."

Her eyes told him to take her into his arms and skip the rest of the speech, but having once started, he had to say it all. He took her hand, a lifeline to her heart, and went on. "I know I've been an ass about the whole thing. I can't really explain it except to say that it just hurt so much."

"I was wrong," she said. "I should have told you. I should have let you come back."

He just shook his head. "That's what hurts most of all," he admitted. "I don't know that you should have. I told myself that I would have been everything that Joe had been and more, but I honestly don't know that it's true. I wanted so badly to leave that I can't imagine I would have come back here and allowed any of us to be happy."

"And now?" she whispered.

"Now, I've seen the world and know this is where the magic is. I want to be an Edwardsburgian for the rest of my days."

"You don't have to," she said quickly. "God knows, along with the whole town, I guess, that I love you. But I'm not going to be selfish about it. Keep your world-roaming job, just as long as you come home to us sometimes."

He shook his head and followed his instincts to pull her into his arms. She felt as warm and soft and welcoming as his heart had always dreamed. "Nope. There's no reason to wander if everything I want is right here."

"Are you sure?"

"Damn it, Tessa. You're going to need help with Shawn. That boy needs a firm hand." He grinned at her. "He's going to be as much trouble as his father was."

Her eyes were wide, searching his. "But he doesn't know that."

He kissed her forehead. "And he may never." Suddenly out here with all this magic, everything was falling into place. "You marry me, and the boys are my sons from now on. They were yours and Joe's for a time, from now on they'll be ours. There's no reason to tell Shawn anything ever." He frowned down at her. "If you'll marry me, of course. If not, there's no telling what I might have to do."

"Oh, Matt. I love you so much."

"Not half as much as I love you."

She fell into his arms, half laughing, half crying, and all he did was hold her. It felt like heaven to him, a heaven he'd given up ever having. Nothing could ever rain on his parade now.

But as he looked up at the western sky, he decided he'd better not take that thought too literally. "Uh, Tess. Are these ornaments waterproof?"

She looked up then, to see the storm clouds gathering in the west. "Oh, Lordy, the widow will kill me if her ornaments get wet."

Matt just laughed, feeling as free as a kid again as they hurried to take down the ornaments on the tree nearest them. "I find it hard to believe she lent them to you in the first place."

"Anything for a good night's sleep, was what she said," Tessa told him.

Matt frowned at her, a tiny golden trumpet in one hand. "But the muffler can't have woken her up. I haven't been by in weeks."

Tessa grinned. "She knows. She says it's the silence that's keeping her up now. She wants us settled in one house so she can sleep."

Tessa was in his arms again. "I'm not sure how many good nights' sleep we'll be getting. We have a lot of years to catch up on."

"And forever ahead of us," she promised.

* * * * *

Silhouette Special Edition

COMING NEXT MONTH

#595 TEA AND DESTINY—Sherryl Woods
Ann Davies had always taken in strays—but never one as wild as playboy Hank Riley! She usually offered tea and sympathy, but handsome Hank seemed to expect a whole lot more....

#596 DEAR DIARY—Natalie Bishop
Adam Shard was falling hard for his childhood pal. But beneath the straightforward, sardonic woman Adam knew so well lay a Kerry Camden yearning for love...and only her diary knew!

#597 IT HAPPENED ONE NIGHT—Marie Ferrarella
When their fathers' comedy act broke up, impulsive Paula and straitlaced Alex grudgingly joined forces to reunite the pair. But after much muddled meddling by everyone concerned, it was hard to say exactly *who* was matchmaking whom...

#598 TREASURE DEEP—Bevlyn Marshall
A sunken galleon, a tropical isle and dashing plunderer Gregory Chase... Could these fanciful fixings finally topple Nicole Webster's decidedly *un*romantic theory on basic biological urges?

#599 STRICTLY FOR HIRE—Maggi Charles
An accident brought unwanted luxury to take-charge Christopher Kendall's fast-paced life—a lady with a limo! And soon bubbly, rambunctious, adorable Tory Morgan was driving him to utter amorous distraction!

#600 SOMETHING SPECIAL—Victoria Pade
With her pink hearse, her elderly companion and her dubious past, there was something mighty suspicious about Patrick Drake's new neighbor, beautiful Mitch Cuddy. Something suspicious, something sexy...something pretty damn special!

AVAILABLE THIS MONTH:

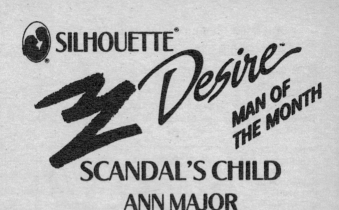